HATE TO WANT YOU

Julia Jarrett

CONTENTS

Authors Note	1
Prologue	2
1. Max	6
2. Heidi	14
3. Max	22
4. Heidi	29
5. Max	37
6. Heidi	45
7. Max	53
8. Heidi	60
9. Heidi	66
10. Max	77
11. Heidi	86
12. Max	94
13. Heidi	103

14. Max	111
15. Max	118
16. Heidi	123
17. Max	133
18. Heidi	141
19. Max	151
20. Heidi	160
21. Max	169
22. Heidi	178
23. Heidi	186
24. Max	195
25. Heidi	207
26. Max	214
27. Heidi	222
28. Max	229
29. Heidi	241
30. Max	248
31. Heidi	256
Epilogue	264
Acknowledgments	270
Also By Julia Jarrett	271
About Julia Jarrett	273

AUTHORS NOTE

Please be aware that this book largely takes place on the pediatric floor of a hospital. There are several instances of sick children, and there is one death of a child due to cystic fibrosis. Dedicated care and attention was put into these scenes, including the use of sensitivity readers (parents of children with CF) to ensure these scenes were accurate as well as sensitive to how these scenes may land for readers.

Please read with caution if reading about pediatric illness is a trigger for you.

Also, I wish to acknowledge that as this book is set in Canada, where health care and the medical school system may seem different to what readers from other countries are accustomed to. Attention was paid to ensure details were accurate for the setting of this story.

Much love, Julia

Prologue

Ten years ago

Heidi

"I can't believe today is your last day." Ginny, who has been more like a mother to me than a boss over the last few years, folds me into her arms for a hug. "We're going to miss you around here, girly."

I squeeze her tightly. "I'm going to miss all of you."

She pulls back slightly, bringing her hands to my shoulders. "Are you sure this is what you want to do?"

I paste on a bright smile, the one that makes my face hurt, but hopefully hides my misgivings. "Of course. This is the right decision for Thad's career, so I'm supporting him."

Ginny makes a sound of derision. She's never hidden her opinions about my boyfriend, but today of all days — my last shift on the pediatric unit of Westport General — it stings more than usual. All my nursing colleagues have made it clear how much they'll miss me and how they wish I wasn't leaving. Even Clarence, the director, told me I'd always have a space here at Westport General if I wanted to come back. It's nice to feel needed and wanted, but it also makes the ache in the pit of my stomach grow bigger.

"I'll come back and visit."

"You had better." Ginny turns and looks over her shoulder at the conference room full of our coworkers who all gathered to say goodbye. My eyes go unbidden to one person in particular. The newest pediatrician to join the department, Max Donnelly.

He's tall, slender yet muscular, with light brown hair that's always perfectly styled. He exudes authority, but also warmth. I've seen him sit down on the floor and play with patients, and I've seen him stand up and face down parents we've suspected of abusing their children. He's strong, and kind, and so freaking handsome.

And I shouldn't be thinking any of that about him. Not with Thad on his way to pick me up so we can go home and finish packing.

But the truth is, I wish I had more time to get to know Max. The little I've seen, he's an amazing man and an amazing doctor. Patients and families love him; he brings a peaceful comfort to them no matter what. He gets along with everyone, and is charming and polite, no matter who he's interacting with. Everyone, from the cleaning staff to his physician colleagues, gets the same respect. It's one of many things I admire about him.

I don't want to leave.

When Thad announced he needed to be on the mainland for his career, what choice did I have but to agree? He's promised me a future, marriage, and a family. And supporting the one you love is what you're meant to do, isn't it?

Even if it does sometimes feel like that support is very

one-sided.

I make my way around the room, stopping to talk with all my coworkers who came out to say goodbye. Gradually, the room empties because everyone is going back to work.

"Seems like you'll be missed." The quiet deep voice vibrates through me. Pivoting on my feet, I see Max Donnelly standing casually to the side, his hands in his pockets.

"They're wonderful people. It's such a great team here."

"It is. I feel quite fortunate to have started working here. Too bad it's just as you're leaving." His lips quirk up into a smile.

"Yo, babe. You ready to blow this place?"

Thad's voice announces his arrival and Max's eyes harden. His lips draw into a thin line. I may not know the man well, but you'd have to be blind not to recognize the walls going up around him. Confusion makes a frown form between my eyebrows, but before I can say anything, Thad throws his arm over my shoulders.

"What the hell are you doing here?"

The low growl surprises me. I've never once heard such anger coming from Max. Thad squeezes me tighter, almost uncomfortably so. "Picking up my girlfriend."

Max's spine goes ramrod straight and I get the distinct impression I'm between two bulls, locked and ready to fight. And I don't want to be in the middle of this — at all.

His eyes go to mine, and there's a coldness in them I've never seen before. "How long have you two been together?" His words sound forced, as if he doesn't really want the answer.

"Three years."

His nostrils flare. He's basically a stranger to me, but it's clear

Thad isn't. And Thad has to be my priority. Pressing gently on Thad's chest, I give Max one final smile before turning to my boyfriend. "Come on, let's go home. There's a lot left to pack still."

"I thought you finished last night?" he says sharply, but thankfully, his attention is on me, not Max, who makes a swift exit. I feel a little bad for whatever just transpired, but at the same time, I'm completely in the dark over what exactly it was. And right now, Thad is my focus.

"I didn't have time to finish the kitchen. We can just order some takeout and tackle it together."

Thad's irritated huff bothers me. Especially since I've done most of the packing on my days off. But I push it aside. It's easier not to engage him when he's annoyed. It's easier to just go along with whatever he says.

Even if the voice in my head tells me all I ever do is go along with what he says. And it's getting louder and louder every day.

As we walk down the hall toward the elevator, I see Max up ahead talking with another doctor. His head lifts, and our eyes meet. And the icy glare he shoots my way makes me shiver. I turn away and try to pay attention to what Thad is saying. But it's difficult when a part of me wants to look back and see if I was imagining the vitriol in Max's eyes.

Because why would a man who's been nothing but respectful and kind turn cold so suddenly?

What could have possibly happened in the last ten minutes to make Max Donnelly act as if he hates me?

CHAPTER ONE

Present Day

Max

Some days my job is heartbreaking, and some days it's just fun. Today, thankfully, it's the latter.

"Boom! I just schooled you, doc," my patient Sullivan cheers, dropping his video game controller down as he pumps his fist in the air.

"Darn, you really did." I put my controller down and push up to standing. "We'll do a rematch tomorrow?"

"Deal." Sullivan's smile fades. "How much longer am I gonna be in here?"

I sit back down beside the teen. He's been stuck here, recovering from open heart surgery, for a week now. And if it weren't for some issues with his blood work, he'd be home. "Hopefully, just a couple more days, bud." I drop my hand on his shoulder and squeeze lightly before standing up again. "I'll see you tomorrow."

I leave the patient lounge, and Sullivan, and head to the nursing station. I might not have planned to be a pediatrician when

I first went into medicine, but I wouldn't have it any other way now. Working with kids and their families, while challenging and painful when it doesn't go well, is so rewarding when it does.

"Dr. Donnelly?"

That voice. I know that voice. I lift my eyes up from the computer screen where I've just pulled up some blood work for another patient and meet the deep green gaze of the most stunning woman I've ever met. Ironically, she's also one of only two women on this planet I want *nothing* to do with.

"Heidi?"

There she is, looking just as beautiful as she was ten years ago. And just as repulsive, given what her presence here means. Her hand lifts to push a piece of hair behind her ear, and that's when I see the flash of a gold band on her finger.

She fucking married him? That means if she's back, *he's* back.

"Dr. Donnelly, there you are." The booming voice of the director for the pediatric program at WGH, Clarence Ross, echoes down the hall. "Ah, wonderful, I see you found him, Heidi. I mean, *Dr. Morgan.*" He winks at Heidi as my jaw drops open.

"Doctor?" I say, as if I didn't hear him clearly, but hearing is different from comprehending, and seeing her again has apparently rattled my brain.

A slight pink tint covers her cheeks. If she were anyone else, it would be cute. But all it does is turn my stomach. "Yeah, I, um, decided to quit nursing and went to medical school. Now I'm in my final year of residency, and I was lucky enough to secure a spot here to finish out my program."

"That's... Wow. That's unbelievable." I can hear the icy tone to my voice, at odds with how my blood is boiling at the thought of Heidi moving back to the area. Or more specifically, the man who almost destroyed my family.

Thad fucking Marshall. The man I was shocked to discover was apparently the love of Heidi's life all those years ago. I knew she had a boyfriend, but never in a million years did I think a sweet woman like her would be with a selfish, slimy asshole like him.

It might be strange to have such a strong reaction to the very thought of a man who, for all intents and purposes, hasn't played a role — directly or indirectly — in your life for years. But no one in our family will forget the night Mom was paid a visit by a police officer who told her Dad had been hit by a drunk driver and was in the hospital. It took months of rehab for him to recover, and to this day, he still walks with a limp. The long days, visiting Dad in the ICU of this very hospital, wondering when the swelling on his brain would go down, and if he'd ever be the same, left a scar on all our souls.

For me, that day is burned into my memory for more than just the accident. I've carried an extra burden by myself for twelve years. Because the day Thad Marshall decided to drive home drunk from a liquid lunch with some coworkers was also the day I found out my girlfriend at the time betrayed me.

But right now, even that betrayal is overshadowed by the onslaught of memories that seeing Heidi is bringing up. She was with Thad when he weaseled his way out of taking account-ability for what he did to my dad. His lawyer got him off on a technicality, never mind the fact that our family was never the same after.

It's a special kind of asshole that can show absolutely no remorse and take no responsibility for something that was completely his fault. And she was with him through it all. Which makes her just as bad as him in my eyes.

Clarence is still talking, singing her praises, I'm guessing. I don't give a fuck if she's top of her class, I don't want her anywhere near me. But I try to focus on what he's saying, given the man is in charge of my paycheck.

"We're thrilled to have her back with us, hopefully to stay, if I have anything to say about it. Now, Dr. Donnelly, you'll have to excuse us. We've got some paperwork to attend to. *Doctor* Morgan has her first shift with you tomorrow." Clarence claps me on the back. Normally, that wouldn't make me budge, but I'm so off kilter, I actually stumble forward, catching myself on the counter just in time. But the action brings me close to *her*. Close enough to hear her intake of breath.

I back up instantly. It's only as the two of them walk away that my brain catches up to something important.

Did he say her first shift with *me*?

Oh, fuck no.

"What's got your tighty-whities in a wad?"

I almost spit out my beer when my younger brother Sawyer thumps me on the back before settling down on the stool next to me.

"And who said you could start drinking without us?" he asks

indignantly.

I choose to ignore the second part of his question because I don't exactly want to go there right now. Admitting that I came straight to the bar after my shift ended isn't high on my to-do list tonight. That would be a dead giveaway to my brothers that something's up. Hopefully, they don't figure it out when I leave my car here tonight and take an Uber back to Westport. Because I've definitely had too much to drive safely.

"Really? Tighty-whities?"

"Sorry, are you more of a boxers kinda guy? It's been a while since I saw your undies." Sawyer signals to the owner of Hastings, the bar in Dogwood Cove I meet my brothers at every month. Dean, who we've known for years, gives him a nod.

"Are you two seriously talking about your underwear?" Sawyer's twin, Beckett, comes up on my other side. "I came in at the wrong time."

"Hey, we won't tell anyone you starch yours."

Beckett leans across the bar in front of me to smack his twin. "You're an ass, Sawyer."

"Nah, just the only one of us to have some fun."

"Can we just drink beer and stop talking?" I say, fed up with Sawyer's incessant antics and teasing. If ever there was a guy who needed to grow up, it's him.

"Shit, settle down, old man." Sawyer grumbles, but he does stop talking. And starts eating the wings I ordered when I got here. That keeps him occupied for a couple of minutes. "But really, why so grumpy? And why are these wings cold?"

"Wasn't today the day for your big impressive speech to the new round of residents at the hospital?" Beckett asks innocently enough, but apparently, I'm shit at hiding my reactions tonight. I blame the shot of whiskey I had the second I sat down at the bar. Thank God it was a different bartender who served it, one who doesn't know how out of character that was for me. Almost as out of character as showing up right after work, but I did at least have the forethought to change out of my scrubs before I left the hospital.

"Oh, fuck yeah, that's it, Beck. It's a resident. Let's see, either they're young and useless, or too cocky for their own good, or… Oh *shit.* You think one's hot, don't you?" Sawyer lets out an obnoxious hoot that has me wanting to just stand up and leave, except beer and nachos night is a monthly thing, and I love my brothers. Most of the time.

I pick up my phone and start rotating it in my hands.

"Max, what's going on? You do seem kinda worked up about something," Beckett asks, and I drop my phone. Fucking observant brother. But at least Beck is way more reasonable than his twin and knows when to just let something go. Which means, I might get out of this without revealing too much.

"Nothing," I answer quickly, but Beckett just tilts his head. "Look, fine. There's an issue with one of the residents. But it's no big deal and I don't want to talk about it. Just drop it, please."

An issue. Yeah, that's one way to put it. Normally, I don't keep much from my brothers. But there's not a chance in hell I'm telling the twins the issue I'm facing is that the guy who almost shattered our family is back in the area. Because if she's back and wearing a ring, then he must be back.

"Sorry guys, I'm waiting on a new keg of Backwoods Amber Ale, so I had to dig in the back for some bottles." Dean sounds harried as he slides three bottles of beer across the counter to us, and I nod at him, grateful for the interruption. Besides, there's nothing better than a new parent to change the topic of conversation, and I plan on taking full advantage of Dean's "new dad" status.

"No worries, man. Hey, how's Riley and Zoey?"

"They're great." Dean's face lights up as he pulls his phone out of his back pocket. He shows off several photos of his wife and their new baby girl, like the proud dad he is.

"Cute kid, Deano."

Dean's eyes cut to Sawyer, who had stolen a look over my shoulder. "What did I say the last time you tried to call me that, Donnelly?"

Sawyer winces. Well, well, this ought to be good; not much makes my cocky fucker of a brother react like that. But Dean measures six and a half feet and looks like a Viking with his long beard, making him intimidating, even to someone like Sawyer. "Sorry man, it slipped out. You need a nickname. I give everyone a nickname, you know that."

"Yeah, fine. Just think of one that doesn't sound like the stuff you take when you need to shit."

Dean walks off to the other end of the bar and I swivel on my stool to stare at my brother. "What did he threaten you with? I need to know, so I remember what to say next time you piss me off."

"Like I'd tell you." He snorts.

"He threatened to replace the tap of Red Frog IPA with a strawberry cream ale and not tell him," Beckett supplies helpfully from my other side.

Knowing how much Sawyer hates strawberries, that makes me laugh. "Dean's a diabolical genius."

"Shut up," Sawyer mumbles, taking a sip of his beer.

I'm just thankful the attention is off me. Truthfully, I shouldn't have bothered coming tonight; I'm too riled up about the Heidi situation to be good company for anyone.

The conversation steers toward Sawyer's constant attempts to get Beckett to join him and some of his firefighter buddies on one of their "hookup excursions," as he calls them. He's an immature fucker, and for a guy pushing his mid-thirties, I can't help but wonder when the hell Sawyer will settle his ass down.

Then again, maybe I do need to go out with him and find some willing woman to fuck. Hell, if I wasn't due back at the hospital tomorrow morning, I'd suggest we go out tonight. I need something — anything — to distract myself and get today's events out of my head.

Because no matter what I told my brother, working with Heidi Morgan is definitely going to be a *big deal*.

Chapter Two

Heidi

Walking through the doors of Westport General Hospital for my first shift as a fourth-year resident feels familiar and yet, so very different. The hard work making it through med school and the first three years of residency, being the oldest student in my cohort, the long nights and longer days, it all lead me back here.

This is my final term for my residency, which is why I begged and pushed to be transferred to WGH. I want to finish my education here, and hopefully, get a job here after I'm done.

I grew up on the mainland but moved to Vancouver Island to get my nursing degree. The job at Westport was my first, and I stayed here three years. I love the natural beauty that is everywhere around me, I love the small towns, the rugged coastline, the mountains and forests; I love it all. This area is where I always envisioned settling down and starting a family.

My ex, Thad, had other ideas. And like the meek little sheep I was ten years ago, I let him uproot my entire adult life and move me back to the mainland for *his* career. Because supporting the one you love is what you're meant to do, isn't it? Shouldn't you always stand by your partner and encourage them to reach all of their dreams?

Apparently, that was a one-way thing with Thad.

But life always gives silver linings. For me that was a patient — Molly.

Who knew a mouthy teenager could be so wise.

Her life was ending just as it should have been beginning. And somehow, she changed mine forever.

Fast-forward to today, and I realize it's not the hospital that feels different, it's me. I loved my work as a nurse, don't get me wrong. The value nurses have, the role we play in caring for sick and injured patients, that's priceless.

But I was a shadow of who I should have been back then.

"There she is!" Ginny shouts as I walk through the sliding doors to the unit after storing my things in the residents' lounge. Several other familiar faces appear, and soon I'm surrounded by my former coworkers. God, I love these people.

"Way to make me the pariah of the residents on day one," I grumble good-naturedly as I hug Ginny. The older woman hated it when we called her mom, but she truly did mother all of us nurses, making sure we drank water and took breaks. "If my cohort weren't worried about me getting special treatment before, they are now. You better bust my ass just the same as we used to any resident in their first week, or I'll never live it down."

"The difference between you and them, honey, is that you know how to start an IV in one shot," she retorts, and we share a quiet laugh.

"Residents, over here, please."

Ginny straightens and gives me a wink. "Better go, hot doc is calling you."

I roll my eyes, even though I don't disagree with her nickname for Max Donnelly. It seems some things never change. When Max started working here, just a few months before I left, many of the nurses had a thing for him. "You're still calling him that?"

"Do you have eyes? That man gets better with age." With a wave, she heads over to the medication dispensing room, and I'm left standing by the nursing desk alone. Taking a deep breath, I pivot and make my way to the back of the small group of residents starting today.

I take advantage of the small distance between us to covertly study Dr. Max Donnelly. Ginny's not wrong, the man is hot with a capital "H." He always has been, but she's right, he somehow got even hotter in the years since I left.

Ten years ago, I wouldn't let myself admit that I too was attracted to him. But now I'm a free woman. Free to enjoy the scenery, as it were. I'll never act on it, not now. Not when my goals are all within reach. And especially not now I have to work with him. Closely. *Intimately*. Make no mistake, real life at a hospital is nothing like *Grey's Anatomy*. We're not all hooking up in storage closets and making rash decisions that break all the rules and moral codes of healthcare. But there is an undeniable closeness that comes from working together to save someone's life. It bonds you in a way that nothing else does. Nurses feel it, and I would imagine doctors do, too.

As Dr. Donnelly's resident, I'll be his shadow for the next several months. Ideally, he'll start to give me more and more opportunities to practice independently, but he'll always be there watching.

That thought shouldn't make me shiver the way it does. The person in front of me asks a question, startling me back to the present moment just in time to hear everyone chuckle at Dr. Donnelly's response to whatever was asked.

Shit, somehow I missed the last few minutes of him talking, and now the other five residents in this rotation with me are dispersing. As a fourth-year resident, I'm technically in charge of our group. I'm the farthest along in the program, not to mention the oldest, even if I am a new transfer to the Vancouver Island residency program. And for me to have zoned out on the first day is not a good thing.

"Dr. Morgan, this way, please." I lift my eyes to see Dr. Donnelly staring at me with his mesmerizing blue eyes. His phone is in his hands, and he's spinning it around.

"Right, yes. Coming. You can call me Heidi still, if you prefer, I mean. Or Dr. Morgan. I don't mind."

Good God, Molly would roll her eyes so hard if she could hear me now.

"Stop being a people pleaser, Heidi. You earned that title, let the hunka hunka man meat call you doctor."

At sixteen, Molly was blunt and to the point. And somehow, I just know that Dr. Donnelly would meet all her requirements for that nickname, the one she reserved for what she called the hottest of the hot.

"Dr. Morgan." The snap of Dr. Donnelly's voice brings me back to reality, and I cringe, wondering how many times he's said it. Crap. *Get it together.*

"Sorry. Yes?"

He shakes his head. "I just said we can use first names when it's the two of us, but in front of patients or other staff, please remember to use professional titles."

His head tilts to the side as those eyes study me. I feel myself start to wilt under his penetrating gaze. Is he judging me, already? I got the feeling he wasn't all that pleased to hear I managed to get placement here, but I'm hoping Clarence at least explained that I didn't take someone else's spot. Yes, Dr. Patel put in a good word for me, but also, there was a last-minute change, not of my doing. *That* was the real reason I got the placement.

"Are you ready to start rounds or do you need another minute to finish daydreaming?" he barks, startling me with his harsh tone.

"I'm ready."

He steps to the side, leaving a large space between us as we take off down the hallway. "Then let's get started. I assume you reviewed your charts before your shift started?"

Thank God I did, because Dr. Donnelly doesn't seem like he's in a good mood — at all. Glancing at my patient list, I say with confidence, "First up is Roberto Alvarez, seven years old, post-op day one of internal fixation to a fractured tib-fib." We reach the patient room and I flip open the binder where the nurses keep track of things like vitals and medications the patient has had. "Looks like he was stable overnight, only needing PRN pain medications."

He nods sharply before walking into the room. And his entire demeanour shifts once again.

"Berto, my man. You ready to blow this popsicle stand?"

I stand back and watch as he does some complex high-five

routine with the little boy in the hospital bed, his casted leg propped up on pillows.

This is the man I remember. The one who connects with his patients in an instant, making them feel safe. I watch him chat with Roberto and his mom for a moment, who's sitting beside the bed, before he motions me closer.

"This is Dr. Morgan, and she's working with me for a little while. She's going to be the one getting everything ready for you to go home, okay? You'll have to come back in about six weeks to get that cast off, but you'll be fine. Just no more jumping from the top of the slide. Deal?" He winks at Roberto, then turns to the boy's mother. "We'll make sure you've got all your follow-up instructions before you leave."

The second we're out of the room, he starts firing directions at me. Luckily, my memory has always been sharp. "Put in a referral for physio to teach him how to use crutches; I'm not sure if they have stairs at home. Ask the unit clerk to book his follow-up down in the cast clinic, and with the nurses to go over signs of infection." His eyes flit to me and narrow. "Speaking of infection, you need to tie your hair up."

My mouth opens to respond, but he's gone, heading to the nursing station to no doubt scribble his orders in Roberto's chart. My hand drifts up to my head where a few strands of my hair have fallen loose from my braid. Not enough to be a problem, so the fact he brought it up irks me. He knows damn well I'm a stickler for infection control. Still, I tuck it behind my ear for now and hurry after him, deciding to take the high road and not push back about his rude attitude on day one.

The rest of the morning flies by in a flurry of checking up on patients, writing orders and chart notes, and two consults in the ER. Throughout it all, Dr. Donnelly — I can't bring myself to call him Max anymore — is brusque and sharp with me, but morphs into a different person around his patients and other staff members.

His Jekyll and Hyde routine confuses me so much that when he finally dismisses me to go and grab some lunch, I find Ginny.

"Hey doll, how goes it with hot doc?" Her cheerful voice hits me as I drop into a chair in her small office just off the nursing station.

"Did he always hate me, or is this new?" I reply dramatically.

"I don't think that man hates anybody," she chides gently. "He's probably just sorting out the different dynamic between you two, now that you're not a nurse anymore."

I consider that for a moment. "But why would that make him treat me any differently? I don't remember him being so harsh toward a resident before, but it's like nothing I do is going to make him happy." I don't mention the glare that was his parting shot to me ten years ago. I've never forgotten how chilling the expression was, or how confusing. One minute we were talking like normal people, the next, my ex-boyfriend showed up, and it was as if the energy was drained from the room, leaving only a void.

It doesn't take a rocket scientist to figure out there was bad blood between Thad and Max. But when I tried to ask Thad about it, he brushed me off.

A familiar occurrence back then.

Laughter filters in from the station, and I look out to see none other than Dr. Donnelly himself, smiling and laughing — with another doctor and their resident, one of my classmates.

"See?" I gesture subtly. "That's not the guy I've spent the day with. I haven't seen a single smile. Those are reserved for patients and anyone who isn't me, apparently. All I've received are frowns and scowls."

Ginny frowns lightly. "Well, shoot. I don't know what to tell you, honey. Maybe he just didn't want a resident and he's annoyed Clarence gave him one?"

"Well, he needs to get over that," I mumble. "I'm here to learn and finish my residency. Not put up with some jerk with an attitude problem." I finish my sandwich and stand up, stretching my arms overhead as I sneak another glance out at Dr. Donnelly. He's still standing there, smiling and talking, like he didn't just run me ragged all morning.

Ginny stands as well and moves to go back to the station. At the door, she pauses and looks back at me. "I'm sure he's just having an off day. Max Donnelly is a sweetheart. You just keep being you, and he'll warm up."

As I make my way over to the man I'm stuck with for the near future and watch his face transform from open and friendly to closed and aloof, I can't help but hope Ginny's right.

Because spending the next several months working with a man who clearly hates me is not exactly my idea of a good time.

CHAPTER THREE

Max

I lost count of the number of times I started to compose an email in my head to send Clarence Ross requesting Heidi Morgan be placed with a different attending. But it was a lot. He'd respect my concerns, I'm sure. There's an obvious conflict of interest, given who she's involved with and what he did twelve years ago.

But Clarence doesn't know that piece of my history. Truthfully, I've compartmentalized it. Pushed the memories of the weeks where we weren't sure how Dad would be into the deep dark recesses of my mind.

It's stayed hidden there, along with one other moment in time that defined me — and not in a good way. And I'm not thrilled about how her return to Westport General has blown the lid off that tightly sealed box.

I could go to Clarence and tell him the whole story. But my professional conscience is getting in my way, telling me to man up and be the bigger person. I can teach her. I can give her whatever respect she *earns* and avoid her the rest of the time. We don't need to get personal; I don't need to see her outside of the hours we spend together within these walls.

But the reality of the situation is unavoidable. In order to do my job to the standard I uphold, I have to spend the next several months with a daily reminder of one of the worst parts of my past.

"Bro, you coming inside?" Sawyer's fist thumps the hood of my car.

"Yeah, gimme a minute, would you?" I grump at him. He steps back and I get out, leaning in to grab the bottle of wine from the front seat.

"Mom's favourite?" he asks as we make our way up to the front door of our parents' house.

"Yup. Hoping she doesn't give me shit for missing the last two weeks."

Our parents host family dinner every week, and it's an open invitation to all five of us — six, if you count our cousin Leo who recently moved to Dogwood Cove. It's rare for us all to be available between mine and Sawyer's shift work, and the fact that our brother Jude plays for the NHL team in Montana and rarely gets to come home. But whenever I can make it, I always grab a bottle of Mom's favourite wine from a local winery, La Lune Rouge. One of the owners is friends with our cousin Leo's fiancée Serena. That's how it goes in small towns. Everyone knows everyone somehow.

"Nah, she'll be too busy pestering Hunter and Kat about their new place. Did you know she bought them a set of pots and pans, like good ones? Shit, when I moved into my apartment, I didn't even get a dish towel. I'm taking those pans when they break up."

"You'll touch my pans over my dead body," Kat says, walking up to us and taking the bottle from me and giving me a quick hug as she glowers at Sawyer. "And stop talking about my relationship ending. It's mean."

Sawyer just shrugs. "Don't say I didn't warn ya. Hunter's cool, but love is for fools." He saunters inside as Kat's eyes follow him for a second before turning to me. There's a small frown on her face. "Will he ever grow up?"

Our younger sister started dating one of the cops in town last Christmas. They had a rocky start, but it would take a blind man not to see how happy they make each other. Personally, I never had an issue with them, but Sawyer likes to take the overprotective brother role to the extreme.

I shake my head slowly. Sawyer has his reasons to be wary of love; hell, so do I. But that doesn't give us the right to be a jackass to our sister and her boyfriend. "Sorry Kat, I don't know what goes on in his head, nor do I want to."

She shudders lightly. "Yeah, that boy's head is a scary place." We both laugh. Out of all of us, Sawyer's the wildest. Spontaneous, reckless, immature at times, but for the most part, he comes from a good place. Except when it comes to Kat's love life. For whatever reason, he can't seem to accept the fact that she and Hunter are happy.

We make our way to the kitchen, where I find my mom stirring something at the stove that smells amazing.

"Hi honey, I'm glad you made it tonight."

I reach for a wine glass and open the bottle I brought, putting it on the counter beside her as I lean in and kiss the side of her head. "Yeah, shifts finally lined up. What's for dinner?" I try to sneak my finger in to taste, but Claire Donnelly raised five kids, and that makes her reflexes faster than anything. She smacks me away with her hand at the same time she picks up her wineglass and takes a drink.

"Fettucine alfredo," she says. "And it's almost ready, so get your mucky hands out of it."

Just then, the front door opens, and more voices fill the air. The telltale sound of little footsteps come running down the hallway, and a blur of purple barrels into the kitchen and latches itself onto my mom's legs.

"Hi there, Miss Vi," Mom croons, bending down to pick up my cousin's four-year-old daughter. "Oof, you're getting big. Auntie Claire won't be able to pick you up soon."

Violet, who's always been a quiet, serious little girl, places her hands on my mom's cheeks. "Dat's okay. I'll stop growing."

A chuckle escapes me, and Vi turns to me, granting me one of her rare smiles. "Hi, Unca Maxy."

"Hey kiddo, hate to break it to you, but not growing isn't an option."

"And he's your doctor, so he's the boss," Leo's deep voice chimes in. "Hey Aunt Claire, smells great in here."

He walks over and drops his hand on my shoulder. "Hey cuz, how's it goin'?"

I lift my shoulder in a shrug. "Can't complain. How 'bout you and Serena?" After moving to town last year to take over as the new deputy chief, Leo discovered his high school sweetheart Serena lived in town. They rekindled things and are happily engaged now.

Funny how Sawyer doesn't have a problem with *their* relationship, only Kat and Hunter's.

"All good man, all good." Leo's words match the smile on his face as he watches Serena come into the kitchen, greet my mom, and take Violet from her, setting her down so she can play with the toys Mom bought just for this reason.

"What are you two handsome boys talking about?" Serena asks as she walks up and nestles into Leo's arms.

"How happy I am," Leo whispers quietly into her ear, but I make out the words anyway. She tilts her head up to meet his and they kiss, which is my cue to go somewhere else.

Dinner is the usual loud and chaotic event. But after, once Leo and Serena take Violet home, and my siblings all leave, it's just me and my parents cleaning up.

"You don't have to stay," Mom says, like she always does, but I just move her aside and keep washing the dishes.

"My hands are wet, so I'm staying." We have this debate every time.

"Fine." Grabbing a towel, Mom starts drying and putting things away as my dad walks in from the garage.

"Max, did your mom mention we had a call from Morag Haynes the other day?" he asks, settling into a stool at the counter. "Hard to believe it's been twenty-seven years since Callum died."

"Oh yes, she called to thank us for the flowers we sent over. It was nice to catch up; we really should make more of an effort to connect. Have you talked to Quinn lately?"

My hands still in the soapy water at that name. Quinn Haynes. My best friend growing up, we were inseparable as kids. The two of us, and his older brother Callum. The truth is hard to admit, but I haven't talked to Quinn in a long time.

"Not in a while," I answer evasively. "How's Morag?" I keep my eyes on the sink of soapy water.

"As well as can be expected. Still grieving, but I suppose she always will. I can't imagine the pain of losing a child so young." Mom's head rests on my shoulder briefly and silence falls over the kitchen.

Callum's death is the reason I went into medicine. Because all those times visiting him in hospital, I was simultaneously in awe of what the doctors could do for him while being so angry they couldn't do more.

I didn't understand it back then, why they couldn't make him better. Now I know better. Now I know cystic fibrosis is a horrible disease that all too often beats any treatment protocol. It's the source of so much pain and frustration from both the medical community and the families affected by it.

When I get home that night, I find myself opening my phone and typing in Quinn's name. I haven't looked him up in years, and I don't know what I would say to him now.

Sorry I disappeared from your life, sorry your brother died, sorry there still isn't a cure for CF. Sorry I never got the chance to try and find a cure like I promised you and your brother I would. Sorry I fell for a woman who stole that opportunity from me.

Cara Andrews.

I flip my phone around in my hand a couple of times. Call it a stress response, or a nervous tick, all I know is that I only started needing to fidget with something after that day twelve years ago. I bet a therapist would have a field day with that.

Dropping my phone, I clench my hand closed and open it again. I repeat the motion a couple of times in a futile effort to clear the tangled web of angry memories. Quinn. Callum. Cara. Thad. Heidi. Five names for five people who shouldn't have anything to do with each other but are forever entwined in my memories.

One taught me that life is fragile and you can lose someone that matters to you in a heartbeat. One taught me that guilt and pain can destroy a friendship. One taught me to never trust a woman, or anyone, with my vulnerabilities. One taught me that the world is full of selfish assholes. And one taught me that beauty and kindness can be only skin deep.

Chapter Four

Heidi

My new approach for dealing with Dr. Max Donnelly is to let his grumpiness roll off my back and give him absolutely no reason to doubt my skills and professionalism.

Our first set together was miserable. He snapped at me over the smallest things, like when I got blood on my plain blue scrub top and I pulled out one of my old nursing ones that happened to have puppies on it. Apparently, that was unbecoming of a doctor, and he insisted I go ask one of my fellow residents if they had a spare set I could borrow.

He didn't seem to have any problem with the colourful scrubs the nurses were wearing, so either he's an elitist jerk or it's just me.

But today is the start of a new set of shifts, and I'm determined to change the way we work together. I'm not the same person I was ten years ago. I'm not weak, easily manipulated, or low on self-confidence. I'm a fully capable resident, almost a doctor in my own right. I did not come all this way, go through all the shit I went through with Thad, only to have another arrogant man push me right back down.

"Donuts anyone?" I proclaim, dropping the box on the counter of the nursing station. In an instant, two of my fellow residents and three of the nurses swoop in and take one each, giving me their grateful thanks. I don't see Dr. Donnelly anywhere, but I straighten my scrubs and check that my hair is pulled back all the same.

Choosing my favourite — the chocolate dipped with sprinkles, of course — I take a bite as I sit down at one of the computers to open an email that came through from my residency program adviser this morning. It's nothing important, but there is one thing that captures my attention. A fellowship opportunity with a leading cystic fibrosis research team. It's not something I'd seriously consider, not when pediatric surgery is my eventual goal, yet I read through the offer.

"Dr. Morgan, when you're ready, I'd like to begin rounds."

I quickly close the email and spin around on my chair to face Dr. Donnelly, who already has a deep frown on his face. He's flipping a pen over his fingers, in what I'm realizing is somewhat of a tell for him. "Ready." I stand up and gesture to the box where two donuts remain and with what I hope is a gracious smile. "I brought those in for everyone, if you'd like one. A bit of sugar is always a nice way to start the day."

The sound of derision and abrupt shake of his head shouldn't sting; it really shouldn't.

"Who's our first patient?"

Glancing down at my sheet and then up to the patient room we've stopped at, I reply, "Susanne Macintire. Twelve years old, came in with acute appendicitis. Post-op day one of a laparoscopic appendectomy, but she's had a fever overnight."

"Possible causes?"

"Surgical site infection, intra-abdominal abscess, peritonitis, or an ileus," I supply promptly.

"Correct. Let's go."

Grabbing a pair of gloves from the box outside of the patient's room, we enter. Susanne is small for her age, and she looks even smaller swallowed up by the bed. Her pale, clammy skin is the first obvious sign this little girl is not feeling well.

"Hey there, Susanne, I'm Dr. Donnelly. This is Dr. Morgan. We're going to be taking care of you as you get better from your surgery, okay?" His voice is gentle, quiet, soothing, and I can see the relief on Suanne's mother's face as she listens to him. "I'd like to take a look at your belly; the nurses said you had a rough night and you're not feeling so good. Is that right?"

The little girl nods, and her mom peels back the blanket. "Her fever wouldn't break, even with medicine. They warned us about infection, especially since her appendix was, what did they call it..." her voice trails off.

"Ruptured?" I supply, and she nods gratefully.

"Yes. Ruptured. We had no idea Suzie was even sick. She never complained of pain or anything until yesterday." Her hands twist together, and I reach over to supply a comforting touch.

"It's okay. Appendixes are tricky, they can have problems and not let us know until the very last minute. The important thing is that Susanne is here, and we're going to make her better."

When I look over at the bed, Dr. Donnelly is looking at me, and for once he isn't scowling. "Dr. Morgan, would you please come and take a look at this incision?"

I make my way over to stand beside him and give the scared

little girl a comforting smile. Her incision is very red, and the skin around it is tight and shiny with inflammation. But when I gently palpate her stomach around the area, she doesn't flinch, which is a good sign that it's only a surface level infection. Still, there's only one way to be sure.

We step away from the bed as Susanne's nurse comes in to give her some medication. Her mother comes over to stand by us, and after Dr. Donnelly nods at me to go ahead, I tell them my assessment.

"There are clear signs of a postoperative wound infection. A course of antibiotics would be my first step."

Dr. Donnelly nods. "Agreed. Let's do twenty-four hours of IV antibiotics and reassess." He straightens and starts to take off his gloves, but I'm not finished.

"Actually, I was also going to recommend an ultrasound along with antibiotics, to rule out any deeper sources of infection."

"Deeper sources?" Susanne's mom says, panic lacing her tone. "Like what? Did they leave something inside of her? I've seen those news stories."

"No, Mrs. Macintire, that is an incredibly rare situation," Dr. Donnelly says smoothly. "Susanne's surgeon has performed this procedure hundreds of times. A wound infection over the incision is the most common complication, and unfortunately, a reality of being in a hospital no matter how hard we work to prevent them. I'm confident a course of antibiotics will have Susanne feeling better in no time."

"But what about the ultrasound? Can we do that? What if Dr. Morgan is right and you're wrong, and there's something more going on?" She gestures toward the bed, her eyes watery. "She's my baby. I...I can't let anything happen to her. Please, do the tests. Make sure she's okay."

"Yes, Mrs. Macintire. We can do an ultrasound to be sure," he says, stuffing his hands in his pockets. "I'll put the order in with a rush on it, and in the meantime, we'll start the antibiotics." With a brief smile toward her, he turns on his heel and leaves the room. I murmur goodbye and hurry after him, ready to write the orders for Susanne and move on to the next patient.

"Don't you ever undermine me in front of a patient and their family like that again." His harsh voice is not exactly quiet as I come to an abrupt stop next to Dr. Donnelly just around the corner from Susanne's room. I can't help but notice the curious glances several nurses, staff, and even visitors are giving us. His anger is palpable, simmering between us like a pot of water about to boil over.

"When you do that, they doubt me. And when they doubt me, they shatter. And these families do *not* need to shatter."

I hate the fact that he's reaming me out in a semipublic spot. However, the fact that he's doing it not because of his ego, but because of his concern for his patient's comfort and trust in him makes me dial down my flare of defensiveness just a little.

But not entirely.

Folding my arms across my chest, I glare right back at him. "I had no intention of undermining your decision, Dr. Donnelly. I was simply trying to suggest a more thorough diagnosis to ensure we don't miss anything." I tilt my head to the side and force an accommodating smile, even though that's not how I'm feeling — at all. "In the future, how would you like me to provide my opinion?"

His eyes narrow. I'm being petty, I know. I should be a good little resident and apologize meekly. But I don't do that anymore.

He leans in closer, dropping his voice down to a menacing whisper. From this distance, I can see his eyes flare wide. "In the future, you'll provide your opinion when it is asked for. And you'll do it before I inform the patient and their family of our plan, not after."

Our gazes are locked. A rational part of my brain knows I was right to suggest the ultrasound. And I know that *he* knows it.

He just doesn't like that I'm the one who suggested it.

"Doctors," Ginny's firm voice interrupts us. "Might I suggest you take your *discussion* somewhere the other patients can't overhear?" Her casual statement is laden with meaning. My cheeks flame with embarrassment. The last thing I need is for my coworkers or other patients to hear me fighting with my attending in the first week. That doesn't bode well for my future here.

I open my mouth to apologize, even as it grates on me to do so when I honestly feel like I'm not the one who's out of line. But before I can say anything, Dr. Donnelly pivots and stalks over to the nursing station. He says something quietly to the clerk and she hands him a chart.

"You okay, honey?" Ginny asks, quieter now. "I didn't mean to get in the middle of anything, but it was getting a little heated."

I choke out a pained laugh. "Heated is one way to put it." She rests her hand on my shoulder for a second, then squeezes lightly before walking back to her office. I watch Dr. Donnelly for a minute longer. He smiles at the unit clerk, then turns and heads off down the hall.

This is what I don't understand. He's capable of being a reasonable, respectful human being.

So why is he so horrible to me?

Thankfully, Dr. Donnelly isn't on call for the entirety of my twenty-four-hour shift. After he goes home, I'm on my own, with only the on-call attending to refer to if I need anything. Who, interestingly enough, greets me warmly, says they've only heard good things about me from my former nursing colleagues, and is more than happy to discuss my thoughts on the new febrile seizure protocols.

Basically, my interactions with Dr. Rollins, who insists I call her Maura, prove that Dr. Donnelly has something against me and only me.

I toss and turn on the single bed in the on-call lounge, sleep evading me at 2 am, and it's all his fault. Because I can't stop obsessing about why he could possibly be angry with me. As far as I know, I've done nothing wrong in the few days we've worked together, and I know we never had an issue when I was a nurse.

But if he's the head of the pediatric department, then do I really want to work here?

As soon as that doubt creeps in, I bolt upright. "No. Hell, no," I mutter to myself, swinging my legs over the edge of the bed. There's no dang way I'm letting another *man* make me change my dreams, my goals, and my plans.

Been there, did that, didn't like it very much.

The island, this hospital, this area — I've wanted to be here my entire life. I have always envisioned myself settling down here, buying a house in the nearby town of Dogwood Cove, raising a family close to the ocean and the mountains.

I almost gave up on that dream when I was with Thad. I was blinded by his manipulations; I couldn't see how terrible of a person he really was. It took a lot of therapy to realize how toxic our relationship was, and even more to start believing again that I was worthy of having my own dreams and goals come true.

Being here is one of those goals. And I'm so close to reaching it and fulfilling the dream of having a life here.

And if Max Donnelly thinks he can force me back into the small, passive person I was, or scare me away from my dream, he's wrong.

So wrong.

CHAPTER FIVE

Max

My head is all screwed up right now, I'm constantly on edge around Heidi, and it's starting to affect my work. When I saw Heidi looking at a fellowship opportunity with the cystic fibrosis research program, I almost lost it. Hell, I *did* lose it.

Fucking Cara Andrews and her fucking study making news all over the fucking world.

Fuck her.

That should have been me. My name, my photo, my research.

What Cara did to me in our final semester of med school is a secret I've never told anyone. I found out she won the position on the research team by capitalizing on a secret I shared with her in a moment of vulnerability, less than an hour before the call came through about Dad's accident. Our family's fear and struggle overshadowed my own pain. As far as they know, Cara and I just broke up because we had drifted apart.

And even now, over a decade later, the one and only woman I've ever let close to me is still stealing from me. Only now she's stealing my sanity and my ability to be a fair and competent supervisor to my resident.

Yesterday was an embarrassment.

Heidi was 100 percent correct in her recommendations for Susanne Macintire. An ultrasound was the best way to definitively know the source of infection. And instead of praising her and encouraging her to take the lead, I yelled at her. I lost my temper in front of our colleagues and treated her like she was an idiot, simply because she questioned my judgment.

So yeah, I'm still angry at Cara, and at the same time, I'm frustrated with myself and my inability to let the past go.

I'm irrationally angry at the fact that Heidi is a competent doctor, and despite how I've been treating her, she's done nothing wrong.

I'm angry that she's friendly, and kind, and fucking beautiful. I'm angry that someone like her is with someone like him.

I'm so full of anger, I feel like I'm going to explode. Which is what brings me here, to the gym, late at night when I really should be sleeping. But Beckett agreed to meet me for a workout, so now I'm on the treadmill, trying to outrun my demons.

"Do I bother asking if you want to talk about it, or should I just let you run like the hellhounds are on your heels?" Beckett asks drily as he steps onto the machine next to me.

"Talk. Later." I pant out, my eyes laser focused in front of me, staring but unseeing.

Beckett starts to run at a much more reasonable pace than I am, and I try hard to lose myself in the repetitive motion. One foot in front of the other. I need to hit that nirvana where my brain shuts off and my body takes over.

That same state of mind I reach when I have really good sex.

Sex with Heidi Morgan would get me there.

Fuck. No.

I stumble and almost bail on the treadmill, grabbing the rails and lifting my feet just in time. I slam the stop button on the control panel and drop my head forward, my chest heaving.

"Max? You okay?" Beckett pauses his own run and turns to me. "Maybe I do need to force you to talk."

I step off the machine and sit down heavily. "I'm fucked, bro. And I can't talk about it. Not even with you."

My younger brother comes to sit beside me. "Can't or won't?"

"Can't."

Out of the corner of my eye, I see his head nod slowly. "Okay. I won't push. But can you at least tell me if you're gonna need lifesaving techniques or bail money? Not that I'm the hero in the family, but I can pull together some cash." He lets out a self-deprecating laugh, and I turn my head to look at him. It's not the first time he's made an offhand comment about himself in a negative comparison to the rest of us.

"Fuck being a hero, none of us are. Except Sawyer on a good day, I guess. But no. I don't need saving or bail money. Just need to get my head on straight." I look back down at my feet. "I'll be fine. I just gotta remember what's important to me."

My patients. My family. Nothing else. Nobody else.

Beckett's hand lands on my shoulder. "Okay. I'm here if anything changes. You know that, right? Don't pull an 'I'm the oldest so I need no one' stunt."

I grimace slightly but manage to give him a nod of acknowl-edgment. "Thanks, man." I don't say anything else. I can't. I'm not ready to unload and unpack all the shit in my head right now.

"Right. Then are we running, or do you want to lift?"

I stand up. "Actually, I think I need to head home. Early start tomorrow, you know?"

Beckett stands beside me, studying me from behind his glasses. "Alright. I'm going to run some more, but I'll talk to you later. Are you coming to Hastings this weekend?"

"Yeah. I'll be there." With a backward wave, I leave the gym. My mind is no clearer and no more settled than it was before. If anything, it's worse.

I wish I could say I found some self-control and figured out how to separate my anger over my past from the reality of my present. But that would be a lie.

I know it's bad when Clarence pulls me aside in the middle of a shift to question if I need some personal time after I snapped at a one of the physiotherapists for not seeing a patient immediately after I placed the order. I've never been that kind of doctor — the kind that lords over everyone else, wielding my authority like a blade. I'm a team player, and I have a deep respect for all the disciplines I work with and their individual workloads.

After the torture of this set of shifts, the last place I want to be right now is walking back into the hospital. I should be on my way to Hastings bar to meet up with my brothers instead. Jude's game is on tonight and we were going to eat wings, drink beer, and watch our brother kick ass on the ice.

But a panicked resident paged me because the attending on

call was busy and they needed help with a patient admitted with asthma exacerbation.

Needless to say, I'm not happy to be here. And that feeling intensifies when I walk onto the unit, heading straight to the patient's room, only to see Heidi come strutting out with a confident smile on her face that makes her so beautiful, I stumble. She might be beautiful, but she still reminds me of too many painful things to count.

"What are you doing here?" I bark, and she turns, surprise colouring her face.

"Mateo wasn't maintaining his oxygen saturation levels. Dr. Chang was worried and wanted a second opinion. Rodriguez is the on-call attending but he's caught up with a multi-trauma in the ER, so I offered to help."

"Shouldn't you be at home? Your shift ended hours ago."

I should be focused on the patient, not the woman in front of me, but all my frustration is bubbling over inside of me. And if Mateo was still in the woods, she wouldn't have left his room smiling.

Heidi folds her arms across her chest. "He's better, in case you're wondering, not out of the woods yet, but I think he's stable. I upped his Ventolin and switched to nebulizers, and he's now maintaining 94 percent with only one liter O2 in between."

Out of the corner of my eye, I see the other resident, Dr. Chang, approaching. He pushes his glasses up on his nose, and I can tell he's nervous. Probably because he can tell I'm not pleased.

"Dr. Donnelly, I'm the one who had you paged. I'm sorry, I

know you're not on call, but the instructions we have are to call you if the attending on call is not available. And I couldn't think of how to improve Mateo's numbers." He shifts back and forth on his feet, and I force myself to take a deep breath in and out. He's only a first year. He did exactly what he was instructed to do, and he doesn't deserve my piss-poor attitude.

"It's fine, Dr. Chang. You made the right decision calling me in. But apparently —" I look to Heidi "— someone beat me to it."

She lifts her chin defiantly, and I'll be damned if the fire in her eyes doesn't turn me on even as it pisses me off.

"What was I meant to do, not help a sick child when I knew I could?"

"And how did you *know* you could?" I ask sharply.

"I spent one of my rotations working at a pediatric asthma clinic," she retorts. "And the other night, I was watching a lecture series with Dr. Cara Andrews from the University of Vancouver's Cystic Fibrosis Research Program. It included a section on using nebulizers in specific circumstances. I know she was referring to cystic fibrosis patients, but the strategy seemed appropriate for Mateo as well."

God-fucking-damnit. Cara again.

"Next time, don't experiment on my patients with protocols that are not designed for their condition. You may have been lucky this time, but that's not an appropriate practice," I snap. "Let's see his latest numbers and make sure you haven't made things worse."

We turn as a group to the screen outside of Mateo's room that displays his continuously monitored vital signs. Sure enough, he's stable. As stable as a five-year-old with viral induced asthma can be. I look back at Dr. Chang, *not* Heidi. I don't want to see the triumphant look that I'm certain is on her face because her judgment call was correct — that Cara's fucking lecture was correct. "Monitor him all night. Keep the nebs going every four hours, don't try to wean off the oxygen until the morning. He and his family need sleep and they won't get it if his monitors are alarming every few minutes."

The other resident nods and then scurries away, leaving me alone with Heidi. She's still holding her defensive posture, and her eyes are still sparking with energy.

"You got lucky, Dr. Morgan. But I mean it. Don't ever assume that what works for one group of patients will automatically work for another, unless you have the data to back it up."

"I did." Her chin lifts. "Like I said, I spent a rotation at an asthma clinic. They still use nebulizers there. So when I thought of Dr. Andrews' strategy, I compared it to my experience at the clinic and made the call."

I grind my teeth at yet another mention of Cara's name. At this point, there's nothing else I can say. If I take her explanation at face value, she weighed her options and made a good call. "You never answered my other question. Why are you still here so long after your shift?"

Her eyes drop to the floor as her body tenses. I feel my own spine straighten in response, even as I wonder what the hell she's going to say.

"I was looking at job opportunities in other parts of the island."

That's not at all what I thought she would say. Frankly, I'm surprised douchebag Thad would be willing to move for her.

"Clarence made it clear you have a job here when you finish your residency. And our surgical program is top tier."

What the hell am I doing, trying to convince her to stay? My response baffles me.

"I'm weighing my options." Her chin lifts in defiance and a small part of me grudgingly admires her strength. Until her next words settle like a lead weight in my gut.

"The workplace environment is important to me, and I don't particularly want to start my career in a place I'm no longer wanted."

Well, shit.

"You're wanted here," I say, forcing the words out. It's only a partial falsehood. Everyone else wants her here; I'm the only idiot whose personal issues are clouding their judgment. She made the right call tonight, and she deserves to know it. "You did well tonight, Dr. Morgan."

She's good, I'll admit. I only see shock colour her face for a bare second before she schools her features into a haughty expression.

"Thank you."

I watch as she pivots on her heel and walks away. It leaves me with my gut churning, feeling like I'm digging myself a hole so deep, I may not be able to climb out of it.

Chapter Six

Heidi

I can't believe I said that to him. I can't believe I told Max that I was looking at other job opportunities because of *him*.

I slam the door to the residents' lounge shut and start pacing the small room.

I hate that he gets to me like that. I hate that he makes me feel like I need to defend myself when I *know* I did everything right. I hate that he's changed from the friendly doctor I knew into this utter jerk, but only with me. I hate that, yet again, a man is making me question my choices, making me want to change my plans to suit them. I swore I would never do that again.

But most of all, I hate how even with all of that, I've never been more attracted to a man.

He should have praised my quick thinking, more than just his meager acknowledgment at the end. Hell, I should be congratulating myself. My quick thinking saved Mateo. Instead, I'm bubbling with anger and confusion, all because of a stupid man.

Again.

"Hey, Heidi, I am so sorry you had to deal with that."

Ryan, the resident who had asked for my help, walks into the room. I didn't even hear the door open; I was so preoccupied. I wave him off as I go over to my locker. "It's fine, not your fault. He's just like that with me. The important thing is, we helped Mateo."

Ryan sits down on the bench, his back to me as I pull my scrub top over my head. Not that I care, I gave up any modesty back in med school, but I appreciate the thought.

"Yeah, I can't believe I didn't think about using a nebulizer. It's just not the protocol these days, so it never crossed my mind."

I sit down beside him. "Protocols are good and important. They're best practice. But that doesn't mean it's the only way."

"Why is Donnelly such a total prick to you, anyway?"

I stand up, not wanting to engage in the change of subject. But Ryan just keeps going.

"I was so excited to work here, you know? I'd heard he was awesome to work with, and even though he never took on his own resident, he'd let you shadow him. I heard he would let senior residents try all kinds of cool stuff. But I've only ever seen him be a total hard-ass to you."

"Maybe he didn't want a resident and got stuck with me, and that's why he's acting so mad." Even though I am positive that's not the case, and I can't believe I'm even bothering to defend him, I do. Because a part of me still remembers what Dr. Donnelly used to be like. "Who knows what's going on in his head, but he's still in charge, and we just have to deal with it."

Ryan looks at me with a mixture of admiration and pity. "I'm just glad he's not my attending. Was he like this when you were a nurse?"

"No, at least, not that I noticed." I sigh, sitting back down to pull on my shoes. "It doesn't matter. At the end of the day, he's a great doctor. He's respectful to the nurses and good with patients and families."

"Just not to you, huh?"

"Guess not."

When I finally get home, I strip off my clothes and step into the shower, thinking about Ryan's comment. If there was any question in my mind that Max's rude behaviour was directed solely at me, there isn't now.

It's embarrassing, really. If my fellow residents can see how unfairly he treats me, who else can? And what does that mean for my future?

I stay in the shower way too long, letting the heat soothe away some of the stress. But with my eyes closed, head upturned to the stream of water, a picture of Dr. Donnelly from tonight pops into my head unbidden.

He wasn't in scrubs, or even the dress pants and collared shirt he sometimes wears. Tonight, instead of the uptight doctor, I saw casual Max. Jeans that hugged his ass and muscular thighs, and a long-sleeved Henley that wrapped around his chest and arms perfectly.

He had the sleeves pushed up, and his strong forearms were far more appealing than they should have been. Even with how annoyed he was at me, there was no denying his attractiveness. The man oozes sex appeal; it really isn't fair.

My hand slips down between my legs, grazing my clit lightly. Shit. I can't do this.

I'm doing this.

Because if he can be that intense in his hatred of me, what would he be like if that passion was for a different reason? What if all his focus and energy was directed toward my pleasure?

I let out a moan as my fingers circle my entrance, dipping in and out shallowly.

I give in and let myself picture him in the shower with me. Towering over me, water dripping down the lines of his body. I can feel the heat of those beautiful cerulean eyes burrowing into me. My fingers speed up, alternating between light flicks to my clit and long thrusts inside. My other hand finds the wall, holding me up as I lose myself to the fantasy.

And when my orgasm hurtles toward me, fast and furious, it's Max's name I call out and hear echoing back to me.

Fighting back threads of embarrassment that I just came so hard to thoughts of my boss, I quickly finish up washing my hair and then get out, wrapping my hair in a towel and pulling on a fluffy robe. I walk out of my bedroom just in time for my phone to ring with an incoming video call from my mom.

I hit answer as I make my way to the kitchen to turn on the kettle for some chamomile tea.

"Hi baby girl!" My mom's large smile fills the screen.

"Hey, Mom," I reply, pulling down a mug. "How are you? How's Dad?"

"Oh, we're fine. Your father's been looking at Alaskan cruises he wants to take this summer. Can you believe it? The man who gets seasick wants to spend a week on a *cruise ship.*"

I chuckle, letting my mom fill the conversation with her endless chatter and updates as I putter around, making my tea.

Once I make it to the couch and sit down, however, Mom shifts the focus.

"So, how is it being back on the island without he-who-shall-not-be-named?"

I roll my eyes even as I smile. Mom always hated Thad. Guess that should have been the first of many red flags.

"It's great. This short-term rental in Westport is lovely, but I'm still toying with the idea of finding a place in Dogwood Cove."

"Oh, is that the cute little town we went to that had the delicious bakery?"

"Yeah, The Nutty Muffin. I wonder if it's still there," I muse, making plans in my head to go to Dogwood Cove on my next set of days off.

"How's work?" she asks innocently enough, but I feel my chest start to flush with heat as I remember what I just did moments ago in the shower.

"Fine. It's good. Yeah, fine."

Mom lifts one eyebrow, but thankfully, doesn't push me. Then again, with her next questions, I find myself wishing we were still talking about work.

"And have you met anyone nice? Gone out at all?"

My head falls back against the couch cushions. "No, Mom. I'm a little busy, you know, learning how to be a doctor and all."

"Heidi, don't be like that. You get days off, don't you? All I'm asking is if there's anyone around you might spend some of those days off with."

A vision of Max lounging at home on days off enters my mind. Only he's not alone in this mental picture. I'm there with him.

What. Is. Wrong. With. Me.

The only answer I have as to why on earth I'd be attracted to a man who treats me like garbage is because I remember the way he was before. When he was kind and respectful. The way he is with everyone else.

If that's not why I find myself still drawn to him, then I need therapy.

"See? You're blushing. Who is it? I knew you were holding out on me!" my mother crows triumphantly and I snap my head forward, shaking my head.

"Oh my God, no one. Mom, stop it. There's no one."

She lets out a small huff. "Fine. Deprive me of possible future grandchildren."

"Really?" I reply, smirking at her dramatics.

"I just want you to be happy. You deserve the best, my baby girl. I know he hurt you and broke your spirit, but you're a phoenix rising from the ashes. You're so much better than he ever made you believe you could be. The right man won't break you down. He'll build you up. I want you to find that. And you'll never find it if you don't at least try."

Well, crap. Now I can't even be annoyed at her anymore.

"I love you. I promise I'm not closing myself off to meeting someone, it just isn't a priority right now."

"It hasn't been a priority in how many years?"

Eight or nine, give or take, but who's counting.

"Like I said, I've been busy."

"I know, and I'm so proud of you, Heidi. Can I say just one more thing, and then I promise I'll stop?"

I nod, gesturing at her to go on.

"At the risk of sounding like my very traditional grandmother, you're not getting any younger, honey. You're in your thirties. I know how important having a family is to you, or at least, used to be. I don't want you to lose that opportunity because you're so busy trying to become the person you've always wanted to be and trying to make up for the years you spent with him."

Sometimes, being good friends with your mom and having her know all the dark and gritty details of your past heartbreaks isn't a good thing. Like when she peels back all the layers you thought were hiding your true desires and forces you to face the things you'd rather ignore.

After Mom and I hang up, I wander into the kitchen, thinking on what she said. Am I going to wake up one day, happy with my career but miserably alone? Grabbing a bottle of tequila out of the cupboard over my fridge, I pour a shot and throw it back. Then I go back to the couch, pick up my phone, and download the dating app I overheard some nurses talking about in the cafeteria earlier this week.

If "Left for Love" is good enough for its own CEO to find love, maybe it'll work for me.

But after I take the personality test and start swiping on the guys their program recommends for me, a pattern starts to emerge.

If they aren't dark and broody-looking, I'm not interested.

If they aren't doctors, I'm not interested.

If their name isn't Max, I'm not interested.

So basically, I'm swiping "no" on everyone because none of them are my very off-limits boss who seems to hate me.

Sorry Mom, my love life is over. Apparently, I'm more messed up than I realized when it comes to men. If the only person I can find attractive is the one that is not only off-limits but has also made it clear he wants nothing to do with me, then I'm truly screwed.

Life of a nun, here I come.

Chapter Seven

Max

"All I'm saying is, if one of you doesn't come with me the next time we hit Last Call for ladies night, I might have to disown you."

Sawyer's pout is so exaggerated, I roll my eyes as I sip my coffee. I came to town to spend the afternoon with my family. It's rare for more than one of us to have a day off together. Most of the time, evenings are the best we get. But today, Sawyer's off shift, Beckett had a short day, and even our cousin Leo agreed to join us for coffee from The Nutty Muffin.

"Sawyer, not everyone wants to be known as a man-whore," Leo says far more patiently than I would have.

My younger brother tries to look insulted but ends up looking even more ridiculous. "Man-whore? I prefer ladies' man. And what's wrong with seeking out a little good ole consensual fun?" He waves his hand at Leo, dismissing him. "You don't count now that you and Serena are attached at the hip, but these two —" he flings a dramatic finger at Beckett and me "— are single, virile men. It's an insult to women that they aren't out there bestowing them with attention."

"Do you even hear yourself?" I mutter. "Mom would fucking murder you in your sleep if she heard you."

"Hey. You know damn well, I don't cross any lines that shouldn't be crossed. I just like to get out and enjoy myself with company of the opposite sex."

"Rationalize it any way you want, bro, you're a player," Leo says matter-of-factly.

Sawyer pivots so he's walking backward, facing us. He focuses on his twin, which he should know by now is a lost cause. If any one of us is a true introvert, it's Beckett. "C'mon, Beck. Think of the hit we'd be with the ladies. Two hot guys for the price of one?"

Beckett blushes fiercely. I feel for him; he is the complete opposite in personality from his extroverted brother. At the same time, he's had over thirty years to get used to Sawyer's antics. "If you're suggesting a threesome, I decline."

Sawyer reels back in horror. "Dude. No. No way." He spins back around and falls in step beside us. "You guys are no fun. If Jude were here, I bet he'd go out."

The thought of our moody hockey player brother going out to ladies night at a bar has me snorting into my coffee.

By this point, we've circled around the town square of Dogwood Cove and reached the police station.

"Well, gentlemen, some of us have work to do." Leo slaps Sawyer on the back before giving Beckett and me a nod. "Good to see you guys."

We each wave goodbye, then carry on back around the square to where I parked in front of the bakery and café that our sister works at when she isn't studying to be a nurse practitioner.

Beckett agreed to go for a hike with me, but Sawyer has plans to hit the gym with a couple of other firefighters.

We're passing by Pages, the bookstore next to The Nutty Muffin, when the door opens and a distractingly familiar head of blonde hair comes out, buried in an open book, and crashes straight into my brother.

"Whoa there, darlin'. Eyes up." Sawyer's flirtatious teasing is innocent but something inside of me rears its ugly head at the sight of his hands steadying her by the shoulders.

"Sawyer, stop being an ass and get your hands off her," I rumble under my breath. Heidi's eyes dart over and widen when she sees me.

"Dr. Donnelly," she says flatly. "Hi."

I guess I deserve that type of greeting, seeing as the last time I saw her, I was giving her shit for doing her fucking job. Still, my hackles raise. She's the one infiltrating *my* town and ruining *my* day off. Not to mention, the proximity of her to anyone from my family has me seeing red. Thank fuck, it's highly unlikely for anyone to make the connection between her and Thad Marshall. Hell, I didn't even realize it until her going away thing at work ten years ago.

"You two know each other?" Sawyer interjects. Fuck. I really do not want him figuring out who Heidi is. Not that she works with me, and not that she's married to *him*. But before I can stop him, he's holding out his hand, his supposedly charming grin in full force. "Sawyer Donnelly. This bastard's younger, handsomer, *nicer* brother. And you are?"

"Sawyer," I growl out a warning, but he ignores me. And to my chagrin, so does Heidi.

"Heidi Morgan. I'm a resident over at Westport General." She shakes his hand, and gives him one of her warm, friendly smiles.

"Lovely to meet you, Heidi Morgan. A resident, you say. That's how you know our Max." He shifts his eyes to me, a knowing glint in them.

I'm fucked.

"Funny, Max was just telling us the other night about how impressed he is with the residents he works with. How professional and skilled they are."

Lies. Well, sort of. I do think that, but I wasn't telling *him* that. What the fuck is he doing?

Heidi's eyebrows lift ever so slightly as she casts a glance my way. I'm scowling, not at her, but at my brother. But the second she realizes it, I see her wince. "That's, well, that's nice to hear. The pediatric unit is a great place to work. I used to be a nurse there before I decided to go to med school."

"I'm sure Dr. Morgan doesn't have time to make small talk with you, Sawyer." I stare at my brother, trying to get him to understand my unsaid meaning.

"Actually, I do have time." Her voice is cold and brittle, and I instantly feel chagrined. "And since I'm not at work right now, I'm quite sure I can control what I do with that time, not you."

Sawyer looks at me like I'm nuts, and maybe I am. "Yeah bro, it's her day off. If she wants to get to know some new people, she can. And can't you call her Heidi when you aren't at work? Pull the stick out of your ass, man."

I haven't had this strong of an urge to punch my brother in years.

They carry on with whatever insignificant small talk or borderline flirtation is going on as my own inner turmoil starts to simmer.

I start to shift back and forth on my feet. Seeing her here, away from the hospital, is not something I was prepared for. Through furtive glances, I take in her appearance. And the fact her hair isn't tied back but is cascading down her back, and the leggings and off the shoulder T-shirt she's wearing, only heightens my discomfort.

Because goddamnit, she's beautiful. And I hate myself for thinking that.

My discomfort is not going unnoticed. Beckett is eyeing me curiously, and I know he's trying to figure out the reason for my moody silence.

"Sawyer, didn't you tell us you were meeting the guys at the gym now?" Beckett interrupts. I hide my reaction, a combination of relief and regret.

Sawyer flashes Heidi another giant smile. "Yeah, gotta keep in top shape so I can rescue the fair maidens." He gives her a wink, and I cover my snort of derision. But Heidi doesn't hold back the same way.

"Let me tell you a secret. Those *fair maidens* won't be interested in your muscles if you call them fair maidens. This isn't Camelot, and you're not a knight in shining armour."

To his credit, Sawyer doesn't take offense. He throws his head back and laughs. "I like you, Heidi Morgan. You'll keep old man Max on his toes."

My glower deepens at Sawyer's use of that stupid nickname. "That's enough, Sawyer, let's go," I say gruffly. I incline my head to Heidi, without meeting her eyes. "Enjoy your day Dr. Morgan."

I make my way to my car, hoping my damn brothers will follow. I hear Beckett murmur his goodbye and Sawyer's more enthusiastic one, then they're beside me.

"What the flying fuck was that?" Sawyer demands. "First of all, why didn't you tell us you worked with total hotties? Second of all, why are you being an asshole to her?"

I glare back at him. "Don't call my resident a hottie. Or any woman, for that matter. You're being borderline misogynistic with comments like that, degrading them to nothing more than their looks."

Sawyer has the decency to look ashamed. "Sorry, man."

"I'm not the one you should be apologizing to — that would be women everywhere." I open my car door and gesture at Beckett. "You ready to go?"

He nods, then turns to his twin. "Max is right. You need to tone down the bonehead comments, bro. Show some respect."

Sawyer's eyes are downcast. "Yeah. Right. I get it." He looks up. "But are we gonna talk about why Max has a hate-on for his resident?"

"No. We're not." I get in my car and slam the door shut. Beckett slides in a moment later, and I peel away from the curb, heading out of town to the hiking trails.

After a few moments of terse silence, Beckett speaks. "I know Sawyer was the bigger issue, but he's not wrong that something was off with you. He wasn't the only one being inappropriate with Heidi. I won't push, but I'm always willing to listen."

I let out a low sigh. "I know. I just don't even know what to say about it, at least not yet."

"Okay. You'll make the right call. Just trust yourself."

Wise words from my younger brother. Too bad they're not so easy to live up to.

Because the right call would be following through on reassigning Heidi to someone else. Someone who isn't automatically biased against her simply because of who she's involved with. And as the days go by, I'm questioning why the hell I'm not doing just that.

CHAPTER EIGHT

Heidi

The universe hates me. That's got to be the only answer as to why I'd run into Max on my day off, my one day away from his glares and scowls.

And for him to have not one but *two* equally attractive brothers, one of whom is every bit as flirtatious and charming as Max is abrasive and rude?

Not. Fair.

On behalf of women everywhere, I curse the Donnelly genes for producing drool-worthy men but shortchanging them in the personality department.

At least the third brother stayed quiet. He wasn't a cocky player like Sawyer, or a mean grump like Max. I guess he's their redemption.

When I get back to my apartment after my trip to Dogwood Cove, I make a cup of tea and curl up on the couch with the book I picked up at the cute little bookstore, run by a woman named Paige and ironically called Pages. It's an autobiography I've been wanting to read for a while but never had the chance.

Yet, no matter how many times I reread the introduction, I

can't get my mind to focus on the words. I keep drifting back to those tense few moments on the sidewalk in the adorable small town I've dreamed of living in someday. Where Max Fucking Donnelly poured salt on the wound that has been my self-esteem ever since we started working together — by showing his disdain for me is not limited to the hospital.

Thad hurt me deeply. There's no question. But Max hating me for no apparent reason is painful in a different way.

I wish I knew what the heck I did to earn his disapproval. The Max I remember from years ago was respectful, kind, and friendly, even. Heck, although I didn't let myself think about it, seeing as I was with Thad, he used to be charming, and I've always been attracted to him physically. We never had an issue — until the day of my going away luncheon, when he met Thad. I know that's what turned him against me, but I don't know why he's still holding it against me all these years later.

It's that very question I moan into my wine glass hours later when my best friend from Vancouver finally arrives.

Skye is here for a work trip, and I'm so glad she managed to extend it by a day to spend some time with me. As much as I feel so good about my move back to the island, I miss my friends and some aspects of living in a larger city.

"Does he know you and Thad aren't together anymore?"

I consider her question for a brief moment. It had never occurred to me that he might not. Anyone who knew me before now knew in an instant that something was different. Ginny and I had stayed in touch over the years while I was gone, so she knew the day after I ended it with Thad. I guess I assumed everyone knew.

"I suppose that's possible. But still, just because he had a hate-on for Thad doesn't explain why he has one for me."

"It's obvious, Heids. He's obsessed with you."

When I first confessed to Skye that my boss was treating me like garbage, she instantly asked what he looked like. I guess my telltale blush gave it away because she managed to get me to confess his attractiveness, and we looked him up on the hospital staff directory. After that, she refused to hear any of my complaints.

"He's not obsessed with me, Skye. He hates me."

"Girl, there's a fine line between love and hate. You make him want things. Things he probably shouldn't want and doesn't *want* to want. All I'm saying is, there must be more to his story than what he's showing you. You're not exactly the kind of person to inspire hatred."

"That's absolutely ridiculous. I'm telling you right now, the man is not attracted to me, he hates me. I just want to know what I did to deserve that."

"Thad was an asshole. You know it now, maybe this guy knew it back then. I'm not saying it was fair for him to judge you based only on who you were with, or that it's right for him to continue giving you crap when you aren't even with douchebag Thad, but guys are idiots, after all."

"Stop making sense." I take a sip of my wine, giving her a wink that says I appreciate her logic. It's true, Skye is seeing things differently and that's helpful, if I'm honest with myself.

"Okay, or maybe he's one of those guys whose own code won't let him mix business with pleasure. And maybe you're the first woman to ever tempt him to break his own code, and that's what is making him angry. He's pushing you away because he hates himself for wanting you. Oh my God, but then, one day his restraint will snap, and he's gonna fuck you in the storage room. This has forbidden romance written all over it."

That's a mental image I won't soon forget. Forcing myself not to dwell on it, I pick up the half-empty bottle of La Lune Rouge Viognier, lean over, and refill Skye's wine glass. "You've been reading way too many romance novels, my friend. That kind of thing doesn't happen in real life."

Skye actually pouts. "You're no fun."

My eyes roll up. "Sorry if my idea of fun doesn't include sexual relations with my jerk of a boss."

"I dunno, I hear hate sex is hot."

"For the last time, he isn't attracted to me," I say, exasperated that she won't let this go.

"We might be in our thirties, but most men still act as if we're on a school playground. 'Pull her pigtails if you like her' kind of bullshit. All I'm saying is, maybe he's one of those twat-waffles who doesn't understand doing that was basically harassment. Maybe he needs *you* to whip him into shape."

I snort-laugh at her insane thought process as I shake my head, my hands plucking at the fringe on the throw pillow I'm holding. "That's not it. He gave his brother shit earlier for being too flirtatious with me. He's not a pigtail pulling kind of guy."

Setting down her glass, Skye throws her hands up in the air. "Well, fine. I have no freaking clue why he's being an idiot. You're a catch. A total hottie, a badass nurse turned incredible doctor, and there is zero reason for him to hate you."

"Thanks, I think," I say drily.

"You're welcome. So, it's settled then. He wants you but doesn't want to want you. So he's pushing you away by being mean. I'm thinking you go on the offense and start dressing a little bit sexier, start leaning in closer, push him over the line so he can't hold back."

"You're drunk if you really think I would ever do that." I toss the pillow at Skye, narrowly missing the wine glass. "Can we please talk about anything other than Max Donnelly?"

"Fine," Skye huffs. "But when you text me and tell me you just boned him in a storage room, I get to say I told you so."

"Not gonna happen."

I take a long sip of my wine.

"Mark my words, someday it will." Skye lifts her glass to me. "Because, as previously stated, you're a hottie and a badass."

I lift my glass and clink it with hers. "Thank you."

"So, what are the chances of finding somewhere for a pedicure tomorrow? Oh, and then you have to take me to Dogwood Cove. I want to visit this café I saw in a travel blog; Camille's, I think it's called?"

"Deal," I reply softly. I needed this, some time with my best friend, away from the pressures of the hospital — and Max.

Skye and I have been friends ever since high school, when she moved in down the street from my family, and we ended up as lab partners in chemistry. She hated science, so I offered to help, and we bonded that weekend over study notes and brownies. We've been there for each other through boyfriends and bad haircuts, prom nights and sneaking into bars underage. She supported me moving to the island years ago, helping me pick out an apartment and everything. When Thad and I started dating, she told me she wasn't sure about him. It was the one time I didn't listen to her opinion.

That was a mistake.

When Thad and I broke up, she had every opportunity to say I told you so. Instead, she offered to let me move in with her and helped me get my life figured out. I owe her more than I could ever repay. So, if she wants pedicures and lunch in Dogwood Cove tomorrow, that's what she gets.

I just hope to hell and back we don't run into those damn Donnelly boys again.

CHAPTER NINE

Heidi

It's been a week since I ran into Max and his brothers. An exhausting and confusing week. Every shift with Max Donnelly is a rollercoaster, except I'm riding it blindfolded. I have no idea what to expect, especially after I caught him looking at me yesterday with something in his eyes that was very much *not* hatred.

The intensity behind the heated way his gaze swept up and down my body made me gasp. And then that heat melted back into the contempt I'm used to.

Sleep did not come easily last night. I tossed and turned, visions of Max filling my head with fantasies I have no right having.

Waking up this morning, I'm determined to call him out on his bullshit. Part of me wants to do exactly that because I know I have every right to wonder why he's being this way. But there's still a voice inside my head telling me not to, that I should keep my head down and just do my job.

Then there's the part of me that wonders what his domineering attitude toward me would be like in bed. Would he be dirty and a little rough? Or would that controlling personality be more sexy alpha?

I'm pretty sure option C, both, is the correct answer. And apparently, my body thinks so, too, and really wants to find out. It's actually kind of inconvenient how my body responds to him, even when he's being an arrogant ass. I never thought of myself as someone who could still be turned on when the man in question is so hot and cold.

But there's no denying the shiver that runs up my spine when he leans in close and his light earthy scent hits me. It's not overpowering at all, but it is intoxicating.

"Caroline, can you please print out a medication record for room twelve so I can finish their transfer orders?" He leans against the counter, giving the unit clerk a charming smile.

I twist in my seat to face him. "I already did that as part of his discharge package."

He spares me the briefest of glances before looking back to Caroline. "And let's make sure his most recent set of lab work is included."

"Also already printed and in the envelope," I say, that drive to call him out growing stronger and stronger. How dare he act as if I don't even exist? This is a new low.

Slowly, he shifts and faces me. "Is that part of your duties as a resident?"

Oh boy, here we go. I put down my pen. "No, but I spent many years as a nurse watching the doctors on this floor work *with* the nursing staff as a collaborative team. In fact, I'm fairly certain I've seen you print out your own discharge package when nurses were short-staffed. I figured it was safe to do the same, seeing as you're meant to be my mentor of sorts."

"Fine. The important thing is that it's done."

I open my mouth, fully prepared to let him have it, to demand respect and gratitude for pulling my weight and then some, when the code bells start going off. One of our patients is crashing and all thoughts of snapping back at my arrogant boss are gone as we move into action.

When we reach the room, the nurse who called the code is leaning over the patient, her stethoscope in her ears. "Shallow breath sounds on both sides and he's tachycardic. His labs are pending."

I take a quick glance at the chart and realize it's a new patient to the unit, here with a chest infection, but he's also an oncology patient. Which makes things tricky.

"His platelet count was low on admission; we're probably looking at a chemotherapy-induced cytopenia which is exacerbating the infection."

Max gives me a nod. "Let's page his oncology team stat." A nurse runs off to do that as Max and I continue a rapid assessment. "Okay, his PICC line is blocked, we need access. Let's get an IV going so we can keep him hydrated and start some platelets. I assume we have his blood type on file?"

"Yes, Dr. Donnelly. I'll call the blood bank." Another nurse runs out as I hand over the tray with an open IV insertion kit. Taking it, Max bends over the patient's arm, but after a couple of minutes poking around, I can sense him getting more and more agitated. The stress in the room is already high and climbing.

"His veins are shot. This is a hard start, I'm gonna need a vein finder."

But that'll take more time that this kid doesn't have. "Let me try," I say, hip checking him out of the way. He steps away, but I know I'll have to accept the repercussions later. Right now, it's the patient that matters the most.

I manage to find a vein and get the IV in just as another nurse runs in with the vein finder.

"Start the saline, full bore, and get the blood going," Max says, and one of the nurses lifts the saline bag onto the IV pole and starts the drip. "Good. Okay, let's call PICU and get him set for a transfer, he's going to need close observation for a while."

I stay back as Max leaves the room, watching as the nurses get the blood hooked up and running, and do one more set of vitals just to satisfy myself that he's stabilized.

Walking out of the room, a scan of the nurse's station doesn't reveal Max. I make my way to an open space at the desk and sit down with the patient's chart, so I can make sure our notes are up-to-date before the transfer.

But just as I'm closing the chart, Ginny sits down next to me.

"We need Dr. Donnelly to do handover with the PICU team," she says quietly. "Do you know where he is?"

"No, I'll find him, though," I say, rising from my chair and looking around the unit. I make my way down the hall that leads to the overflow storage area, and that's when I see him. He's leaning against the wall in a small alcove that normally holds a photocopy machine but is currently empty. His eyes are closed, but there's a furrow to his brow and a tightness in his jaw.

"Dr. Donnelly," I say softly, and his eyes fly open. And in that split second, I see a flash of something. Fear? Worry? Angst? Guilt? I don't know what it is, but it's gone in an instant.

"Yes?" he says stiffly.

I step closer. The tension is still radiating from him, and my hand starts to lift, but I drop it quickly. What am I doing? He won't accept comfort from me.

"The pediatric ICU team needs a handover call for the patient we just transferred."

"Right," he sighs. "Okay."

He moves to walk past, and this time, I do put a hand on his arm to stop him. "We stabilized him. He's going to be okay."

He snorts quietly. "You of all people know we can't guarantee that. We see it every day. Kids whose bodies just give out on them. The only reason he's still with us is a combination of miracle and medicine."

"Right, and you gave him the medicine," I say, hoping to soothe him somehow. He's wound tighter than a drum, and I realize it's the first time I've ever seen him show a sliver of vulnerability. Approaching carefully, as one would a wounded animal, I opt for humour to lighten the mood. "Well, I guess technically, I did, since I'm the one who got the IV in. Takes a nurse to do the hard stuff, I guess."

Clearly, that was the wrong thing to say. His eyes darken with what looks dangerously close to rage. "You're not a nurse anymore, Dr. Morgan."

The way he says my name, laced with derision, makes me wince and my hand drops from his arm. He's lashing out, and yet again, I'm getting the brunt of his anger. I don't know why, but this man cannot handle letting anyone see weakness in him, least of all, me.

But too freaking bad. Because I am not someone else's

punching bag anymore. And I made a promise to myself that I never would be again. He takes another step to walk past me as I speak, not bothering to disguise the sharpness of my tone.

"You're right, I'm not. But I still have all those skills and years of experience, and it wouldn't hurt you to remember that. Lord knows, you seemed to respect me more when I was a nurse."

I'm fully prepared to do battle. He's going to let me have it, I know it.

But then the frustration of the last several weeks bubbles up and out of my mouth before I can stop myself.

"Tell me, Dr. Donnelly, why the heck have you treated me like garbage since the day I returned? Correction, worse than garbage. Like the gum that you step in and can't wait to scrape off your shoe. What the hell did I ever do to you? Is it because of my ex? Good God, if Skye was right and this is all because of Thad, I'm going to scream. Why are —"

"What do you mean 'ex?'" His sharp voice interrupts my rant. When I look up, he's staring at me with such intensity, if I weren't already fired up, I might shiver.

"Thad Marshall. You met him my last day here as a nurse."

"I know who fucking Thad Marshall is," he bites out. "Why did you say 'ex?'"

I lift my chin. "Why does that matter? You're my supervisor. Who I date shouldn't matter."

He gestures to my hand. "Don't you mean who you marry?"

I look down at the ring my grandmother gave me years ago, then back to him in confusion. "This? This was my grandmother's wedding band. I wear it on this hand to remind myself that my first commitment is to me, not to a man." His eyes widen with something that looks suspiciously like respect. I put my hands on my hips, unwilling to bend until he explains himself. "But you don't deserve to know any more than that. So, I'll ask again, why does it matter if I'm with Thad anymore?"

He steps closer. So close, I can see the flecks of green in his blue eyes. And the storm of emotions brewing in them. "Thad Marshall destroyed my family twelve years ago. And you were with him when it happened."

My jaw drops open. "What the hell are you talking about?"

Max steps back and rakes a hand through his hair as he pivots and moves a few steps away. "Twelve years ago. You were with Thad, weren't you?" He whirls back to me. "That's what you said. That day you were leaving. You said you were with him."

There's a desperation lacing his words. Does he want me to confirm what he's saying or challenge it?

"Yes, I started dating Thad twelve years ago." I lean back against the wall, attempting to look relaxed instead of radiating the tension building inside of me.

Max starts to pace, only a few steps in each direction, thanks to the small alcove we're in.

"Twelve years ago, Thad Marshall got behind the wheel drunk and crashed his car into my father's. Landed him in hospital with a brain bleed, multiple fractures to his leg, and a ruptured spleen. He was in the ICU for two weeks, hospital for another two weeks, and then rehab for a month."

My heart starts to pound so loudly, it's as if I can hear it. Can he? I remember this incident, but not the way he's saying it.

"Any decent person would show remorse, right? Take responsibility for almost killing a man? But not your Thad." Max snorts with derision. I want to interrupt and tell him he's not *my Thad,* but this isn't the time. "He lawyered right up and managed to skate by on a technicality. A fucking *technicality* while my father faces lifelong repercussions of Thad's decision to drive drunk. And you were with him through it all."

"Hold on. What the hell do you mean I was with him?" I interrupt. "I can assure you; I was not. I remember Thad telling me he'd been in an accident a few months *before* we even started dating, only because I asked about a scar on his arm."

I stop and think back to the early days of my relationship with Thad. How he often had meetings and phone calls that he didn't want to talk about. How he insisted I be the designated driver if we went out with friends. He said he wanted to be safe and blamed it on a low alcohol tolerance. But what if it was more like a license suspension — or worse? I don't want to admit to the possibility I was so blind I didn't know there was more to his story about hitting a pole from being too tired. But then again, I was so naive, so stupid when it came to Thad. I was so charmed by his good looks and sweet words, I didn't realize I'd been in a controlling, borderline emotionally-abusive relationship for years until I'd almost lost everything that mattered to me.

With startling clarity, I realize Max's story must be the truth. It explains his visceral reaction to seeing Thad the day of my going away luncheon. And if he assumed I knew about the accident, then of course, his pain and anger spread to include me, given his mistaken belief that I was a part of it all. I can even understand his confusion over my grandmother's ring. God, he must have thought me being married to Thad and being back in town meant Thad was back as well. No wonder he spiraled.

I don't like it, but I can understand it.

"Max, I can assure you, I had no idea about the circumstances of the accident. I know that makes me sound naive, or oblivious, but I truly didn't. Thad —" I pause and suck in a deep breath "— Thad was really good at fooling me. He was a master manipulator and knew exactly what to say and do to make me blindly follow his lead. I'm not proud of how long I was with him, or how long it took for me to fully recognize how toxic things were with him. I don't doubt for a second that he pulled that kind of move and got out of taking responsibility for the accident."

This is where I get stuck. I suspect Max wants me to apologize, but for what? How can I possibly apologize for something I had no idea even happened, much less had any involvement?

But this feels like the opportunity for Max and me to start over with a clean slate. With no more demons or baggage between us. And part of that is acknowledging not just my own pain and frustration but his as well.

"I'm sorry your family went through that. I'm sorry your father was injured, and that you all had to deal with the stress and anguish we see families fighting every day. But..." I choose my next words carefully. "Any regret I have over my relationship with Thad is for me and me alone. I can't apologize for being with him ten years ago, or even twelve years ago after the accident happened. I had nothing to do with any of that. Me being with Thad had nothing to do with what he did to your family. I hope you can see that." I suck in a deep breath. "And stop giving me shit for something that was not about me in the first place."

The bustling sounds and activity of the hospital carry on

around us, but it's as if time has suspended right here in this corner of the hallway. Max is staring at the ground, giving me no read on his reaction to everything I've just said. Internally, I start to squirm. Part of me wants to keep going, to apologize more profusely, to try and fix something that I never broke in the first place. The old Heidi, the one that let Thad pull the wool over her eyes, probably would do just that. But not anymore.

I've owned my piece, now to see if Max can own his. I let my eyes shut as I take several deep, calming breaths. No matter what he says or does after today, I've done what I can to fill the void between us. I've explained my truth.

"Heidi, I'm sorry," he says it so quietly, I almost miss it. But when I open my eyes, he's looking at me, and the haze of anger and criticism with which he normally looks at me has lifted. There's clarity and remorse there instead. "I misjudged you." He shakes his head, his brow furrowing. "No, that's not right. I didn't misjudge you. I made an assumption based on nothing but my own rage. And worse, I let that assumption affect my role as a physician and as a mentor. I have been unfair to you since the day you started, for a completely untrue reason, and I'm sorry. You deserve better, and if you want to go to Clarence and request a different supervisor, I would support you in that."

This moment feels pivotal. As if I'm on a tightrope and what I say will determine my future in more ways than one. The air between us is vibrating with indescribable emotions and energy. Whatever anger I held toward him dissipated the moment he explained himself. As Skye would say, men are idiots. This is a supreme idiot moment for Max, but I wouldn't be who I am if I didn't admit I understood where he was coming from. He screwed up, and he's owning it. The least I can do is give him a second chance. Now that he knows the truth and has acknowledged the errors in his judgment, I know Max will respect me, not just as a doctor, but as a person. I could rage about the injustice of needing to explain myself the way I did, I could hold onto a self-righteous anger that he misjudged me in the first place, but that won't accomplish anything.

"I don't want a different supervisor. I want the head of the department. I want the doctor who can help me become the best doctor I can. I can let go of whatever misunderstandings we had if you can. I just want you to see me as the capable resident I am."

I hold my breath, waiting to see how he'll respond. When he does, those deep blue eyes are staring straight at me, wide open, transparent, and full of honesty. We've laid bare our wounds, our barriers, anything that was between us. And what he says next proves that.

"I do see you. I see all of you."

Chapter Ten

Max

A few weeks ago, I would have gladly passed off responsibility for Heidi's residency to someone else. But that was before she said she didn't want anyone else.

She wants me.

Even after I was reprehensible in my treatment of her, and even after finding out why — the truth being that I misjudged her entirely — she still wants to work with me.

Professionally, I'm flattered. Personally, I'm humbled.

Her grace and forgiveness are astounding. I'm not entirely sure I could be the same way were the roles reversed. Could I forgive someone so quickly for treating me like shit, simply because of an assumption they made about me and my personal life?

When I break down the tangled mess that existed between us to that simple explanation, it's embarrassing. I pride myself on having a sound mind and an ability to judge a situation fairly, yet I did the exact opposite of that with Heidi.

I've had all of yesterday away from the hospital to process our conversation and untangle my feelings when it comes to Heidi.

And while clarity has been reached in so many ways, a new layer of complication has been added.

Because now that I know the truth, that she had nothing to do with Thad and what he did to my family, I'm forced to face another uncomfortable realization.

Heidi is beautiful, just as beautiful as always. She has a girl-next-door softness that belies her inner strength. And now that her beauty is no longer tainted by my incorrect assumptions about her, my thoughts about her have gone down an entirely different path. An entirely inappropriate path, given my role as her supervisor.

But that's a worry for another day. Today is my second to last day off before I have to return to the hospital, and I just want to be outside.

Beckett and Sawyer were meant to join me for the hike to the hot springs just outside of Dogwood Cove, but Sawyer picked up an extra shift last minute, and Beckett is down with one of his migraines. Which leaves me alone on the trail with nothing but my thoughts to keep me company.

Naturally, those thoughts keep drifting back to one particular woman. I can't help but wonder what she's doing on her days off, if she's gone out with anyone, or how she's spent her time.

And that is exactly why I should be texting the lawyer from Victoria that I occasionally meet up with for some casual, meaningless, mutually satisfying sex and setting something up for tonight. Clearly, I'm not thinking straight if I'm wondering what my resident is doing on her day off. It's been too long since I got laid, and the only answer is to hook up with someone who is *not* Heidi. But every time I've picked up my phone to send the message, I've stopped — for reasons I'm not sure I'm ready to explore.

After all, the last time I got involved with someone tied to my work, it ended in betrayal. There's not a chance in hell I want to risk that again, especially not with the added complexities of my working relationship with Heidi.

Breathing deeply, I focus on the inhale and exhale, feeling the slight strain in my lungs at the uphill nature of the trail I chose to take. It's not the most direct path to my destination, but it's the more scenic route, and the one that gives me the physical exercise I'm craving.

The hot springs carved into the rocks nestled in the mountains just outside of Dogwood Cove are one of those natural wonders. As a local, I simultaneously want everyone to experience it and no one to ruin it. Today, especially, I'm hoping for peace and quiet.

There's a series of pools, the first one being the largest and most popular, with natural benches carved into the stone, and a shallow entry point. This is the one the public knows about. Today being a workday for most, it's empty except for one older couple, who give me a nod as I walk past. I'm not stopping here; my destination is further down the trail.

I turn off the trail onto a path that's hidden enough so not as many people know about it. When I reach the small pool tucked in the trees that I was headed for, I exhale. Nature has this uncanny ability to lift the tension from my body, sometimes without me even realizing it. And sure enough, after an hour of hiking, and now being surrounded by trees and the sound of bubbling water, I finally feel my head clearing of the chaos that has been in there lately.

I open my backpack and pull out my towel and water bottle, then start rummaging for the swim shorts I packed. But they're nowhere to be found.

That leaves me with two options. Wear my boxer briefs into the springs and hike down commando with all the fun chafing that will bring or forego clothing completely for a soak in the warm water. Given the fact that I'm reasonably confident the trail will stay empty and that this pool, hidden as it is, should be undisturbed, the decision is an easy one.

I strip down, leaving my T-shirt, shorts, and underwear in a heap beside my pack. Then I slide into the hot, lightly sulphuric-scented water. This pool doesn't have the natural benches of the larger one, but there is one spot where a rock juts out enough to make a seat. So, after dunking myself under a couple of times, I go and sit, letting my surroundings put me into an almost meditative state.

Some time later — who knows how long, but the air has definitely cooled around me — I stand up and stretch, feeling the bones and muscles of my back pop and crack with the movement.

"Oh, I'm sorry, I didn't mean to disturb you."

I whip around at the sound of the one voice I'm trying hard not to think about. Only at the last second do I remember my naked state and drop down low enough to make sure I'm covered by the water.

"Heidi."

"Max," she says, her breath catching in surprise, whether it's at finding me here, or hearing me say her first name. I must admit, hearing my name come out of her mouth, especially in that tone, is making my dick stir. Thank fuck it's under water. "I didn't know... you... I... oh. Okay. Wow. Sorry." She's adorably flustered, and if I weren't in such a compromising position, I'd probably find it even more endearing. But instead, all I can do is pray inside my head.

Please don't decide to get in the water. Please don't decide to get in the water.

Because when I decided to go nude into the hot springs, I never in a million years expected to be caught by the one person I came out here to clear from my mind.

Her chest is heaving, those most likely perfect tits constrained by a bright pink sports bra. Unbidden, my eyes travel the length of her, but only as far as the tight black shorts that barely cover her ass before I snap my gaze back up to her face. Her own eyes flick down to the tattoo on my chest and then back up, then down again and up.

"No need to apologize, you're allowed to be here. It's a public place."

Just don't decide to get in the fucking water.

"Right. Yeah. Anyway, I'll um, keep going. I must have taken a wrong turn." She gestures randomly behind herself. "See you at work."

The speed with which she takes off back down the small trail through the trees is astounding and makes me wonder how I didn't hear her approaching. But I certainly hear her leaving.

And that peace and tranquility nature had given me? Also gone, right along with her.

Two days have passed since the hot springs. Two days of hoping Heidi didn't realize I was naked under the water, but also fighting the curiosity of wondering what she would have done if she *did* realize.

As I make my way to the nursing station, coffee in hand, I pause and lean against the wall, pretending to look at something on my phone. But in reality, I'm looking at her.

Really looking at her. Not as my resident or someone connected to painful memories, but as a woman I'm slightly ashamed to admit, I fantasized about last night. About feeling her underneath me, writhing with passion.

The clearing of a throat next to me startles me so badly I almost drop my phone, catching it at the last second. One of our head nurses, and one of Heidi's friends, Ginny, is standing beside me. She's the backbone of this unit, an experienced nurse who takes no shit from families or doctors. She runs this place, and I've always had nothing but respect for her. Up until now, I would have said that respect was mutual.

"Far be it for me to comment on how you handle your residents, but you need to decide whether you want to have sex with her or fire her. Because you can't do both."

I choke on the sip of coffee I've just taken, my eyes widening as I look down at the diminutive, yet no less powerful woman in front of me.

"Excuse me?"

She places her hands on her hips and cocks her head at me.

"You heard me. I might be the only one who's noticed your ogle session today. But I'm *not* the only one who noticed that, up until last week, you were treating Heidi like she's nothing more than a thorn in your side. She's a damn good doctor, and I think you know that. Which begs the question why the lovely Max Donnelly, who charms everyone and always has, is being the grumpiest, most foul human ever to our sweet Heidi."

My mouth opens and closes in disbelief. And shame. And panic.

"I..."

Ginny holds up her hand to stop me. "I don't want to hear it, Max. I don't need to. I trust you to do your job as a doctor and as the head of this department, the same way you always have. We've got many years working together under our belt, and so far, you've never given me cause to question your judgment. But if you don't figure out what's going on in your head —" her eyes sweep me from top to bottom "— either of them, then we might have a problem."

"Ginny," I start lamely, feeling utterly chastised. Of all the nurses, she's the only one who's never pushed me or made comments about my personal life or my rejection of all the attempts to set me up with someone. So for her to see right through me, and to call me out in such a blatant way, is a hot poker straight to my gut.

"I've said my piece, Max. And all I have to add is this: Heidi is one of the most wonderful women out there. And she doesn't deserve whatever messed up game you're playing. So figure yourself out, and stop being an ass."

I stand there, dumbfounded, as Ginny walks away, heading

straight to Heidi and the other nursers. She claps her hands and says something, and they all disperse. Heidi makes her way over to me, a guarded expression on her face.

I hate that I did that. That I've dulled her glow, her energy, her vivacity in any way. Because Ginny is right — about a lot of things — but most importantly, that Heidi is one fucking incredible woman, and a damn good doctor.

Somehow, I need to get my brain to accept that and find a way to keep appropriate boundaries in place around her. She deserves that and more.

"Hi, Dr. Donnelly," she says softly, and for the second time in a short period I almost choke on my coffee. This time it's simply from the sound of my name and her voice. "Are you okay?" she asks, her hand lifting as if to touch me. She doesn't, thank God.

"Yeah. Yeah. Sorry. I'm fine." I give her what I hope is a reassuring smile.

"Listen," she starts, glancing around before settling her gaze on my face. Her spine is ramrod straight and her voice is firm. "I just want you to know that running into you at the hot springs was completely unintentional, and I have no plan to tell anyone about it. As far as I'm concerned, it never happened."

My mouth flaps open and closed a couple of times before I can stop it. Of all the things I thought she might say, that wasn't even on the list. And the idea of her pretending she never saw me, even though I *know* I didn't misinterpret the attraction in her eyes when she saw my bare chest, well that just fucking stings.

But. She has a point. We have to be professional.

"Right. Of course. That sounds fine."

Our gazes stay locked on each other. Something passes between us, crackling in the air. But it's gone in an instant. Yet, I don't stop myself from lifting my hand up to slide a piece of her hair through my fingers. Fuck, it's soft. As is the tiny gasp I hear from her. I drop her hair. "Tie this up," I say gruffly. "And let's go."

Her wide green eyes are locked on mine as she loosens her ponytail. The second her hair cascades down her back, my fingers twitch at my side. *Don't. Don't think about wrapping that hair around your fist and...*

I shake my head to clear the dark and dirty thoughts clouding my mind, just in time for Heidi to finish tying off her hair.

"Let's go."

But something has shifted between us. Something significant.

I'm not the only one affected by whatever passed between us in those fleeting moments at the hot springs. And I'm clearly not the only one who's unsure what to think about it.

The stakes have been raised. There's a line we cannot cross, not without it possibly having consequences on both our careers. But that line is looking very blurred right now.

Chapter Eleven

Heidi

"Oh, I'm sorry, I didn't mean to disturb you."

"It's fine, Heidi." Water droplets cascade down his torso as Max slowly emerges from the steaming water. I trace the path of one drop down his tattooed chest, over the hills and valleys of his abs, until it's lost in the thatch of neatly groomed hair at the base of his deliciously stiff cock. My tongue darts out and licks the corner of my lips. It's impossible not to look at it, jutting out from his lean, muscular body, demanding my attention.

"Max," I breathe as he comes closer. He reaches his hand out and I take it. My clothes are gone. I don't remember taking them off, but they're gone.

"Your body makes me want to do some very dirty things to it, Dr. Morgan."

I let out an embarrassing whimper. "Like what?"

"Why don't you come here, and I'll show you."

I step into the water, gasping slightly at the warmth. It matches the heat building inside of me.

"Good girl," he rumbles. "I worked up an appetite on that hike. Your pussy is gonna be the perfect snack, and I'm gonna make you

scream my name so fucking loud, everyone in this forest will know what I'm doing to you."

"Max!" I bolt upright in bed, my heart pounding so hard, I swear I can hear it in the dark of my bedroom. My sheets are a mess. I'm damp with sweat. And there's an ache between my legs so intense, I have no choice but to deal with it.

My fingers slide underneath the waistband of my cotton sleep shorts. The instant I graze across my clit, my hips lift, seeking more. I try to extend it, draw it out, but I'm so turned on — from a dream — that it takes no time at all before I'm moaning, embarrassingly loud, as my orgasm cascades over me.

I pull my hand out and lay there for a minute, panting heavily. Good Lord.

A part of me can't believe I just got off to a dream where Max called my pussy a perfect snack. How freaking cheesy was that? God only knows why my imagination conjured *that* for dirty talk.

Then again, I've also, apparently, got a little unexpected praise kink inside of me. Because Max calling me a good girl was definitely hot. Who knew two words could make me horny, even while sleeping.

And now I have to get up and go to work with him. Which won't be awkward at all, I'm sure. Oh, who am I kidding? I know I told Max I would act as if the hot springs never happened, but the truth is, there's not a chance in hell I'll forget the sight of him glistening with water and dappled sunshine. His hair slicked back and every inch of him on display.

And I do mean every inch.

Even obscured by water, what I saw was enough to make my

panties damp.

Apparently, my subconscious mind is determined to make it even harder for me to remember that I'm not here to cross the line with my boss, I'm here to become the best doctor I can. I'm here to start over and build the life I've always wanted.

I wonder what it would take to get him to hate me again. Maybe that would make it easier…

As luck would have it, Max is off-site today at a pediatric trauma medicine conference in Vancouver. Being able to work a shift without worrying about whether he'll snap at me or — after last night — worrying that I'll somehow let it slip that I'm having sexy dreams about him is great, and yet, also disconcerting.

I miss him, the grumpy, confusing, sexy man.

I take an overly large bite of my veggie wrap and chew slowly, forcing away those annoying fleeting memories of my dream.

"What's got you all worked up?" Tina, one of my nurse friends, sits down beside me.

"Nothing," I mumble around my mouthful.

"Yeah, right," she says cheerfully, but she doesn't push. "We totally need to plan a night out soon. There's so much to catch up on."

"I'd like that," I say, smiling gratefully. And it's the truth, even if my life is so insanely busy right now, getting our schedules to line up will most likely prove impossible.

"Great! Do you have any plans this weekend? Any hot dates?"

I let out a little snort. "God, no." Then, in the interest of reconnecting with an old friend, I launch into a story about one of the messages I received on the dating app I signed up for.

"Did you know guys are sending dick pics instead of greetings? There's no 'hi, nice to meet you.' It's just, bam. Dick pic."

In no time, we're both cackling with laughter, and a couple of my other former colleagues are joining us.

"They can't be all bad. Come on, let's find someone for you to go out with this weekend." Tina wiggles her hand, demanding my phone.

I mean, maybe it's not the worst idea. A date might give me something to take my mind off my very inappropriate crush on Max.

"Fine, but I get power of veto."

Ten minutes of laughter and swiping later, we land on one guy who actually shows some promise. A few taps of the keyboard later, and Tina has somehow landed me a date. For tonight.

"Wait, shouldn't I talk to him first? Over messages or something?"

Tina shrugs. "Why waste time? Meet the guy in person, see if there's any sparks; if there are, great. If not, move on. Time's a wasting, babe."

"Are you calling me old?" I say drily, and Tina giggles.

"No, but you've been here a month and haven't gone on a single date. Come on, Heidi. You're a young hot doctor. Get out there and live!"

"I don't know, I still feel like I should be able to talk to the guy a bit first," I grumble.

"Talk is cheap. Instead, now you've got a hot date to look forward to after work today."

"Yeah, when I'll be tired and gross from a full day of work,"

I grumble half-heartedly, but Tina just gently shoves my shoulder.

"C'mon, go for a drink, maybe dinner, and just see what happens."

I look at her pointedly. "Nothing is going to happen, Tina. Nothing."

Curtis, who was always my favourite nurse to work with, given the stories he'd share about his wife and two kids, chimes in. "Because our girl has standards. Look, Heidi, just go and have fun. Be safe and let me know if you need a ride home."

I drop my head down onto his shoulder. "Thank you. I guess I'm dating again."

Tina and Curtis both let out a little whoop, and I try to muster up the excitement to match. But it's hard. Because the man I'm meeting tonight is not the man I *wish* I was spending an evening with.

"Of all the freaking self-absorbed, idiotic —"

"Hope you're not talking about me."

The rumble of Max's voice brings me to a stop, and I spin around to face him. It's been over twenty-four hours since I last saw him — dream not included — and I hate the fact that my heart leaps a little at the sight of him.

"No!" I say, but even I can hear the aggravation in my voice. I temper it and try again. "No." I wave in the direction of the restaurant I've just left. "Bad date."

His eyebrows raise, but he doesn't say a word. Which I take

as an invitation to keep ranting about the situation I just walked out on.

"I realize, thanks to Thad and then med school and residency, it's been a while since I dated. But is it common practice to basically treat a first date as a really terrible job interview? I'm talking no conversation, just a guy telling a girl how awesome he is and how lucky she should feel to be with him? Because that's not what I remember. Where's the romance? Where's the chemistry? Where's the *trying to get to know each other?*"

I whirl back when I realize I've stomped on down the sidewalk and Max isn't beside me. "Word of advice. If you're on a date, try to pull your head out of your ass and talk about something other than your classic car obsession."

His throaty chuckle reaches me at the same time he does, his hands casually stuck in the pockets of his sweatpants. Dark grey sweatpants. That show an outline... My eyes dart back up to his face, and that's when reality hits me like a tonne of bricks.

Did I really just vent to my attending — and the guy who starred in a very dirty dream of mine — about a horrible date from hell?

Shit.

"I'm sorry. This is incredibly unprofessional of me to be talking to you like this." He's my boss. Not my friend.

Just being friends is the last thing I want with him.

"It's fine," he says, amusement colouring his tone. "I'm sorry you had such a terrible experience...for your first time back in the dating game?" There's a question in his words, and I nod to answer it.

"Yeah, well, if that's what I'm in for, I'll stay single."

"Most men don't know what to do when they're faced with a beautiful, intelligent, capable woman. They expect them to melt at their feet in a puddle," he says wryly. I manage to hide my surprise at his candid comment, but there's no fighting the blush that flames up my cheeks when he continues.

"You're intimidating to those kind of men, Heidi, simply because you're better than them."

"Are you intimidated by me?" I ask, not sure where the bold words come from.

His eyes flash with something. "No. I'm surprised by you."

The world comes to a standstill as we stare at each other for a moment before Max clears his throat and the moment is over. "Can I walk you home?"

"No need, I'm close by." And the thought of walking next to him in the dusky evening light has my insides tied up in knots. Because it feels too much like my date should have been with him.

"Heidi, let me rephrase." I startle at the command in his tone. It's not the same as how he sounds when he's running the show at work, but it's powerful, nonetheless. "I want to walk you home. You shouldn't be walking around alone at night."

I bristle at that, even as a part of me swoons at his protective instinct. I'm sure it has something to do with his father's accident, but still, there's no need for him to be this way with me. "I can take care of myself, you know."

"I do know. But I couldn't live with myself if I didn't see you home safely and something happened. Please. Let me do this." His quiet request takes me by surprise, yet again. God, this man keeps me on my toes like no one else.

"Okay. Thank you." I reply quietly, and we start walking in the direction I was headed. "What were you doing out at this time, finishing a hot date yourself?" I regret asking the question as soon as it comes out, and I hold my breath to see how he'll respond.

But he just chuckles. "Nope. No date, I was out for a run."

"That explains the sweatpants," I blurt out.

Max's head turns to look at me. "What is it with women and sweatpants, anyway?"

"You don't want me to answer that," I say quickly, hoping he won't push for more.

"Humph." His noncommittal grunt is a relief. What the hell am I doing flirting with him about his freaking sweatpants?

Apparently, I'm losing my grasp on any semblance of self-control around him.

This should make work *very* interesting...

Chapter Twelve

Max

"You don't look comfortable."

"Thanks, Captain Obvious." I glare up at Cyrus, a colleague from the cardiology department. He leans against the counter in the small coffee shop that's a part of the hospital lobby. Normally, I'd walk across the street to the café and get a *good* cup when I have an actual break like I do right now, but my back is telling me not to move anymore than necessary.

"What did you do and why are you here?"

Cy always gets to the point. It's one thing I appreciate about him: there's no pretense, no beating around the bush, just blunt honesty.

"Tweaked something at the gym, and I'm here because it's my job," I grumble, barely managing to flash a smile of thanks to the girl who made my coffee. I make my way out to the hall, working hard not to make it apparent I'm in pain. Cyrus has a point; I shouldn't be here. Of all the days to use a sick day, this would be it.

Except, I received a notification from the nurses. The one thing that would bring me in to work, no matter what, has happened.

"Did you at least take something so you stop walking around like you got railed in the ass last night?"

"Seriously, Cy?" I bark at him in a loud whisper, my eyes darting around. "Come on, man, we're at work."

Blunt and no filter. That's Cyrus.

He just shrugs as his pager goes off. "All I'm sayin' is, you look like hell, Max."

With a parting wave, he takes off toward the emergency room. I, on the other hand, slowly make my way to the elevator, trying to take stock of how obvious it is that I'm in pain. Crude as his description was, Cy wasn't totally wrong about the location of my pain. After all, it is my sacroiliac joint that I irritated with a late night gym session trying to exorcise the vision of Heidi, in that dress she was wearing for her date from hell, out of my goddamn head.

The muscle relaxers I took just before going to get coffee are weak, because the last thing I need is a fuzzy head today, but I'm hoping they take the edge off. Because as soon as I get to the unit and see the worried looks on the nurses' faces, I know it's not good.

Teagan is what we call a frequent flier. Only instead of reward points, she just gets to see our faces way too often. I've known her since she was five, which is when I first started at Westport General. We've had good years and bad. Years when her disease is under control, and years when it isn't.

This year was looking good, she hadn't had an infection that landed her with us in months. But that's changed, apparently.

"Where are we at?" I ask Ginny quietly as I gingerly sit down in a chair opposite her.

She types on the computer for a minute, pulling up Teagan's chart, I'm sure, then she spins the screen around so I can see the initial results from the ER.

"She came in last night, febrile, with a productive cough and audible wheeze. Mom said it started as a cold, and they were able to manage at home for a couple of days, but she worsened quite suddenly, became short of breath, so they brought her in."

"Okay. Are the nebs helping?"

Ginny grimaces. "Somewhat, but her mom said they haven't been as effective lately. Dr. Giustino is coming in as well to do a consult."

Good. Her respirologist is always welcome on our ward. Because while our staff can manage a lot, Teagan's cystic fibrosis is advanced, and when she's here, she needs attention from the experts.

"Dr. Donnelly, hi, I didn't expect you until later."

I look up to see Heidi standing across the counter from me, a slight smile on her face. I give her a brusque nod, partly because of pain and partly because I can't get distracted right now.

"We've got a VIP patient on the ward. Do you remember Teagan Narusaka?"

Heidi's face falls. "Yes. Of course, I do. Is she in with an exacerbation?"

"Lung infection brought on by a cold virus, from the sounds of it. I was just getting the update on her admission record from Ginny."

We both turn our attention back to the head nurse. While she finishes her report, I gently move and stretch my back, realizing gratefully that the meds are starting to have an effect on my back pain. Enough so that when I go to stand, intent on starting my assessment of Teagan, I'm not quite as stiff as I was before.

But either I'm still walking funny, or Heidi is exceptionally perceptive.

"Are you alright, Max?" She keeps her voice pitched low with her question.

"Yeah, just tweaked my lower back at the gym. I'm fine, let's focus on the patient." I know it's a brush-off, but I saw her lift her hand, as if she were going to touch my arm. And I can't lose focus on the priority, which is the girl waiting for us in a hospital bed.

As we walk into the room, the nurse is just helping Teagan hook up her specialty vest that will provide a specific type of massaging and rhythmic thumping to her chest, in an effort to try and clear the fluid buildup in her lungs, so we get the chance to hear Teagan's cough firsthand.

"That's good, T, clear it all out," I say encouragingly, pasting a smile on my face just before I cover up with a mask and a gown. A pump of hand sanitizer follows, and only then do I approach her bed.

Teagan looks up at me from the bed, and I take in her flushed skin and hollow eyes. She is definitely not feeling well.

"Hey Dr. D," she rasps before turning to Heidi. "Heidi, hey, I remember you."

"Actually, Heidi here is now *Doctor* Morgan," I interject. "She's a resident working with me for a while."

"You can still call me Heidi, Teagan," the woman in question interrupts, reaching a hand to lay across Teagan's. "We've got enough history with me being your nurse, no need to mess it up now with formal titles."

"A doctor? Well done, Heidi, that's impressive," Teagan's mom, Maya, a lovely woman we all have come to know well, pipes up.

Heidi dismisses the compliment with a slight shrug of her shoulders. "Thank you. And as lovely as it is to see you both again, I wish it were under better circumstances. Can you tell us some more about how things have been the last few weeks? Ginny mentioned you had a cold for a day or so, but then it worsened?"

Maya nods and fills us in on the last week. As is to be expected, the initial infection was a simple viral cold, likely passed on at school. Kids like Teagan struggle to live life as normally as possible, and for T, that means still going to school when she can. She's always been good about wearing a mask, but that's not a foolproof barrier.

"You did all the right things," I reassure Maya when she finishes, because I know she's beating herself up for the inescapable fact that her daughter is yet again in a hospital bed. My own mother has confessed to me how Morag used to be filled with guilt when Callum got sick. That parental guilt is so common with genetic disorders. I know my words don't even chip away at it, but I'll do what I can to alleviate it every chance possible.

Heidi and I finish our physical assessment and discuss the treatment plan, even though it's a familiar routine for Teagan and Maya. Insertion of a central line for antibiotics, nebulizer treatments, aggressive hydration, feeding via an NG tube if needed, chest physio, and movement.

As we're finishing up, Teagan starts another coughing fit. I go to her side, sitting gently on the bed and supporting her frail body as it's racked with coughs. Heidi comes to the other side and holds the collection tray underneath, so all Teagan has to do is spit any sputum out. Our eyes meet over our patient's head, and I know the worry I feel is reflected back at me.

When her frail body eventually sags back against the pillows, Teagan opens her eyes. The familiar strength I've come to respect in my young patient is still there, but it's layered with fatigue.

"Okay Dr. D, let's see them."

I smile, knowing this question was coming.

"See what?" Heidi asks, confused.

"His socks," Teagan replies, a twinkle slowly coming into her eyes. "Don't tell me you haven't noticed?" She turns to Heidi and grins. "His socks are the best. But they never match."

Heidi tilts her head at me, but I see the open curiosity. Standing up, I lift first one pant leg and then the other, revealing just as Teagan predicted, two mismatched but equally ridiculous socks. One with corgis on it, the other slices of pizza.

"Awesome. The dogs are the best. Do you still have the rainbow ones?" Teagan asks, then she's hit by another coughing fit. I wait until it subsides to reply.

"Sure do. I'll wear one tomorrow."

"Thanks, Dr. D." She gives me a wan smile, and Heidi and I make our way out to the hall.

"I have to ask. What's with the socks?"

I chuckle. "It started a few years back; I was so exhausted after a night shift, I didn't realize I put on mismatched socks. One of the patients noticed and thought it was so funny. Then I started doing it on purpose. These kids need any reason possible to smile."

Heidi stares at me for so long, it starts to feel like she's examining me, trying to make sense of what she sees.

"That's really sweet of you."

My shoulders lift in a shrug. "It's no big deal." I might sound dismissive of her compliment, but in reality, the opposite is true. I like that she admires something so small about me.

I like it a lot.

The rest of the day is a blur. We see our other patients, respond to consults, but our minds never leave Teagan for long. Over the course of the next eight hours, her respirologist comes, adjusts the treatment plan, and confers with me, then leaves. He'll be back tomorrow. All of us on shift today are in and out of her room.

That's the thing in pediatrics. Certain patients just stick with you. They find a way into your heart, and they never leave. Oftentimes, it's the sickest ones that we connect with. It could be because we know subconsciously that they need the human connection and compassion even more than the kid who's in for a day with a broken leg and can then go home, never to be seen again, God willing. Or maybe it's because we know this young soul may not be around much longer.

And the death of a child equates to the death of infinite possibilities. A future that never gets to happen.

That's something you never get over, no matter how many times you experience it.

Later that night, well past the end of our shift, there's still no change in Teagan's status. If anything, her numbers and vitals are slightly worse.

I find Heidi buying a chocolate bar out of the vending machine. She looks as weary as I feel. "Listen, I'm going to stay overnight and keep an eye on Teagan."

She nods, unwrapping the bar and holding it out to me. I shake my head.

"Okay, I'll crash in the residents' lounge."

I don't know why I'm surprised she would stay. After all, I know how dedicated she is to the job, and she's also got history with Teagan.

"You don't have to, if you'd rather go home. I'll page you if anything urgent happens."

Heidi quirks her brow at me. "Max. Teagan is a VIP. You said it yourself. I'm staying."

I stuff my hands in my pockets. "Okay. Well, let me walk you to the residents' lounge."

Her soft chuckle is a soothing balm right now. "It's just downstairs, I think I can make it by myself."

"Well, I'm going that way anyway. It would be weird to not walk together." Okay, that's a stretch and I can tell she sees right through it, given the tiny smirk on her face.

When we get to the door of the lounge reserved for residents, Heidi hesitates just outside. "Will you text me when you go to check on her?"

I nod. "Of course."

"Okay." She pushes the door open, and from our vantage point, we can see that both bunks are already occupied. "Crap," Heidi says softly as she closes the door. "Two beds among all the residents in this dang hospital is just not enough."

"Take it up with administration," I say wryly. There's really only one other option, and I don't even give myself the briefest of moments to consider if this is a dumb idea before I say it.

"Come and sleep in the attending's lounge."

"Isn't that the ultimate taboo?" she whispers teasingly. I arch a brow at her word choice, my mind going down a much different path.

"Taboo? Really?" Heidi blushes slightly and I soften my response with a grin. "It's fine. Come on."

But when we reach the on-call room for attendings on our floor, I realize the fatal flaw in my suggestion.

There's only one fucking bed.

Chapter Thirteen

Heidi

"I'll take the chair," I say quickly, moving to the small, yet thankfully, padded chair.

"Don't be ridiculous. You take the bed. I can stretch out on the floor."

I look at Max like he's crazy. "Says the man who's been wincing and limping all day? Dream on, Donnelly."

His lips split into a brief smile. "Resorting to last names only, Morgan? I see how it is."

I let out a huff, but secretly, I'm loving this relaxed intimacy between us. "Okay, compromise. We can share the freaking bed. We're adults, aren't we?"

Max's eyes flare with something indiscernible in the low light of the on-call room. Do I regret offering to share the small bed? Not really, if I'm being honest with myself. The alternatives both suck if we want any hope of getting some sleep in between going to check on Teagan.

"You don't think that's a little inappropriate? You're my resident," he says softly.

"We both need to get some sleep, Max, or we'll be no good for

Teagan. I promise you, I'm fine sharing the bed. I trust you."

Those three words seem to help, but I forge on, determined to diffuse his tension. My shoulders lift and fall, and I give him an impish grin. "But if you really want to sleep on a hospital floor —" I let him see me shudder slightly "— go for it. But that's pretty disgusting. You know what's on that floor."

He stalks over to the bed, standing there with his hands on his hips, staring at it, as if he could will it to be bigger, or make another one materialize. I cautiously approach and sit down on the mattress in front of him, patting the spot beside me.

"It's fine, Max. I won't bite."

His tongue darts out to moisten his lips as his stare zeroes in on my mouth. I might not bite, but I might want *him* to...

Oh boy. Time to stop this train of thought. I kick off my shoes and shuffle back until my head is leaning against the headboard.

"Come on. I'm not tired yet, so we can just sit and relax for a while before we check on T."

Finally, I see some tension leave his body. He toes off his shoes and sits down at the foot of the bed. Seeing him there, his legs crossed in front of him, his body leaning sideways against the wall, it's easy to forget this is the man who treated me so poorly these last several weeks.

"What made you decide to become a pediatrician?"

His lips tip up in a smile, but it's tinged with sadness. I wait and watch as he flips his phone around in his hand. I'm coming to realize that's his thinking habit. He's a fidgeter, always needing something in his hands to move around.

"The human body has always fascinated me. I was the kid

who wanted to play doctor and loved going for checkups and seeing all the instruments in the clinic. When my brother broke his arm, I begged my mom to let me save the X-ray films. I thought it was amazing that we could see inside our bodies like that. So, medicine was always my plan."

He pauses, and I can tell from the faraway look on his face that he's caught up in memories. But the haunted expression that comes over him is unexpected and makes me yearn to offer comfort.

"My best friend growing up had a brother. The three of us were pretty tight. Hell, most of the time I preferred them to my own damn brothers. Even though he was older, Callum was small, and he always preferred to play with us rather than kids his own age. He couldn't always keep up if we were playing tag or soccer, but he was a great scorekeeper. Except he got sick a lot. If any of us had a cold, he couldn't play; we couldn't even go to their house. He kept going in and out of the hospital, and Quinn — my best friend — would come and stay with us. I didn't really get it until we were older, when he had a particularly bad episode. That's when my mom sat me down and told me Callum would never get better."

"He had CF," I say quietly, all the pieces of the puzzle that is Max Donnelly clicking into place. "That's why Teagan is so special to you."

Max just nods. "I got to see him just before he passed. I promised him I'd be a doctor, and I'd help kids like him get better. Fuck, he was so wise, he knew that was impossible, but he just smiled at me and told me I'd be a great doctor. I didn't think I'd actually end up in pediatrics, though"

I want to ask why, but I also don't want to push things. As silence falls between us, I'm struck by the similarities in our stories of how we ended up as doctors. Even though my path had a few more twists and turns, the underlying motivation — to help kids — was because we couldn't help *one particular kid*.

"When we moved to the mainland, I got a job at BC Children's Hospital," I start to say, then stop, unsure how Max will handle even an offhand mention of Thad. But he just gives me a nod to continue. "There was an opening on the oncology ward, so I did the upgrades in training so I could work there. At the time, I thought it would be a great experience, something I could take with me to any hospital if Thad decided we had to move again."

I give Max credit, he says nothing. Just gives me the space to get it all out.

"While I was there, I met Molly. The brightest, boldest, most optimistically realistic teenager I've ever come across." A smile creeps across my face as my head fills with images of Molly. Her smile, the colourful scarves she loved to wear, and the way she always had us all laughing. "I knew better than to let myself get attached, but she made it impossible not to. Every shift I'd request her assignment if she was admitted, which sadly, was often. Leukemia ravaged her body over the course of a year and a half."

Max's hand lands on my leg, startling me. I look up to see compassion and sympathy etched into his features. My voice takes on a hoarse quality, and I'm not surprised to feel tears burning my eyes. Thinking of the profound impact this one girl had on my entire life always gets me emotional.

"She's the one who pulled the wool off my eyes about my relationship with Thad. In her blunt, unassuming, filter-free teenage way, she pointed out that he was holding me back, controlling my entire life, and that I was miserable as a result."

The hand on my leg tightens imperceptibly.

"As soon as she pointed it out, I could see it all so clearly. How he slowly and systematically built up his authority over my entire life, leaving me no choice but to go along with his move to Vancouver. He promised me a future, a pretty picture that I should have known he'd never deliver on. But somehow, I got wrapped up in the lies, thinking if you love someone, then that is what you do — you follow them, no matter if you want to or not. I had mentioned wanting to go to med school to him a couple of times, but he always had a reason why I shouldn't do it. Not enough time, not enough money, whatever. Yet, there I was, encouraging him to go for a promotion at work, to take all the out-of-town trips he needed, and hosting all the dinner parties he wanted. I wasn't his partner. I was just, heck, I don't know. I'm not hot enough to be arm candy or a trophy, so maybe I was just a tool."

"Don't say that." His growl interrupts me.

"What?"

"Don't call yourself a trophy or a tool. Any man would be lucky as hell to have you by his side. And you deserve to be a partner. More than that, even. You already know how I feel about your ex. But I'll add this. He's even more of a fucker if he couldn't see that."

My heart beats faster in my chest. We're crossing lines with this conversation. And once we go over them, I don't know if we can go back.

That thought, along with my promise to Molly, brings my focus to where it should be.

"Thank you," I say softly. Then, even though I desperately want to keep his hand on my leg, I pull away, needing some space. "Anyway, once I ditched Thad, Molly pushed me to submit my med school application. I got my acceptance letter two days before she died."

The filtered sounds of the hospital at night are the only noise I hear when I stop talking. Max's head is bowed slightly, his gaze fixed on his hands.

We've both bared a piece of our souls tonight. And I'm slightly terrified how that might change things. I can't let Max get too close. I can't lose myself to a man again.

I won't.

My eyes are so dry, they're stuck to the inside of my eyelids. It's a struggle to blink them open, but the incessant vibrating of my watch on my wrist is driving me insane. And I'm hot, like majorly overheated, as if I've been under a weighted electric blanket all night.

Okay, that part actually feels kind of good.

I shift my head slightly, then freeze. There's a strong arm banded around my middle, a leg tangled between mine, and warm breath tickling the back of my neck.

Oh, shit.

As gingerly as possible, I start to move my legs away from

Max's, sliding my upper body away from the heat of his solid wall of muscle at my back. But I don't get far before his arm tightens, and he pulls me back flush against him.

His lips find my neck and he nuzzles me.

Nuzzles me.

He's got to be sleeping still, right? There's no freaking way Max would let this happen if he were awake. I close my eyes and let my body soften into his embrace. Those lines I was so worried about crossing earlier have clearly been destroyed. Besides, it's been so long since a man held me like this. I don't even remember when Thad last did, if ever.

If I pretend he's anyone but my boss, then there's no harm in taking just a second to enjoy this, is there? He won't remember a thing as long as I get out before he wakes up.

"Heidi." A whispered rumble against my skin causes goose-bumps to break out. His hand grips me tighter, then, I feel him stiffen behind me.

"Shit." Max pulls away and sits up abruptly. "Fuck, I'm sorry. God, I can't believe I did that. Heidi, I'm so sorry." I roll over and sit up in one movement, so I'm facing him.

"It's fine. Nothing happened. We fell asleep, it's a small bed, our bodies touched. All good."

All I can do is pray he doesn't remember kissing my neck or whispering my name. Because the guilt he is clearly experiencing is written all over his handsome face. And it's making me feel a little uncomfortable for enjoying that split second of intimacy with him — even if he was unaware of it.

"We should go and check on Teagan. My alarm went off a couple of minutes ago."

He scrubs a hand over his face, then checks his own watch. "Right. Yeah, let's go."

We stand up, and I stretch my arms overhead to ease the kinks in my back that are normally there after sleeping on the notoriously uncomfortable on-call beds. But there are no kinks. No soreness or stiffness.

Because, of course not. Of course, sleeping with *Max* makes even the thin, rock-hard mattresses of these beds feel like a luxurious cloud.

Damn it, now the man has ruined any chance I could hope to have of sleeping on one of these beds without thinking of him.

My arms drop back down to my sides, and I spin around to face the door. And in doing so, I catch Max staring at me. He looks away immediately, but not before I see something sparking in those deep blue eyes.

There's no denying a shift has happened in our dynamic. And falling asleep all tangled up in each other has made that shift even more pronounced.

I just wish I knew what to do about it.

Chapter Fourteen

I allow myself to wallow in equal parts guilt and satisfaction, but only until we hit the pediatric ward.

I knew sharing that goddamn on-call room bed was a mistake. I knew my self-control would shatter when my conscious mind, the only part of me with any semblance of sanity, apparently, went to sleep.

What I didn't expect was for it to feel so fucking right to have her in my arms. To wake up with her hair tickling my chin, her hand holding mine tightly against her body, and her soft sighs of contentment.

That sense of rightness lasted up until I came fully awake. Then the impact of what transpired between us hit me with the force of a ten-tonne truck.

I slept with my resident. Yeah, fine, we literally only slept, but still.

My baser desires took over, and I can't bring myself to fully regret it. Hence, the guilt.

"I'm going to check Teagan's overnight reports," Heidi says when we reach the double doors that lead to the pediatric ward.

I can't mistake the fact that her voice sounds softer now, more intimate. All I can do is hope no one else notices.

I incline my head, and we split, her to the desk and Teagan's chart, and me to the coffee pot that's always brewing overnight. It's only when I find myself pouring a second cup and adding the amount of milk I've seen Heidi add to hers that I realize she's found her way past my defenses. Even deeper than I anticipated.

I suppose it's to be expected; we shared parts of our past last night, secrets that bonded us. But this also means Heidi is even more of a risk for me than before.

As inappropriate as my hatred of her was, especially since it was based on misunderstandings and incorrect assumptions, it kept me safe. Because that anger masked my undeniable attraction to her.

And now that I know how she feels in my arms, I don't think I can resist her anymore.

Now, she could break me.

We complete our check on Teagan, and her sigh of relief echoes my own when we see her maintaining her oxygen levels and that she's now fever free. She's not out of the woods completely, but for tonight, we can rest more easily.

"Let's continue the nebs and antibiotics for another twenty-four hours, but I'm happy she's responded quickly," I say quietly to Teagan's mom as we stand in the doorway to her room.

"Thank you, Dr. Donnelly," she replies, tears shining in her eyes. "We're going to need to adjust her home regime, aren't we?"

I weigh my words carefully. "I'm not her respirologist, Maya, but I suspect so."

"I should probably pull her from school. But she's so happy being around other kids. I hate taking that piece of normalcy away from her."

The heartbreak is evident in her words. I can't begin to imagine the pain she has lived with, knowing her daughter will die from a genetic illness that no one can control.

"Dr. Donnelly."

Heidi's voice washes over me like a wave of warmth. Her hand on my bicep sears me.

"I've got the latest lab results from earlier this evening. Her white count is lower. But there's something else."

Her eyes dart to Maya, then back to me. We don't keep important information from families, but we do proceed with caution with how we share it. Something tells me what Heidi is about to say might be hard for Maya to hear.

"Her creatinine is elevated. I was surprised by that, so I've already called the lab to ask them to repeat it, but I wanted you to know."

"What does that mean?" Maya turns to me, folding her arms across her chest, as if she can somehow protect herself from bad news. Her eyes dart over to Teagan, who's sleeping fitfully.

"It means her kidneys are under stress," I explain. Glancing at the printout Heidi has, I scan the numbers. "It's not too high, so we don't need to wake her for anything right now. We'll see what the numbers are after the retest. In the meantime, let's also monitor her fluid intake." I place what I hope is a reassuring hand on Maya's shoulder. "This is not necessarily a significant problem. Try to get some rest, and we can reassess in the morning."

Maya takes in a deep breath and nods. "Okay." She looks up at me and then back to Heidi. "I'm really happy to see you back here, Heidi. You and Dr. Donnelly make a great team."

Logically, I know Maya means a team of doctors, nothing more. But that doesn't stop the tightening in my stomach. I give her a stiff smile and turn to leave. I need some space.

But Heidi falls into step beside me. Of course. The scent of her shampoo brings back the memory of feeling her in my arms. Was that really only an hour ago? Our path down to the doctor's lounges is silent. We reach the residents' lounge first and come to a stop.

"I should see if there's a bed available now."

She speaks softly, and there's an unspoken question in her words. A dangerous question, so I don't answer it. "Yeah."

She pushes open the door, and the room is empty. I shouldn't feel disappointed by that.

I shouldn't.

"Are we going to check on her once more before morning?" Heidi asks, her eyes hopeful. For what? I don't want to know. This is all feeling too much. My attraction to her, it obviously being reciprocated, how close we came to crossing a line earlier tonight, and the fact that Heidi seems eager to cross it again.

"I'll go up again. You can sleep." The words come out harsher than I intend them to, and I close my eyes when I see the flash of hurt cross her face. "What I mean is, there's no need for us both to be disturbed. I can do the next check and call you if there's anything urgent."

"Okay." Heidi steps inside the residents' lounge, then stops, turning back to me. "Max," she starts hesitantly. "I hope I'm not speaking out of turn, but I appreciate you opening up to me like you did earlier. And I truly don't feel anything inappropriate happened, and I don't regret anything." Her hands twist together, at odds with the strength in her voice. "What I'm saying is, I would very much appreciate if we were able to not let what happened affect how we work together."

"Nothing happened," I say gruffly.

"Right."

"But it almost did," I continue, my mouth spewing words before my brain can catch up to whether it's smart or not. "And that would have been highly inappropriate. We're not just colleagues, Heidi. I am your superior. Something like...whatever happened earlier...could be perceived as more than it was. Could land one or both of us in trouble, and compromise not only our careers, but our integrity."

It's bullshit, all of it. I know it and I'm pretty damn sure she knows it. But I need to regain control. I need to rebuild the walls that keep me safe. I can't let myself be vulnerable to someone, anyone, ever again.

"Oh, for fuck's sake," Heidi mutters before pulling me into the residents' lounge and locking the door.

"What the hell are you doing," I bark out, backing away. She stands in front of me, her hands on her hips. Not that fluorescent lights could ever be called romantic, but from this angle, the lights hit her hair and make it look on fire.

"Nothing, Max. I'm doing nothing. But you, apparently, are beating yourself up for falling asleep. That's all we did. We fell asleep."

God, she's incredible when she's fired up like this. Her eyes sparking with ire, her luscious tits heaving under her scrub top.

Fuck. No. Stop thinking about her breasts. Of course, that self-reprimand only makes my eyes drop to them again.

"Eyes up here, Donnelly," she says, sarcasm lacing her prim tone. My head snaps up and for the first time in years, I feel heat covering my cheeks at being caught.

"Sorry."

"Don't be."

I arch my brow. "You just caught me checking you out."

Her braid falls off her shoulder as she tilts her head. "Maybe I liked it."

My hand scrubs over my face as I groan. "Heidi."

"Max."

Fucking hell, when did she become an impertinent brat? Where's the quiet, kindhearted nurse? Or the calm, collected, confident doctor?

"Max." She steps closer. I can't go anywhere with the door at my back. "I'm attracted to you, Max, but I respect that you don't want to cross any boundaries with me. I admire your ethics and your commitment to your job. I'm not trying to cause trouble, but I do want you to stop carrying any guilt over tonight or anything over the last few weeks. Because there are two of us in this..." She pauses, pursing her lips. I want to bite those lips. "Relationship is the wrong word. Dynamic? Sure, dynamic. There's two of us in this dynamic. You're not the only one responsible for making sure we keep things appropriate and professional. Or not."

Jesus, fuck, what am I meant to say to *that*?

"Heidi." My voice cracks. I clear my throat and try again. "Heidi." My hand starts to lift to the piece of silky hair that's fallen from her braid.

The obnoxious beep of my cell phone interrupts us. A glance at the screen displays an unfamiliar number, but I have to answer, just in case. When a robotic voice comes on the line, I exhale and hang up. But by now, Heidi has stepped back and is over by what I assume is her locker.

"I'm going to go," I say quietly. She nods. And as I turn to leave, I can honestly say I've never been more grateful for a spam phone call giving us a reprieve from whatever is starting to grow between us.

Because as fast as I try to rebuild my defenses, she seems to be smashing them to pieces. And I don't have a fucking clue what to do about it.

CHAPTER FIFTEEN

Max

"What the hell are you doing here?"

Sawyer claps me on the shoulder as he pushes past me into my apartment. "Nice to see you, too, bro."

Beckett follows, then our cousin Leo, and then to my surprise, Hunter trails in. He gives me a sheepish smile. "Hey, Max."

I close the door and turn around slowly to see my brothers and cousin setting bags down on the coffee table. A set of poker chips comes out first, then decks of cards, then a case of beer. Leo walks over and hands me one. "You guys showed up at my house, bringing guys' night to me when I needed it most. I don't pretend to know why the twins decided you needed guys' night brought to you, but family comes first." He lifts his bottle, and dumbfounded, I lift mine in return.

"I appreciate the gesture, but I'm fine." I move into the kitchen where Hunter is opening pizza boxes I hadn't even realized he was carrying.

"Sure, y'are," Sawyer calls out. "That's why you missed drinks at Hastings last night and why you've been ignoring all of our texts."

I blink slowly as his words settle over me. With the pressures of work — Teagan's declining health in particular — plus the strange shift in things between Heidi and me, apparently, I've been a bit distracted. Absent, even.

"Sorry, guys." I take the plates of pizza Hunter hands me, tucking my beer bottle in the crook of my arm, and head back to my living room where Leo and the twins have set up a poker game. "Is this, like, a tradition or something now?"

"If beer and poker is what's needed, then beer and poker is what we do."

Leo chuckles at Sawyer's attempt at being wise. "Okay, Yoda."

"Actually, if Sawyer were pretending to be Yoda, he'd say 'beer and poker, we need.'" Beckett's wry voice interjects.

"Look, I have a little girl. Sorry I'm not up-to-date on my nerd fandom references," Leo gripes.

"Dude, Vi is no excuse to not know how Yoda talks." Sawyer shakes his head, and I chuckle as well.

"He's not wrong."

"Yeah, even I know you butchered that Yoda reference," Hunter chimes in, wincing as Leo scowls at him.

"I can still put you on highway patrol, Callaghan."

The rest of us fall silent. Leo and Hunter have some figuring out to do on where they're going to draw the line between their work dynamic — with Leo being Hunter's superior — and their off-work dynamic, with Hunter dating our little sister, Leo's cousin.

The parallel to Heidi and I is not lost on me. We've also got a steep hill ahead of us in trying to figure out if we can exist as anyone other than Dr. Morgan and Dr. Donnelly to each other.

But I must admit, I'm no longer willing to avoid the idea quite as desperately.

"We're not here to give Hunter a hard time. We're here to play poker. Deal 'em, Beck."

"To be fair, we're also here to figure out what's going on with Max," comes Beckett's oh-so-helpful reply.

I narrow my eyes at him. "Traitor. You're meant to be the brother with boundaries."

"Boundaries are only good when they help, not hinder. You've made it clear that not pushing you to talk about whatever is bugging you isn't helping anymore." He lifts his shoulders in a shrug. "We're worried about you, Max."

I sink back against the couch, thinking about what he just said.

Boundaries are only good when they help, not hinder.

Could the same be said for my boundaries with Heidi?

"It's my resident," I blurt out. Beckett's hands still mid-deal. The silence is deafening, and when I lift my head up off the back of the couch, I find four sets of eyes staring at me.

"Heidi. She's getting to me. Drawing me in, making me want things I haven't wanted in a long time — if ever," I start, trying to decide how much to tell them. I won't explain her connection to Thad. Not yet. "But I'm technically her boss, and no matter how attracted we are to each other, it feels wrong. The problem is, I don't think either one of us cares if it's right or wrong, and it's only a matter of time before we cross that invisible line. Hell, we've already blurred it."

"Is there a written policy about interprofessional relation-ships at the hospital?" Beckett asks.

I shake my head slowly. "No. There would be no way to enforce something like that with such a high number of staff. But this isn't a nurse dating a physical therapist. Or even two attendings starting a relationship. She's my subordinate. I'm in a position of authority over her, and a relationship between us could be construed as abusing that."

"Max, you're the last person anyone would ever accuse of taking advantage of someone."

I turn to Leo. "Thank you, but it wouldn't matter. People would talk and wonder. That's not fair to Heidi or me."

"So, don't do anything until her residency is over." Sawyer bites down on a piece of pizza, his next words mumbled around his mouthful of food. "Just keep it in your pants until then."

"Or could she ask to get reassigned to someone else?" Hunter chimes in. Even though the two ideas have merit, I hate the thought of them both.

"There's all manner of ways to handle things appropriately by taking necessary steps to protect the integrity of both your careers. I'm more concerned with why this is the first time I can remember Max expressing interest in a woman beyond some casual fling, and why he sounds so torn up about it."

As usual, Beckett hits the nail on the head, first try. I shift on the couch, uncomfortable with how close they're getting to uncovering parts of me I've kept hidden for years.

"It might not have been at poker night, but you guys pushed me to face my fears and figure out what was holding me back with your sister. And it was the best thing you could've done.

So, consider this me returning the favour. Whatever it is, let it out. Move forward."

I stare at Hunter, remembering how he almost let his deep-seated anxiety destroy his relationship with Kat. But he's right, he faced his fears head-on. I'm just not ready to do that yet.

"Message received. I'll think about it, guys. Now are we gonna play poker?"

My attempt at redirection is weak at best, and part of me fully expects them to push back and demand I tell them more. But to my immense relief, Leo comes to my rescue.

"Yeah, let's play. Five-card draw or Texas hold 'em?" He turns to Beckett, who resumes dealing.

"Five-card, obviously," Sawyer replies, standing up. "I'm going for more pizza. Anyone need a refill?"

The energy shifts, thankfully, and I force myself to relax and enjoy some time with the boys. But it weighs on me that they don't know the full story.

Which is why, after they leave — not before making me promise to join Hunter and Sawyer at Hastings tomorrow night — I find myself wandering my apartment, feeling no less confused about what to do with Heidi than I was at the beginning of the evening.

Chapter Sixteen

Heidi

After close to two days of monitoring Teagan, Max somehow manages to get us both a day off. I'm grateful for it. Not only because I'm tired, but also because I could use the distance from him.

My head is a mess of confusion, and I feel so unsure about what's going on between us. Am I attracted to him? Of course. Do I think he's attracted to me? Yes. But do I want anything to happen...

I don't know.

The *lonely* part of me says yes. The *determined to live life my way* part says no. The last thing I need when I'm so close to my goal of becoming a pediatrician is a man to come in and think he can control me or my choices. And Max definitely seems like the type of man who'd want his partner to do things his way.

I find my way over to Dogwood Cove. This town charmed me when I lived on the island before, and it still does. If anything, I feel like I'm seeing it with new eyes, not held back by Thad. He never wanted to wander and explore, go in and out of small stores and see what treasures were around. But today,

I can do just that. Heck, maybe I'll even peruse the rentals here and find somewhere cute to live.

I buy coffee and an apple nut muffin from The Nutty Muffin and take a seat at an empty table outside. Every time I was here in the past they'd been sold out of their signature muffins, so to get one today feels like an auspicious sign. The woman who rings it up proclaims them orgasmic, and as soon as I take a bite, the moan that escapes my mouth tells me she wasn't lying.

"They're really freaking good, aren't they?" I glance up to see a pretty brunette smiling at me as she gathers plates from the table next to me.

My mouth is full, so all I can do is nod until I swallow. "Seriously, I didn't believe her when she said orgasmic, but embarrassing as this is to admit, that was the most action I've had in a while." The brunette laughs, her blue eyes shining. She's familiar, somehow. "I'm sorry, I haven't lived on the island for a few years. Have we met? I feel like you're familiar but I can't figure it out."

She comes to stand beside me, a friendly and welcoming expression on her face. "Don't apologize. It could be me you recognize or one of my brothers." She sticks out the hand that isn't balancing a stack of dishes. "Kat Donnelly. I work part-time at Camille's when I'm not doing my practicum." She gestures over to the café that is right beside the bakery. It's new since I was last living on the island, and looks to be busy.

I shake her hand, the pieces falling into place. "You must be Max's sister. Studying to be a nurse practitioner, right?"

Her smile remains in place, only it's slightly guarded and curious now. "Yeah, that's me."

"Sorry," I hurry to fill in the blanks. "I'm Heidi Morgan. I used to be a nurse at WGH with your brother. Now I'm his resident."

"Oh." Kat's eyes widen dramatically. "Oooh…" she draws it out the second time, and my brow furrows. "So much is making sense now."

"Hey, Kitty Kat." A handsome man in a police uniform walks up, snaking his arm around Kat's waist and kissing the side of her neck.

"Hunter," she says almost dreamily before pivoting in his arms and kissing him deeply. Another man, this one older, with lighter hair but a faint resemblance to Kat, walks up.

"Seriously, Callaghan? What did I say about making out with my cousin in front of me," he gripes good-naturedly before turning to me. "Hi, sorry, did we interrupt?"

"No," Kat waves him off, disentangling herself from Hunter, who I think it's safe to assume is her boyfriend. "This is Heidi Morgan. She's Max's *resident*."

There's a heavy emphasis on the word resident, some underlying meaning I'm clearly not aware of, which is only magnified by the look the two men exchange with Kat.

"Yep, that's me," I say, standing up. This is feeling weird, and I don't know why. Not a bad weird, just, weird. "And I'm going now. Nice to meet you all." I start to walk away.

"Wait!" Kat calls out, and I stop, not wanting to be rude. Turning back, I see Hunter and the other guy heading inside the café, leaving just Kat out here with me. She seems nice, like someone I could be friends with. If only she wasn't the sister of the one man who's got me tied up in knots. "What are you doing tonight?"

I shrug because the truth is, I don't have any plans.

"Want to meet up for a drink later, get to know each other? The bar in town, Hastings, is super chill. I can give you all the dirt on Max you could possibly want."

There's a hopeful expression on her face, and I find myself wanting to say yes. Besides, there isn't really a good reason why I couldn't be friends with Max's sister.

"Sure. What time?"

Kat grins. "I've got family dinner at my parents' house, so how about eight?"

"Sounds good."

"Great. Let me give you my number." We exchange info, and then I finally walk away. The peaceful day I had hoped for, exploring the town, still lies in front of me. Only now, at the end of it, instead of my only company being a glass of wine and my favourite true crime podcast, I have plans. Plans that could turn out to be very interesting.

After all, it isn't much of a stretch to assume Kat will tell her brother about meeting me, and possibly about going out tonight. Which leaves one question. Will Max join us? Or will he keep his distance? I pushed the line last night. I know it, he knows it. What we don't know is, who's going to push it — or cross it — next?

I leave Dogwood Cove after an afternoon exploring and wandering along the beach. Back in my rental apartment in Westport, I quickly heat up a deeply unsatisfying frozen dinner, then get in the shower.

Opting not to drive so that I can enjoy a couple of drinks, I grab an Uber back to Dogwood Cove.

Kat Donnelly turns out to be a force of nature, just like her brother, only in a very different way. As soon as I arrive at Hastings, the brew pub where she suggested we meet, she pulls me in for a strong hug and introduces me to her best friend Lily. The three of us order a round of drinks and spend the next half hour getting to know each other.

They're a riot to hang out with, and when they drag me out on the dance floor, I don't protest. It's been forever since I let myself just have fun, med school and residency doesn't exactly lead to a lot of down time. But country night at a local bar is the perfect opportunity to do just that. Have fun.

A few songs later, we collapse at our table, all of us laughing and breathing heavily.

"Whoever made tonight's playlist deserves an award," Lily huffs out. She twists in her chair and gives a wave to the guy behind the bar. At his nod, she turns back. "We'll have to tell Dean that country night is a success."

"Consider me told, ladies. And I'm glad to hear you're enjoying it. You've got my wife to thank for the idea," a deep voice says in amusement. The bartender sets down three glasses of water with a smile before looking down at me in particular. "You're new. I'm Dean, welcome to my bar."

I swallow the sip of water I was drinking and grin up at him. "Thanks. I can't believe I haven't been here before."

"Heidi just moved back to Westport; she's working at the

hospital with Max," Kat supplies, leaning forward. "Dean and his wife Riley have the cutest little baby," she says to me before smacking her hand on the table. "But right now, we need another drink, Hastings!" Dean chuckles and heads back to the bar.

"I take it he named his bar after himself?" I ask, then we all giggle at how stupidly obvious my question is. Clearly, my lightweight tendencies with alcohol haven't changed. I make a mental note to pace myself. I don't want to make a complete fool of myself in front of my new friends.

Dean delivers another round of drinks, but this time he puts down three extra glasses.

"You're about to have company," he says, nodding toward the door. Our heads all swivel around. Lily groans, Kat sighs, and I suck in a breath.

"Kat, why do your brothers always have to crash girls night?"

"Because I can't stand being away from Hunter that long." Kat giggles in reply to Lily's half-hearted complaint.

Max, Hunter — who I remember from earlier today — and one of Max's twin brothers that I remember meeting the last time I was in town are heading our way. Hunter leads them straight to our table where he sweeps Kat out of her chair before sitting down and pulling her into his lap. The brother — Sawyer, I'm assuming, given the carefree grin he gives me — drops into a seat next to Lily and nudges her with his shoulder before picking up a fresh glass of beer and drinking deeply. His twin is nowhere in sight.

I sense Max at my shoulder and I lift my chin in greeting.

"Is it okay if I join?" he asks quietly, and I nod. He sits down next to me, and I stifle the urge to lean into him.

"Maxy! Why didn't you tell me Heidi was so freaking awesome. I love her!" Kat leans over, slapping his hand. "We're besties now, FYI."

Max lifts one eyebrow. "How many drinks have you had, Kat?" But she just scoffs.

"Hush. You can't crash girls night and then question my choices."

I see the tick in Max's jaw out of the corner of my eye. Knowing what I do now, I can assume his siblings' drinking is a sore point for him. Kat has clearly experienced his protectiveness before because she gives him a soft smile. "Besides, Hunter will take care of me and Lily. You just worry about Heidi."

Max smiles back at her, and something special passes between the two. As much as I want to protest that I don't need anyone worrying — especially not Max when our relationship is so up in the air — I don't dare interrupt them.

Just then, the song changes, and Kat jumps up, grabbing Hunter's hand and dragging him out to the dance floor.

Lily stands as well, staring at something on her phone. "I'll be right back," she mumbles before hurrying off. I watch her with a frown, until a playful voice interrupts me.

"Great to see you again, Heidi." I look across the table at Sawyer. Just as he was the first time we met, the guy's got *flirt* written all over him.

"You too, Sawyer," I say, choosing *not* to engage with his attempts to charm me. Not only because he isn't my type, but also because of the man sitting next to me with a glower on his face.

"So, how's work going? If this one —" he jerks his head toward Max "— starts giving you grief, come find me at the firehouse." His flirtatious wink is obvious to everyone.

"Back off, Sawyer. She's my resident, remember?" Max growls through clenched teeth. Sawyer lifts his shoulders in a nonchalant shrug.

"So? Does that mean I can't be friendly?"

"Not your kind of friendly."

Sawyer and Max stare at each other, and I get the sense an unspoken conversation is happening.

"Right, anyway, as thrilling as it is watching you two throw daggers at each other with your eyes, I'm gonna go find Lily." I push my chair back and stand, fully intending to go and find her. But Kat appears out of nowhere and apparently mistakes my standing up for a different reason.

"Oh my God, you have to come and dance! Max, dance with Heidi," she shrieks excitedly. I hadn't even noticed her and Hunter come back to the table, but sure enough, Kat has me in one hand and Max in the other, and she's dragging us both onto the dance floor.

She drops our hands, only to push us together so strongly I stumble, and Max has no choice but to put his hands on my hips to steady me.

"Dance!" Kat whirls away and into Hunter's arms.

"We don't have to —" Max starts to say but emboldened by alcohol, I decide to throw caution to the wind. Taking his hand in mine, I move my other to his shoulder.

"I want to."

The sounds of Chris Stapleton singing "You Should Probably Leave" fill the room, and our eyes lock. The significance of the two of us dancing to this song is not lost on me.

We start out slow, figuring out our rhythm. There's enough space between us for a third person, but over the course of the song, we slowly draw closer together, like an unseeable magnetic force is in control of our every move.

My awareness narrows down to the feel of his strong hand spanning my back, his muscles bunching under my touch, and the way he's firmly gripping my other hand.

It's undeniable: Max is in control. He's leading this, us, and I'm just along for the ride. And for once, the idea of a man controlling me fills me with heat, not dread. Maybe because a part of me trusts him, trusts that he isn't controlling me to hurt me, but to bring me happiness. Pleasure, even. My hand tightens on his shoulder at the thought of Max leading me to a different kind of pleasure...

"Heidi?" his questioning rumble blows warm air against my ear. I don't reply, I simply shift slightly closer to him, reveling in how his hold on me tightens.

We stay in that bubble of trust and connection that apparently slow dancing can create for another minute or two. When the song ends, and the more upbeat sounds of Luke Bryan's soulful voice comes over the speakers, it's undeniable that I'm disappointed. I fully expect him to drop my hands. But to my surprise, Max gives me an almost impish grin.

"Think you can keep up, Morgan?"

My eyes narrow with confusion, but that quickly morphs into surprise as he begins to spin me around the dance floor. This is no slow dance. This is a fast-paced, full of tricks and surprises two-step that I did not see coming. Thank God for that session of two-step classes I took after my breakup with Thad as a way to fill my evenings, or I would be flat on my face.

Except, no, I wouldn't be. Because Max is so masterful with leading me, guiding me through every move, it's as if we've been dancing together forever. My body instinctively knows how to respond, twirling and shifting to his every command.

I find myself mouthing the lyrics to myself, and then I see Max's eyes zeroed in on mine just as the chorus line hits.

"All I know is, I don't want this night to end."

Chapter Seventeen

Max

"You're just full of surprises, Dr. Donnelly." Heidi's breathless teasing tickles my ear as I lift her up from a dip at the end of the song.

I don't hold back my chuckle. There's a lightness inside of me I haven't felt in a long time. Dancing with her was fun. Easy. Right. Taking a step away from her and losing the physical connection we had? Not so fun, but necessary, if I don't want her to feel exactly how affected I am by having her in my arms.

"Kat decided she wanted to learn how to two-step in high school and none of our brothers would go with her, so I agreed to. Can't say I've had much opportunity to practice since then, but I guess I remembered a few things."

We make our way back to the table. Sawyer looks up from his phone and gives me a knowing stare. "Done cutting a rug out there, you two?" He passes over two glasses and a fresh pitcher of beer. "Figured you might be thirsty. Max, I'm surprised you still remember how to do all of that. But I guess a pretty lady is good motivation." He winks at Heidi, ignoring my glare. Thankfully, he stands and pockets his phone. "Anyway, I gotta get going. See you around, Heidi. Max, gym tomorrow?"

"Yeah man, I'll see you then. You good to drive?"

Sawyer nods. "Of course."

My siblings are used to my obsessing about their safety when we go out. It's why we all have Uber on speed dial, and why they know I'll always check in to make sure they're okay to drive. The guys and I know our limits. But even still, I can't help but check in with them.

I nod, Heidi says goodbye, and Sawyer makes his way to the exit, leaving just Heidi and me at the table. She picks up one glass filled with beer and pushes the other to me, but I wave it off, choosing water, instead. I've had one beer, that's my limit.

"That was fun, Max, thank you for dancing with me." Her hand lands on my leg for an instant before she snatches it away.

"I think I should be thanking you," I say, stretching my arm out across the back of both our chairs. My fingers catch a loose curl of her hair that came free from her ponytail while we were dancing, and I twist it around. "It's been a long time since I danced with anyone. I could've stomped all over your feet."

Her eyes sparkle. "I doubt that. You wouldn't lose control."

Fuck, if only she knew how much I'd like to lose control with her.

"We're going home." Kat and Hunter stumble up to the table, arms wrapped around each other. Hunter's lips are pressed to Kat's neck.

"Hunter, you good?" I ask, and his head lifts. His eyes are clear, and he gives me a sharp nod.

"Absolutely."

Heidi and Kat hug. I can't deny it does something to me to

see her get along with my family so easily. Since Cara, I've never let another woman get close enough to me to warrant meeting my family. But Kat and Sawyer are both taken by Heidi, I can tell. I briefly wonder what they'd think or feel if they knew who her ex is, but that thought is dismissed quickly. My family is far better at forgiveness than I am, that's for sure. They wouldn't jump to a snap judgment the way I did, assuming she had any part of Thad's destruction. They would give her the chance to explain.

Because my family, they're all better people than I am.

After they leave, Heidi sits back down, closer to me this time, so that our legs are almost touching.

"I guess I should probably head out soon as well," she murmurs softly, her finger drawing circles in the condensation left on the table by our drinks.

Now that the adrenaline rush from having her in my arms is starting to subside, it's being replaced by a seed of misgiving. All the lines, all the boundaries and rules I've set for myself when it comes to relationships are being obliterated, one by one. It's disconcerting, confusing, and maddening, even. Because I'm not entirely certain I want to go back to my old way of living — behind those lines, boundaries, and rules.

"I'll drive you home," I say gruffly. I walk up to the bar and settle the rest of our tab, paying for mine and Heidi's drinks. When I make it back to the table, she's waiting for me, and I can tell she's just as disconcerted by tonight as I am.

We make our way to my car in silence, and I open her door. She mumbles her thanks under her breath as she slides in, and I close the door. In the few seconds it takes for me to walk around to the driver's side, I decide it's up to me to dispel the tension.

Except I can't. Because in the close confines of my car, all I can think about is how close she is. How alone we are. And how badly I want to pull over and find out if she's as desperate for me as I am for her. Dip my fingers underneath her panties and see if she's wet to match the ache of my hardening cock. Kiss her and feel her mouth open to me and her body melt under me.

Fuck.

That ache? It's now a sharp throb as my angry dick presses against my jeans.

Thank fuck, the drive to Westport is quick at night. We manage to fill the time with superficial topics about work, and before I know it, I'm pulling up in front of her apartment building. Shutting off the car plunges us into a silent darkness, but the air is charged with something indescribable. I can sense it like a living being in the car with us, begging to be set free.

I open my door and get out, discreetly adjusting myself to try and hide the evidence of how badly I want her. Walking around and opening her door, I realize my mistake in standing so close when she brushes against me as she stands.

Her intake of breath tells me I didn't manage to hide fucking anything. And when those mossy green eyes turn up to look at me from under long dark lashes, I know I'm lost.

My hand lifts to stroke her cheek, tucking her hair behind her ear.

"I really want to kiss you," I admit, my voice sounding hoarse with need.

"Why don't you?"

At her bold question, my heart fucking stutters in my chest.

"Because...I shouldn't." That sounds pathetic, even to me.

"There are no rules against this. I checked." Shit. Her boldness is sexy as hell. The admission that she wants this, wants me, enough to have looked into whether we can be together? The last shards of my resolve are dissolving rapidly.

"Heidi," I say warningly, but it comes out half-hearted. We both know where this is headed. My hands cup the back of her head and I pull her in until our lips are barely an inch apart. I need to know she's certain. This is a line we can't go back from. "Are you sure?"

Heidi answers by closing the distance between us. The second our lips touch, the ripples of sexual tension and attraction that have been growing between us turn into a tsunami-sized wave of lust. She moans into my mouth, and I take the opening, teasing her with my tongue, nibbling on her lips, and consuming her with my kiss.

This is unlike anything I've experienced in my forty years on this planet. One touch of her lips and I'm gone, spiraling into the unknown. She was tempting before, now she's irresistible. Our kiss turns deeper, more intense. Her hands are clutching at my shirt as if she, too, is desperate to get closer.

A car alarm going off startles me back to reality. We're outside her apartment, this is anything but private, and we're bordering on indecency with this kiss.

"Wow," she gasps when we reluctantly separate. Her hands are still gripping the front of my shirt, just as mine are still tangled in her hair.

"Yeah. Wow," I reply. My heart is thundering as I try to regain some sort of control.

"That needs to happen again. And again and again and again."

We both laugh at her enthusiasm, and I duck down to press a firm but closed-mouth kiss to her luscious lips. "Agreed."

Our foolish smiles match as we stand there staring at each other. "But next time, maybe we go somewhere so we won't offend your neighbours."

Heidi's head darts from side to side. "I don't see anyone offended." She gives me a wink. "But private sounds good, too."

Private. Because we shouldn't let anyone know about whatever this is, not yet.

"The optics of this won't be great for you if people at work find out." My thumb strokes her cheek. "Are you sure you want do... whatever this is we're doing?"

I give her credit; she does seem to pause and consider it for a second. "First of all, let me be clear. *I want you*. Second of all, I appreciate your concern about how this will look for me, so yeah, we'll keep it a secret for now." Her hand lifts to cup my cheek as she stares into my eyes. "But are you sure *you* want to do this. I know I said it's not against the rules of the hospital, and it's not. But you're right, it could look wrong to anyone on the outside. I don't want to cause any problems for you or me."

I truly didn't think it was possible to want her even more than I already do, but somehow, I do. Her transparency, her authenticity, her willingness to be open and bold about what she wants... Fuck, it's sexy.

I kiss her again, partly because I can't help it, but also because I'm having a hard time coming up with my own response.

Normally, I'm fully in control. I know what I feel, what I

want, and what I'm going to say. But Heidi manages to somehow erase all of that from me and turn me into a simple man who wants to worship at her feet.

"You're a temptress, Heidi Morgan. I think while I was so busy hating you for all the wrong reasons, I didn't realize just how much I wanted you. But I don't want to hate you anymore. Not when wanting is so much more fun." Our lips crash together in another kiss, this one a little more desperate and messier than the last. "Tomorrow night, after our shift, I'm picking you up and taking you out. You deserve nothing less, hell, you deserve a lot more than some secret rendezvous with your ass of a boss. But I'm a selfish man. And I want you."

Her face splits into the widest smile I've ever seen.

"A little clandestine romance never hurt anybody..." The seductive, teasing lilt to her voice has me sliding my hand around to the back of her neck as I tug her in for another kiss.

I kiss her once more because now that I've had a taste, I don't know how I'll ever stop. Then I reluctantly step back. "I'll see you tomorrow at work."

Her lips — that I know now are exactly as soft as they look — curve up into a satisfied smile. "Okay."

Walking backward, I keep my gaze connected with her until I bump into my car with my ass. Her hand lifts to cover her soft giggle, and I give a rueful smile in return before finally turning away to get in my car.

The drive home is short, and that citrusy smell I'll now always associate with Heidi lingers inside my car. The dumb smile that's been on my face since I kissed her is locked in place. It's only when I get inside and dump my phone and keys on my kitchen counter that I notice a message waiting for me from Sawyer.

SAWYER: She's hot man, don't mess it up.

MAX: I thought you didn't believe in relationships

SAWYER: I don't. But fuck, the way she looked at you almost made my pants tight.

MAX: That is so wrong.

SAWYER: You're tellin me. Look, Heidi seems great. I'm just saying, you might have your reasons to not want to get close to someone, but she might be worth breaking your rules.

He's right.

She is.

Chapter Eighteen

Heidi

Walking into work the day after kissing Max feels a bit like the first day of school as a kid. The nervous anticipation, the excitement for the unknown, the overthinking of what to wear, all of it.

We agreed to keep things a secret for now, but how hard is that going to be now that I know what it's like to be held by him? I've felt his lips on mine, his hands on my body, and I've heard his rough voice whispering filthy, perfect things into my ear.

The fantasies and dreams he used to exist in actually have a chance of coming true. Which is exhilarating and terrifying. That fear has me clinging desperately to wanting to keep whatever this is strictly physical. No emotions. Because the last time I let a man into my heart, he ruled my life for far too long.

I'll be damned if I ever let that happen again.

When I get to the peds nursing station, he's not there. There's no mistaking the flash of disappointment that brings.

Instead, Tina comes rushing up. We haven't had a shift together since the failed online dating experiment. "You're glow-ing," she states dramatically. "Am I that good of a matchmaker?"

Of course, just as she's saying that last word, Max appears. Our eyes connect instantly, and he quirks a brow at me. I give what I can only hope is a subtle shake of my head.

"Sorry to disappoint, Tina, but no. He was a total dud. Spent more time talking about his wish list of classic cars, and how his high-paying job as — get this — a real estate agent was going to get them for him. Pretty sure he mentioned his 'fucking awesome stockbroker' a dozen times and how they were 'making a killing in bitcoin.' I left before dessert."

Tina covers her mouth as she laughs. "Oh God, I'm sorry. Did he call his stockbroker 'bro?'"

I nod slowly, sneaking a glance over at Max, who's doing a really good job of pretending to focus on a patient chart. But I see his lips tipping up slightly.

"Anyway, no more online dating for me. If I'm going to find a guy, it needs to be someone who understands the demands of our work, and someone who sees *me* and wants *me*. I don't think a little worshipping is too much to ask."

Max's eyes flare wide, and I see the subtle clenching of his jaw. But it's not anger or frustration. Nope, I know better now. That's desire.

And it's directed at me.

He's flipping a pen around in his hand, a sure sign he's thinking about something. A full body shiver comes over me at the thought that I could be the subject of his intense concentration. I turn away from him slightly, because if I don't, there's not a chance in hell of hiding my body's response to him.

"If anyone deserves to be worshipped by a hot guy on his

knees, it's you," Tina says seriously, placing her hand over mine. "Bonus points if his tongue is doing the worshipping."

Thankfully, she whispers that last bit because — talk about a *not suitable for work* conversation. But the clatter of a pen on the counter has me peeking back at Max. He heard her, alright.

"Dr. Morgan, if you're ready, I'd like to get started on rounds."

I stand up quickly, too quickly, apparently, because the chair I was sitting on rolls across the station. Tina gives me a weird look, but I recover and avoid her attention.

"Yup, I'm ready." Crap, do I sound breathless? I force my steps to be normally paced as I make my way around the desk to him when what I want to do is to run to him.

We set off, presumably to our first patient, but then Max veers down a hallway. He opens the door to an empty conference room and ushers me in.

The second the door closes behind him, he spins me around, so my back is pressed against it, my hands above my head, pinned in place with one of his as the other trails down my cheek.

"Worshipped by a guy on his knees? Is that what you want?" he growls in my ear, nipping my earlobe with his teeth before soothing it with a press of his lips. The feel of him, combined with the mental picture he paints, sends a rush of wet heat between my legs. Christ, I'm going to need to start keeping extra panties at work.

I bite back a moan as he trails kisses along my jaw before covering my mouth with his. His tongue plunders my mouth. He's holding his body back from mine, and if my hands were free, I'd be pulling him in to meet me.

"I'll worship you, Heidi. You've already brought me to my knees metaphorically, but if it's my tongue you want, you'll have to wait until later."

"Max," I sigh, pushing against the hand holding mine. "I need to touch you."

"No. If you touch me, I won't be able to keep this under control. You're too tempting, sweetheart."

The endearment makes me pause. That's not keeping things physical. But before I can say anything, he kisses me again, hard and fast. Desperate. Then he steps back, drops my hands, and backs away even farther. His stare is locked on me, his hands in his pockets.

"Tonight."

He says that one word like a promise. I lick my lips as I nod. Slowly he steps forward, withdrawing one hand from his pocket to stroke a finger down my cheek.

"I knew it would be a challenge working with you now that we've given in to this. But fuck. Not being able to touch you when you're next to me is..."

"Anticipation?" I supply with an impish smirk, my worry over the pet name forgotten. "Foreplay, even?"

His deep chuckle brings him closer, and his forehead drops to meet mine. "Sure, let's go with that. Twelve hours of torturous foreplay until I get you alone again."

Needless to say, over the course of our shift, the anticipation continued to build. He didn't kiss me again, there were no stolen moments, but our physical chemistry is undeniable. I could feel it, vibrating between us, the entire day. It's a miracle no one else did.

But a voice in my head became louder as well, warning me to hold back. The intensity of the last few days hits me in the shower while I'm shaving my legs and thinking about tonight. We've gone from enemies, to a fragile understanding, to confessing our secrets, and finally, giving in to our attraction — in a matter of a few days.

It's a lot, and my head is spinning, to say the least. For all that keeping it casual and only physical feels safer, I must admit, I want him. *All of him.*

If he wants all of me. Which, I realize, I don't even know. We were so caught up in the physical pull between us, and in setting the ground rules for how to handle our attraction at work, we never actually spoke about what this is. For all I know, he's just looking for a casual forbidden fling.

The possibility of that, along with my mixed reaction to the idea of being nothing more than a fling, even though it would be a hell of a lot smarter for me, has me chewing on my thumbnail as I open up a video chat with Skye.

"Hey, baby cakes," she says cheerfully once the call connects.

"I have a date with Max Donnelly and I don't know what to wear," I blurt out. Skye's mouth falls open and her eyes bug out, and the whole look is so amusing, I snort-laugh.

"Hold on. Wait. What the heck did you just say?" she sputters. "Wait. Do I get to say I told you so? Oh my God, did you have storage room sex?"

"No, no, no." I laugh, already feeling less nervous. "No sex.

Just a kiss. And a dance. And now a date."

"That's a lot! Shit, okay. Deep breaths, Skye."

"I'm the one who needs to breathe, woman, I'm the one with the date."

She flaps her hand in the air. "Hush. I'm doing some calming breaths."

I sit down on the edge of my bed, aware that my drama queen of a best friend needs a minute. Sure enough, a few seconds later, her eyes open and she looks at me, her excitement for me palpable, even through a phone screen.

"Okay. Let's hit the closet. You need to look hot."

Several outfits and plenty of laughter later, we settle on a wide-legged black jumpsuit that drapes off one shoulder nicely.

"Now, you have fun tonight, and don't do anything I wouldn't do."

I roll my eyes at Skye's parting shot, knowing full well that she'd do whatever the heck she wanted. "Thanks for your help, I'll talk to you tomorrow."

"I expect a full report."

After hanging up, I suddenly realize Max will be here any minute. A final swipe of lip gloss and mascara is all I have time for before grabbing some shoes and a clutch just as my phone rings the tone for the front door buzzer to my building.

I grant Max access, then do a final check in the mirror before going to the door of my apartment and opening it.

Crystal blue eyes travel up and down my body, devouring me with their intense gaze. His hand comes up to scrub across his jaw. "Heidi, you're stunning."

Unfortunately, I blush easily. Most of the time I can control it, but apparently, one compliment from Max has my skin heating and becoming pink instantly.

"Thank you." I drink in the sight of him in slim-fitting pants and a dark shirt he's left untucked. Something about that untucked shirt with the sleeves rolled up to show his muscled forearms stirs the needy lust inside of me. It's a far cry from the scrubs or slacks and collared shirt I'm used to seeing him wear at work. My tongue darts out to lick my suddenly dry lips.

Max reaches down and takes my hand, guiding me out of my doorway and into the hall, and into his arms. His head dips forward and he kisses me lightly. "Ready?"

We go down to his waiting car, he opens the door for me, and closes it after I'm seated. I'm not used to a man being considerate like this, doing these small gestures that are just the right amount of chivalry. It could feel controlling, but with Max, it doesn't. It feels right.

The entire drive, Max has my hand in his. His thumb gently strokes across my wrist as we talk, and it's so distracting, I have no clue what the conversation is about.

Pescado, the seafood restaurant Max chose for tonight, is a beautiful upscale place right on the water in Westport. The warm wood accents, candlelight, and acoustics designed for intimate conversations far surpass any other date I've been on. We're led to a smaller room at the back of the restaurant with high-backed booths that seem to guarantee privacy. Once we've each ordered a glass of wine and our dinners, Max settles back in his seat and smirks.

"Do I still make you nervous?"

I'm caught off guard by his question, so take a sip of my cool, crisp sauvignon blanc before responding. "You, no. Us, yes."

Max leans forward, placing his elbows on the table, and locking his eyes on mine. "Tell me why."

It's not a question, it's a command. A gentle, respectful one, but I feel the power behind the words. Where my ex was conniving with his control, Max is considerate. He wants to be in charge because he wants to take care of me.

I choose to be honest and transparent. "You said it last night. A relationship with you has the potential to have a negative impact on me and my career if it goes poorly. And truthfully, a part of me is still trying to navigate the shift in you from jerk supervisor to seriously sexy date." I leave it at that, hoping the door is open enough for him to step in and give me an indication of how he'd define us.

He steeples his hands under his chin. Something tells me if he had a pen in hand, it would be flipping over his fingers as he processes what I've said.

"I was awful to you, and I'm sorry for that. An apology is the least of what you deserve from me, but it's also the most I can give. That and a promise to never be like that to you again. No matter what happens tonight or in the future with us. You're an incredible doctor, and it wasn't fair for me to take out my own issues on your performance."

I want desperately to ask what those issues are, to try and understand, but something stops me. This isn't the time. Instead, I wait, my eyes never leaving Max's face.

He takes in a deep breath and expels it slowly, closing his eyes as he does so. When he opens them again, I see his soul laid bare, and it makes my heart crack open. "You make me feel weak with how attracted I am to you, and how much I want you. I've never felt so out of control of my emotions and desires, and it terrifies me. Any negative outcome from a relationship with me would be limited to your work. And I swear to you, I would do my utmost to prevent anything from affecting your future. But for me, its not my job on the line. It's my heart."

To say I'm stunned into silence is an understatement. "Max," I croak out in a whisper. His confession has me overwhelmed. He's laying all his cards on the table. He's making it clear that being with me is both the thing he wants, and the thing that scares him. That openness, that willingness to show his vulnerability, that says more than any words. Because if there's one thing I've learned, it's that Max Donnelly doesn't show his soft side to anyone.

Max reaches over and lifts my hands in his, drawing them up to his lips and kissing them sweetly before laying them back down on the table, his eyes downcast the entire time.

The powerful, intelligent, perfectly imperfect man in front of me has been brought to his knees by his feelings for me. The realization opens a floodgate in my mind and in my heart, and the emotions I thought I'd kept at bay come rushing in. He might have admitted to his feelings first, but that doesn't mean I don't have them, too.

But he is the one laid bare before me. He is the one who needs to know he's not alone right now.

"You aren't weak because you have feelings for me," I start softly. "Because it's not weakness to let someone in. It's strength. Because it takes trust."

Max nods slowly.

"Do you trust me, Max?"

There's a long, drawn out second in which I hold my breath waiting for his reply.

"Yes."

Chapter Nineteen

Max

To my surprise, the world doesn't implode now that I'm dating Heidi in secret. Fine, it's only been a week, but that week has been...dare I say, good?

After our first official date, cliché as it was to simply go for dinner, we made plans to hike the trails of Dogwood Cove on our next day off. This time, we're avoiding the hot springs and the memories held there. When she admitted over a fucking text message that she knew I was naked in the water, I just about lost it and drove to her house to make good on the fantasy she described having that night.

It's gone unspoken that we're taking it slow, given both of our past experiences with relationships. But that goes against everything my body wants, even though it is exactly what my head says I need. Unfortunately, the stolen kisses in supply closets, brief touches of our hands as we walk down the hall, and text messages that are becoming increasingly risqué are only serving to increase my primal desire to have her in every conceivable way.

It's been months since I was with anyone intimately. And my hand is a poor substitute for the tight, wet heat of a woman's body. I've increased my runs in distance, speed, and frequency.

But even that isn't enough to outrun the continual list of filthy things I want to do with Heidi.

Take right now, for instance. She's bending over my shoulder to read an MRI report with me, and it's taking all my self-control not to pull her into my lap and kiss her senseless.

And she knows it, the little temptress. Because when she reaches out to point at something, her hand drags across my bicep. When she turns to say something, she doesn't shift away, no, she keeps her mouth close to my ear, tormenting me.

"Dr. Donnelly? Dr. Morgan?"

We spring apart as if we were caught in the act. Curtis, one of my favourite nurses to work with because of his calm, steady demeanour, is standing on the other side of the desk. His eyes look troubled, which is unusual for him.

"Yes?" I say, standing up and casually stepping away from Heidi.

"I think you need to come and see Teagan."

An ominous sense of foreboding comes over me. We both hurry over to her room, pulling on masks, gowns, and gloves before we go in. Maya is hovering over the bed, clutching Teagan's hands.

Heidi goes to her side, while I go straight to Teagan. Her breathing has slowed to a disturbingly slow rate, and I can hear the fluid rattling around with every inhale. She's semiconscious, her eyelids fluttering open when I gently squeeze her shoulder and say her name before closing again. The effort it's taking her body to breathe is clearly taking a toll.

This is the part of cystic fibrosis that I hate the most. The way everything can seem to be improving one moment, and then crash the next.

After listening to her heart and lungs, I don't need to look at the monitor to know what I'm going to see. But I do anyway. Her oxygen saturation is horrendously low. She's febrile again. And when Curtis silently hands me the results from her latest blood work, it confirms my sinking suspicion.

Teagan's body is shutting down, and there's not a fucking thing I can do. As a responsible minor, she has the legal right to express her wishes for resuscitation. And last year, after a particularly bad bout of infections, Teagan and her family came to an agreement. If her body began to not respond to treatment, and her prognosis was poor, she didn't want extraordinary measures. No breathing tubes, no CPR, no ICU admission. Teagan's family knew from the outset that her diagnosis was a life sentence. But none of us could predict when the end would come.

We've staved this moment off for over a decade. And while so many CF patients go on to adulthood, I know in my gut that Teagan's end is coming sooner than any of us wanted.

I remove my gloves and walk over to Maya, whose shoulders are shaking with silent sobs. Heidi has her arm around her, and when she meets my gaze, I give a subtle shake.

"Maya, I'm sorry. Our options are limited," I start, fighting back my own emotions. I have to hold it together until I'm alone. Teagan and her family need me to be strong. "We can try a few runs of dialysis to pull off the excess fluid, but the microbiology report came back on the sputum sample, and it's not good."

"It's that one we can't pronounce, isn't it?" Her voice is shaky as Maya lifts her gaze from her daughter to me. "The one that starts with 'P.'"

"Pseudomonas aeruginosa. Yes. And she's not responding to the antibiotics anymore." I give her a sad smile, remembering different times when Teagan came in with lung infections that she'd recovered from. She'd always want to know how to pronounce the technical names.

"If you can name it, you can tame it," she'd say, and we would fist bump.

But there will be no fist bump this time. No taming of this bacteria.

"She hated dialysis," Maya says. *"'No more tubes, Mom.'* That's what she said last night. I didn't understand why, but now I suppose it makes sense. She knew she was getting worse." Teagan's mom sinks down into the chair beside the bed and drops her head to the mattress, overcome with tears.

I drop down to my haunches next to her. "We'll do everything we can to make her comfortable, Maya." The words are hollow-sounding, even to me. The end of a child's life, whether it's sudden or expected, is a gut-wrenching experience for everyone involved. Even us practitioners — nurses and doctors and therapists — it breaks our hearts every time. The helplessness as we stand by, offering what little comfort we can, watching families say goodbye to their kids far too soon.

Heidi leans down to Maya. "Can I call your husband for you, Maya?"

She nods and Heidi steps out to contact Teagan's father. From what I remember, he works out of town a lot. I can only hope he's not far away right now. From the looks of things, she doesn't have much longer.

I step back a bit and murmur some instructions to Curtis about adjusting medications and moving toward a palliative approach. We've gone over this with Teagan's parents before when we had a scare on a past admission. They know not to expect her to regain consciousness, especially since part of the comfort measures we will use will keep her sedated.

Before I leave her room, I do another check of Teagan's vitals. I know what the monitors and lab results are telling me, but I need to hear it, see it, and feel it for myself. If anything, her breathing sounds even more laboured than just a few minutes ago. The wheezy congested sounds coming through my stethoscope have me cursing inside my head at this demon of a disease that is robbing a young girl of her life and her family of her very existence.

The next few hours are tense. By now, all the staff on shift know Teagan is dying. Her family and friends are with her, and all we can do is check in to make sure she's comfortable and wait.

Heidi and I make our way to all the rest of our patients, but I hold myself back from leaning into any comfort she might try to offer. I'm detached. Distant. I have to be. I have to compartmentalize right now while a beloved patient is dying in one room, a dozen others are waiting for my attention, and the woman I'm coming to care for far too much is looking at me with a worried expression. As if she fears I'll break in two.

When the monitor at the nurse's station displaying Teagan's vitals finally shows the flat line where her heartbeat should be, we all hear the cries of grief and pain coming from her room.

Nurses turn and hug each other, Heidi included. I watch

Curtis fold her into his arms, and I see the tears on all their faces.

Still, I stay strong. Cool and in control, disconnected from the flood of sadness looming inside me.

I go through the motions of Teagan's final assessment and pronouncement of death. I hug Maya, shake hands with her husband who thankfully made it here quickly, and offer the trite words of comfort that are all I *can* offer now.

Back at the desk, I fill out the necessary paperwork, file everything, and ensure Curtis knows where it's all located when Teagan's body is taken down to the morgue. Only then, when I've done all I can do and all I must do, I make my escape.

There's a back stairwell at Westport General that's rarely used. It's meant to be a fire exit, and all the doors have signs that say an alarm will sound if you open them. But most experienced staff know that's not the case. Instead, this stairwell has become an unofficial refuge for us. A place where we can go when we need to get away from patients or coworkers. At any given time, there'll be someone walking up and down the flights of stairs, muttering under their breath. Or someone simply sitting on the stairs, lost in thought.

It's an unspoken rule that you don't disturb anyone who's in the back stairwell unless it's an emergency.

So when I sense someone sitting down beside me as my head hangs low and tears well up in my eyes, I know it can only be one person.

"Max, what can I do?"

Even if I come to regret this moment, I don't care. I need her. I turn and drag Heidi into my lap, bury my head in the crook of her neck, and just hold on tight. Her hands run soothingly up and down my back. I can't hear what she's murmuring over the sound of my own grief in my head.

Losing a patient always hits me hard. Clarence pushed me to talk to a therapist last year about it when he became aware of just how hard it was for me. That helped me learn the skills to be able to function after a loss, but it's a struggle every time.

Yet somehow, Heidi being here in this moment is lessening the tidal wave of pain, guilt, and questioning what I could have done differently.

Time passes. We probably need to go back to work. Some small rational part of me knows that if someone sees us like this, it will look suspiciously intimate for two coworkers. Even if comforting each other is a natural act after a patient loss, it's not like I'm about to hold Curtis or Ginny like this.

Eventually, my shuddered breathing calms, and I manage to find a thread of my normal self-control. I lift my head to meet Heidi's worried gaze.

"I'm sorry." My voice is a rasp, hoarse with emotions. She simply lifts her hand up to cup my cheek before leaning in and kissing my lips sweetly.

"Don't be. You have nothing to apologize for. Thank you for letting me be with you right now, I know it probably isn't easy to let someone in when you're feeling like this."

Fuck, this woman. Does she even know the power she holds over me? One sentence and I swear I would go to the ends of the earth for her.

"It's easy to let you in," I reply honestly, bringing her lips to mine for another taste. This is reckless. I know it is, she knows it is, but we both need the connection.

Her fingers are raking gently through the hair at the nape of my neck as she pulls back to study my face closely. There's no judgment, just open curiosity, and compassion.

"I normally go home and eat a popsicle after a death."

A bark of laughter escapes me at her seemingly random comment. "A popsicle? Why?"

She shrugs. "I don't really know. I guess because it's a childhood treat, it's what we give our patients when they can't keep food down or need a sweet treat or a reward for undergoing something difficult. So I guess in my head, having one is a way of honouring them. I spend the evening thinking about them, their lives, and their struggles. If I knew the patient well, I might spend a few days thinking about them and honouring them in my thoughts, but even if they were a new patient, I still feel like they deserve to be remembered, even if only for a short while. Sometimes, when I was on the mainland, a few of us nurses would meet at a park and plant a flower somewhere. Why, what do you do?"

I'm too stunned by her beautiful and compassionate nature to answer right away. Because my way of coping is a lot less romantic and sweet.

"I used to be devastated for days. It got to the point where I questioned if I could continue working in peds. Then Clarence hooked me up with a counsellor to work through the guilt I'd always feel. Now I go home, pour a large shot of whiskey or two, go to bed, then get up the next day and force myself to move forward."

"Alone?"

I nod. "Always."

She tilts her head to the side, a worried furrow to her brow. "You shouldn't be alone tonight, Max. Teagan was special to you."

I draw in a ragged breath. "Yeah, she was."

"Can I be with you tonight?" she asks quietly. And there is only one answer.

"Yes. Please." Her lips find my forehead, then my cheek, then my lips. "Heidi," I say hoarsely, pulling her back in for a deeper, more intense kiss. "I can't promise anything. But tonight, I need you."

"I know," she says against my lips. "I need you, too."

I groan into her mouth once more, my hands tangling in her hair. Voices in the hall outside the stairwell force us apart.

"Tonight."

Her tongue darts out to lick her lips. "Tonight."

Chapter Twenty

Heidi

I pull up to Max's apartment building and turn my car off but make no move to get out just yet.

The silence is deafening.

I know why I'm here tonight, and it has nothing to do with any romantic notion about Max and I taking our relationship to the next level. Whatever happens tonight is between two people who need a release, who need a way to process the incredibly heavy emotions that lingered like dark clouds over our entire shift.

When he told me how he normally spends his nights after a patient loss, my heart broke for him. Of course, losing a patient would hit hard for someone who almost lost their father. I'm grateful he got some help, but that doesn't mean his coping strategy is the healthiest. For some reason, Max doesn't seem to think he deserves a partner — in anything. It makes me wonder about his family. I know he's got siblings, and I always assumed they were close. But if so, then why does he hold himself back from everyone at work? Did someone in his past really fuck him up that much emotionally, scar him so permanently that he's resigned himself to a life alone?

My phone vibrates on the seat next to me, and I glance over to see his name. Picking it up, I open the message and huff out a short laugh.

MAX: I can see you thinking from here, Morgan. If you're having second thoughts, just go. I promise it won't change anything between us. But if you're planning on coming in, then get that perfect ass out of the car.

My face heats. First, because he caught me overthinking everything, and second, due to the comment about my ass. I'm suddenly realizing tonight might be the night I learn just how dirty Max Donnelly can be.

And that's what makes me get out of the car. I look up, and several stories in the sky, I see the silhouette of a man looking out a window, and I shiver. I'd know the cut of that torso anywhere; the image is permanently imprinted on my mind ever since the day at the hot springs.

As soon as I get to the front door, I hear the telltale buzz of it unlocking. He's definitely watching. And waiting.

Knowing that sends a wave of wet heat between my legs, and I clench them together.

The elevator takes forever, or at least it feels like it does. I suppose anticipation makes everything seem longer than it really is. When the doors finally open on Max's floor and he's got one arm up leaning against the opening, my sharp intake of breath causes a dark smirk to cross his face.

He reaches out and pulls me from the elevator car, straight into his arms, his mouth crashing into mine right there in the hallway. His hands lower to my ass and squeeze tightly as he growls into our kiss.

"Perfect."

We stumble to what I assume is his apartment. As soon as we're inside, Max spins me around to face the now locked door and lifts my hands up over my head, his nose running down the column of my neck.

"Are you sure you want this?"

His voice is quiet, and I know he's asking me to confirm my consent, but I can hear how close he is to the edge. How flimsy his hold on his control is right now. And the thought that I'm the cause of that, of Max Donnelly letting loose, is the thing that erases any lingering doubt in my mind.

"I want this. I want you."

Six words are all it takes to light an inferno.

Max's hands go to the hem of my shirt, and it's lifted up and off, all while I'm still facing the door. His hands travel down my sides, coming to my pants. The entire time he's undressing me, his lips are moving over every bare inch of skin, kissing, sucking, nipping, and licking his way across my body.

"Do you even know how fucking hot you are? The madness you inspire in my head with your beauty?" he rumbles against my skin in between presses of his lips. "You stunned me that first day. Fucking stunned me. I'd wanted you before but couldn't have you because someone else did. But then, there you were. And even more beautiful than before. The fire in you now, it's fucking hot, Heidi. I haven't been able to stop thinking about you for months."

My pants are down around my ankles, and I sense him crouch down. His hands trail down my legs, then he's lifting my feet, one by one, to fully remove my pants. I expect him to stand up, but he doesn't. He stays down on the ground. Instead, his hands lift up to my hips, sliding back onto my ass again as he slowly kneads the globes with his hands.

"Fucking. Perfect."

"Max," I moan, finally finding my voice after pushing through the initial haze of pure lust that has clouded me ever since he first pushed me against the door. "I need…"

"I know what you need."

His teeth, *biting* my ass, make me gasp. Then he's spinning me around, lifting one of my legs over his shoulders and bringing his nose to the gusset of my panties.

"You're soaked. Jesus, Heidi," he groans, nuzzling my sex.

"Max. Please." I can't keep the whine from my voice. I'm so full of pent-up need, I feel like I'll explode soon.

His finger tugs my panties to the side and then finally. *Finally.*

The first swipe of his tongue is quick. The second is slower. The third he takes his time, his tongue finding every crevice of my pussy, licking and swirling around, whipping my already high arousal into overdrive. He growls, and the sound reverberates across my sensitized skin.

"Oh God," I pant, my hands tugging on his hair, pushing his face into me. I should maybe be ashamed by my actions, but somehow, I know. This is what he wants. What we both want.

"Lick." Max lifts two fingers up to my mouth and I eagerly suck them in, swirling my tongue around. "Fucking hell, Heidi. Your mouth needs to get on my cock." I nod, releasing his fingers with a pop.

"Yes, please."

"Later. I'm not done with you yet." He slides those two

fingers between the folds of my pussy, not quite entering me, just teasing with shallow dips. "You're going to come on my face and my fingers first."

He plunges his fingers in at the same time as he sucks my clit into his mouth, and I keen out his name. My head is thrashing back and forth, the hard wood of the door providing the only grounding I have right now.

I'm certain that anyone walking down his hall will hear us and know exactly what's going on. And I don't care. Because this man, with his magical tongue and magical fingers, is bringing on an orgasm that already feels more intense than anything I've ever experienced.

"Max. Max. Oh God, Max. Fuck, yes, oh my God. Max, *Max*!" I become a babbling, boneless mess when I finally break apart. Forget fireworks, I'm blinded from lightning strikes of pleasure as my release pulses through me. If he wasn't holding me up, I'd sink to the floor.

Before I've even managed to come down from the high, Max is standing up and sweeping me into his arms, carrying me through his apartment. By the time he lays me down on his bed, my brain is finally feeling functional again. I lift onto my elbows to watch him peel off his clothes.

"That was the sexiest thing I have ever experienced. I knew you'd be amazing. But the way your body responded to me? Shit, Heidi, you almost made me come in my fucking pants like a teenager, instead of having the control of a forty-year-old man." His intense stare is locked on me. I can't look away, it's like I'm caught in a tractor beam. Until he pulls down his black boxer briefs, and his cock springs free.

Good glory God. I had a tantalizing peek at him when he was in the water at the hot springs. But based on that, my imagination did *not* do him justice. Long, thick, and rock hard, my mouth waters. I want that very impressive cock in my mouth. I lick my lips and reach for him, but he steps back.

"Trust me. I want that too, gorgeous, but I don't have a hope in hell of lasting more than a minute if you put that pretty mouth on me. And I need to fuck that sweet pussy."

He strides around to the side of the bed, opens a drawer, and pulls out a strip of condoms and some lube. I arch my brow at him. "Pretty sure you made me plenty wet."

His lips quirk into a cocky grin. "Yeah. I did, didn't I."

He unwraps the condom and rolls it on, and I've never found that to be sexy until now. But watching him squeeze and tug his length sends a fresh wave of moisture to my sex. And he knows it, the filthy man, because instead of climbing onto the bed and making good on that promise to fuck me, Max just stands there, smirking as he plays with himself.

"I thought you wanted to be inside of me when you came?" I say pertly, lifting my knees up and letting them splay open. I drag one hand down my torso, circling around one of my nipples before dipping between my legs. My back naturally arches when I flick across my clit. But my actions have the desired effect. Because Max lunges across the bed, covering my body with his own. He grabs my hand and pins it over my head with the other.

"Hands off," he growls. With his free hand, he shifts me underneath him so that he's perfectly lined up. His head dips down to meet my lips for a hungry kiss. "Your orgasms are mine."

"Yes," I gasp.

In one movement he plunges his dick into my aching core with enough force to send me sliding up the bed. He grabs my hip, digging in hard enough, I suspect I'll have marks left by his fingers. The thought of him claiming me like that sends a fresh wave of heat pulsing through me, making my pussy clench around him.

"Christ, Heidi," he groans, dropping his forehead to meet mine. "You feel like heaven."

"Don't stop."

"Fuck. You gorgeous girl." Suddenly, Max pulls out and flips me over, manhandling me in a way I never expected to enjoy as much as I do. He lifts my hips before swatting my ass lightly. "Goddamn, this ass." He sounds almost reverent, and I know that's his lust talking, but God, it feels good. His slick cock slides between my legs, nudging against my clit with every thrust. "You make me lose control like nothing else. I don't know who I am around you except for the man who wants to possess every inch of your body."

"I want that, Max. I want you to take me." I turn my head to try and look at him. "Take me."

He bends over and plunges his tongue into my mouth, in a messy passionate kiss as he plunges his cock back into my pussy. It's so much deeper this way, I'm full in the best possible way, and when he rocks his hips slowly but surely into me, every stroke hits my inner walls, lighting up nerve endings I didn't even know existed. He bands his arm around my stomach, lifting me up so that my back is flush against his front. Somehow, he's still moving in and out of my dripping sex. We're sticky with sweat, but when he puts his hand on my cheek and turns my head to the side, any discomfort from the position is gone.

"Mine." His hand travels down from my cheek to gently cup the base of my throat. "You're mine." It's so possessive. And so, so sexy. The feel of his hand gently squeezing my neck has me so close to the edge. I start to writhe against him. His hand tightens, just slightly, as his other fingers come to my clit.

"Milk my cock, Heidi. Take everything," he growls in my ear, tugging my earlobe between his teeth. The sinful combination of sensations, the bite of his teeth, the squeeze of his hand, and the pinch of his fingers on my clit, all of it combined send me hurtling over the edge of oblivion as my climax hits me. I cry out his name, my head thrown back against his shoulder, my own hands scrabbling to find a grip on him. But he's holding me in place so firmly, I'm not going anywhere.

I hear him grunt my name, and his thrusts grow impossibly harder and frenzied, until I feel him pulse inside of me.

Eventually, his movements slow, and he sags against me, still somehow holding me up against his body. I can feel the heave of his breathing against my back as his grip on me softens, and his lips begin to press gentle kisses across my shoulders.

He steadies me as he pulls out, and I let him move my body so that I'm laying down again. There's a tenderness in his eyes I've never seen before.

"Are you okay?"

I nod dreamily. I'm tired, but the good, satisfied kind of tired. "So much more than okay."

"Thank you for being here tonight."

My hand lifts to cup his cheek, and I melt when he leans into my touch. "I wouldn't want to be anywhere else. Thank you for letting me be here with you."

His lips float across my forehead, whispering soft kisses over my skin. My eyes start to close as the emotional and physical exhaustion of the day hits me.

Vaguely, I'm aware of him shifting off the bed. He's gone for a minute, but then he's back, drawing the sheets over me and gathering me into his chest. Sleep is taking over, but even in my semiconscious state, I hear him.

"You are so much more than I expected."

Chapter Twenty-One

Max

I wake to the feel of hands sliding down my body and lips toying with my nipples. It takes a second for my brain to register that I'm not still dreaming. The sunlight filtering in from between my blinds is real, as is the woman currently wrapping her hand around my cock.

The juxtaposition between the pleasure building inside of me and the sad memories of what happened yesterday is hard to reconcile. But there's no denying the absence of the overwhelming grief and guilt that normally surrounds me after losing a patient. Especially one like Teagan. Instead, there's a peaceful acceptance filling my soul. And it doesn't take much to realize the difference is the woman in my bed.

"You're a hell of a lot nicer to wake up to than my alarm," I mutter, my voice still laced with sleep.

She hums her agreement, her lips vibrating against the skin of my abs.

My morning wood is starting to throb in her hand as she slowly rubs up and down its length. The friction of her hand on me with no lubrication is an exquisite form of torture. But it's nothing compared to the feel of her mouth enveloping me in her heat.

"Fuck. Heidi." I gather up her hair in one hand so I can see her face. When I see the blissed-out expression she's wearing as her head bobs up and down, my own head falls back against the pillow with a groan. "You're so good at that, sweetheart. Watching you suck my cock is the hottest thing I've ever seen."

Her answering moan is accompanied by her swallowing my dick as deep as I've ever gone with a woman.

"Jesus Christ! Fuck, yes." My back arches off the bed. It takes some restraint not to thrust my hips up into her mouth, but for once I'm letting someone else be in control. And it feels fucking amazing. Because Heidi needs no direction, no guidance on what feels good. Which is why, when her hand comes down to cup my balls and she tugs them gently, I shouldn't be shocked. Yet, the second I feel one finger stroking the seam that runs under my balls, I know I only have a minute before I'm going to be coming down her throat. "Heidi, I'm gonna come." I ground out the warning, but she doesn't pull off. Her head keeps moving up and down, her tongue swirling around the tip, and then I'm coming. Shooting off into her mouth, exploding with a roar of her name.

Heidi lifts off my cock, sitting back on her heels. I crack one eye open to see her smirking and that talented tongue darting out to lick a drop of my load from the corner of her mouth. I muster the energy to sit up, reach for her, and pull her down onto my chest.

"Such a good fucking girl. Holy shit, I don't think I've ever been sucked off like that," I say, still trying to catch my breath.

Heidi snuggles in and giggles. Fucking giggles.

"I don't think I've ever enjoyed sucking a cock that much." She looks up at me through her dark lashes. "It was really hot. Watching you let go and knowing it was because of me? That's really freaking hot, Max."

I flip us over and pin her underneath me. "Time to even the score, Morgan."

But of course, my alarm chooses that fucking second to go off. Normally I'd call in sick. It's something I'm a little ashamed of, but I typically take the day off after losing a patient. I'm normally hung over, and not functioning, as I wallow in grief and guilt.

Heidi wiggles out from underneath me, dancing out of my reach. "Nope, *now* we're even, Donnelly. I owed you one from last night. And you better not make me late for work. My boss is a real grump."

"You minx," I growl, lunging out of bed to follow her, but she dashes into the bathroom with a shriek of laughter. I pound on the locked door, my face split into a wide grin. "Your grumpy boss will be a lot grumpier if you don't at least let him shower with you."

I hear the door unlock, then it opens a crack.

"Shower, only. No funny business."

I push into the room and grab her around the waist, lifting her into the shower stall and straight under the steaming water.

"Sure. No funny business."

But the smile she's fighting to contain tells me she knows just as well as I do — there will be funny business. After all, what fun is a shower if you don't get a little dirty before you get clean?

Shockingly enough, we're not late for work. Granted, if Heidi didn't have the spare set of scrubs in her car, she would've needed to go home first and *that* would have made her late. But instead, we arrive at the same time, pulling into parking spots right next to each other and exiting our cars with knowing smirks.

"If I thought it was hard working with you before I knew how fucking sweet your pussy tastes, now it's going to be impossible," I mutter under my breath as we walk toward the front door of the hospital. She stumbles and I take her elbow to steady her.

Any excuse to touch her.

Of course, as soon as we get inside, I have to let go. We split off to go to our respective lounges and get ready for the day, and I'm immediately swept into department meetings for the morning.

I wish I could say I participated fully in those meetings. But I didn't. For all I know, Clarence asked me to work seven twelve-hour shifts in a row, and I agreed. Or fuck, maybe I signed off on doubling surgical slates. I don't have a clue. I was too busy remembering the feel of sliding my dick into Heidi's fucking pussy.

Not exactly appropriate work time musings, that's for damn sure.

Finally, the meetings end and I decline Clarence's invitation for lunch, claiming I need to check in on some patients up on the ward.

It's not entirely a lie. I do need to complete my rounds, but

I also have complete faith that Heidi has managed anything important so far. Clarence doesn't need to know that, though. Just like he doesn't need to know the real reason I'm taking the stairs two at a time is because I feel like a junkie searching for my next hit, except my drug of choice is five and a half feet of stunning blonde.

When I reach the nurse's station, she isn't there. Ginny is, however, and she takes in what I assume is my disheveled and desperate appearance, having just run up six flights of stairs, with a confused tilt to her head.

"Everything okay, Dr. Donnelly?"

I nod abruptly. "Yes. Fine. How are things up here?"

Ginny's face relaxes into a smile. "Just wonderful. Heidi made sure the other residents checked all the lab results, updated orders, and touched base with our new patients. She really is a wonderful doctor." Her eyes narrow. "I hope you've sorted yourself out so you can see that?" It's framed as a question, but I know she doesn't mean it as that, but as more of a command.

"Of course. Yes. I have. I mean, I do." I try not to be too obvious in my scanning of the ward. "Is, ah, is Dr. Morgan here at present?"

"She just went down for coffee." Ginny folds her arms across her chest. "She is allowed a break, you know."

It's in this moment that I realize something. While I can't exactly let on that Heidi and I are now sleeping together, I do somehow need to make it clear I'm not out for blood anymore. Dropping down into a chair next to my favourite head nurse, I adopt what I hope is a remorseful expression.

"Ginny, thank you for calling me out on my shit the other

week. I can't get into details, but you were right, and I needed to get my head out of my ass and see Heidi for the professional she is." I lean in closer. "You're the only person who could get through to me like that. So, truly, thank you."

Every word is the truth. Ginny cut through my bullshit better than anyone, even my own brothers. Maybe because she only knew what she was seeing, maybe because she's the most insightful woman I've met — aside from my own mother. Either way, she has no idea just how grateful I really am.

A laugh that has become intimately familiar to me drifts down the hall and my head jolts upward, seeking her out.

Ginny says something, but I don't even hear it. Because she's here, but she's not alone. And instantly, some possessive demon inside of me sits up and takes notice.

She's coming down the hallway with another resident. He's not on peds this rotation or I'd recognize him. And given the way he's leaning down into her, his shoulder brushing hers, I'd instantly put him on the worst cases. Stomach flus and stool collections.

They reach the unit, and Heidi still hasn't acknowledged my presence. She's too wrapped up in whatever this dickwad is saying. Something about neuropsychology. She's giving the pretense of being fascinated, but I'm starting to know her tells. The way she keeps twirling that rogue lock of hair around her finger tells me she's not fully paying attention to him. And when her eyes jump over to meet mine, *finally*, her tongue darts out to lick her lips.

Yeah, she's not listening to him. She's too busy remembering how good it felt when I sucked her clit between my teeth.

I'm vaguely aware that my thought processes today are no better than those of a sex-obsessed twenty-something man who's just tasted his first pussy. Hardly suitable for a grown ass man who's meant to be a respectable doctor and has plenty of experience with women.

But that's what she does to me, I guess. Dissolves my veneer until I'm nothing but basic primal instinct. And right now, that instinct is driving me to do something about the way this jackass isn't getting the message.

"Dr. Morgan, I'd like to review a case in the conference room, now that you're back from your break." I stand up and stride over to them, noting with some satisfaction that I'm taller and broader than the young resident trying to talk up my girl.

My girl.

Jesus fuck, when did I start thinking of her that way? But there's no time for an existential crisis because Heidi is giving me a grateful look, then turning to the jackass and saying a hurried goodbye. We turn and go down the hall into the empty conference room.

As soon as the door is closed, I pull her in, cupping her chin, not exactly gently, and tilting her face up to meet mine. I'm not used to feeling this way, obsessed and territorial over a woman, much less in the face of someone I know I'm superior to.

My arrogance should perhaps be alarming, but right now my rational thought has left the building, and all that's left is this need to remind her of who I am. Who we are.

"What was that all about?" I ask in a low growl.

Her eyes roll up. "Oh God, he followed me up from the cafeteria. We had one class together last semester. One class.

Thank you for getting me out of there."

Even though I know the eye roll was for him, not me, that sass sparks something inside of me. I plunge my hand down the front of her scrub pants and cup her pussy. It's warm and wet already.

"This is mine, Heidi. Mine. Got it? I don't share."

She moans, arching into my hand. "Take it, Max. Take me."

"Shit," I grunt. I thrust one finger into her heat, then two. Then I start up a punishing pace, pushing in and out of her. It's tight and awkward, given she's still fully dressed, but neither one of us cares in this moment. When her mouth opens on a cry, I cover it with my own, drinking down the sounds of her release even as my fingers milk it out of her.

When she sags against me, I slowly withdraw, lifting my fingers to my mouth and licking them clean.

"This sweetness is for me only."

Her head nods up and down against my chest and I feel the band of jealousy ease slightly. I tilt her head up and kiss her firmly, relishing the fact that she opens to me immediately. "It's torture not being able to claim you in front of bastards like him." There's an uncomfortable thread of vulnerability in my words, and I tense slightly, wondering if she hears it.

Her arms snake around my neck as she pulls me back in for another kiss. "You don't need to claim me in public, Max. I'm not about to flirt or entertain anyone else when I can go home with you."

The relief I feel at her reassurance is somewhat surprising. I guess I hadn't realized how invested I was in her, nor how much I needed to hear that she is seemingly just as invested in me.

"Are you coming home with me tonight?" I ask, my voice much calmer than before.

"I hope so." A saucy grin creeps across her face. "I can't have you getting too far ahead on the orgasm tally, now, can I?"

I chuckle drily. "Sweetheart, you don't have a chance in hell of ever getting ahead. Not when making you come has become my number one hobby."

She's fighting back laughter as her fingers thread into my hair. "Well. I guess I can't stand in the way of your *number one hobby* then, can I?"

I shake my head, trying to be serious when I can feel my own amusement bubbling up. "No. Definitely not. After all, hobbies take a lot of practice and dedication. I really shouldn't be distracted."

"Right, right... So, tonight then, I guess you'll need to focus on this hobby. Perfect it, maybe."

My lips turn up. "Yes. Exactly. I may need several tries, but perfection is the goal."

Her lips press to mine lightly before she murmurs against my mouth.

"Far be it for me to stand in the way of perfection."

"Especially when it truly serves both of our best interests."

With a stifled groan, Heidi steps back and makes a show of looking at her watch. "How many more hours do we have to work?"

I don't bother hiding my adjustment of my stiff cock in my pants, loving the way her eyes widen as she catches me doing it.

"Too many, sweetheart. Too many."

Chapter Twenty-Two

Heidi

Somehow, Max and I settle into a routine. We work together as Dr. Donnelly and Dr. Morgan, exchanging nothing more than heated glances. Then we go home, mostly to his place since mine is still a basic furnished rental, and we're Max and Heidi. Two adults who can't seem to get enough of each other.

On our days off, we've gone all over Vancouver Island. There's an unspoken agreement to avoid Westport, but we've visited Dogwood Cove, headed down to Victoria, and one weekend, we went inland to hike some trails in the national park.

I won't lie and say it's a comfortable routine because it's not. I hate having to hide, even as I rationally understand the need. In my head, I have a countdown to the end of my residency. But not because of my excitement to finish the program and be a doctor — no. Because of my anticipation over not having to hide how I feel about Max anymore.

Because moments like tonight, where we're stretched out on Max's far too comfortable couch, his head in my lap as we both read — me, an academic journal, and him, some patient charts he's auditing for a colleague — these moments feel surreal. As if we were always meant to end up here.

"Have you ever had a case of measles come to Westport General?"

Max puts down the chart he was reviewing and tilts his head up to look at me.

"No, not in my years there. I heard of an outbreak over on the mainland a couple of years ago, but thankfully, it never made it to the island." He shifts to one side and sits up, drawing my feet into his lap. "Why?"

My eyes are still focused on the article I'm reading about the resurgence of some childhood illnesses in the wake of a rise in numbers of unvaccinated children. The seminar I'm attending next week on pediatric outreach in remote communities has an entire panel discussion dedicated to increasing vaccination rates.

"This article I have to read before my seminar — the number of measles cases over the last few years is surprising. And the kids that get sick but maybe don't get diagnosed or treated by a doctor; those aren't included in the statistics." I pause, thinking through what exactly is troubling me. This is one thing I never expected to appreciate so much about having a partner who works in medicine — the ability to discuss things and have my opinion valued. "Parents have so many difficult decisions to make, I can't begin to fathom how they make them all. But I guess it's just baffling to me that vaccines are such a hot topic. Medicine has come so far, and can do so much, but the one thing we can't eradicate is fear."

Max nods thoughtfully. "True. And remember, there's always going to be a certain amount of mistrust in medicine. Our job as doctors is to respect everyone's different opinions while still doing our best to educate them on what we believe is best practice."

His response astounds me. So many doctors and nurses get incredibly frustrated when faced with families that choose not to take the simple measures that would protect their children. But not Max. His capacity to see both sides and to compassionately respect different opinions, even those that go against everything he stands for as a physician, is so freaking sexy.

"Do you want children, Max?" The question spills out before I can think about whether it's too soon to ask. "Sorry. Wow, brain to mouth filter isn't working." I blush furiously, attempting to pull my feet out of his grasp, but he just tightens his grip.

"It's okay, I don't mind," he says casually. I make myself relax back into the couch, filled with curiosity about how he'll reply. "The answer is, I don't know. I've seen a lot in my career that makes the idea of having children of my own absolutely terrifying, but at the same time, I love that I have a big family. Having one of my own might be nice someday."

"I get that. Children bring such joy, and I've always wanted a family, but at the same time, knowing what we know makes it even more scary." I fall silent, my mind automatically tracing back to the last conversation I had with a man about starting a family. A conversation that was nowhere near this respectful and open. "Anyway, I guess somewhere along the way, I accepted a family wasn't going to be in my future."

"Why?"

I shift on the couch, really not wanting to say why. I hate bringing up Thad with Max.

"It was him, wasn't it. He made you set aside that dream."

Keeping my eyes downcast, I nod.

"But you're not with him now, are you?"

My head lifts, and I meet Max's crystal blue eyes that are focused intently on me. The air between us is crackling with some indescribable energy. My tongue darts out to moisten my lips.

"No. I'm not."

The conversation has shifted into something that feels precarious. Suddenly, I'm nervous. Do I want to define our relationship right now? Things have been so good; will it be ruined if we try to make this more? Either way, I'm not sure what I expected as a reply from him, but it wasn't for him to abruptly lift my feet off his lap and stand up. He starts to head into the kitchen, and it's only when he's halfway across the room that he finally says something.

"How do you feel about soy-glazed salmon and some roasted vegetables for dinner?"

I scramble to stand and follow him. "Sounds delicious." I come to a stop on the other side of his kitchen counter and wait for him to close the fridge door. Things are awkward all of a sudden, and I'm desperate to go back to the easy comfort of before. "Max. I'm sorry I brought up kids, I shouldn't have. We don't have to talk about that, we just started seeing each other and I don't want you to think I was implying anything."

He freezes, a bag of asparagus and bottle of soy sauce in his hands. I watch as he slowly, methodically places them on the counter, then walks around the end of the island, spins me around, and pins me in place with his hands on either side of me.

"Heidi, I said I didn't mind the question and I meant it. Our relationship might be new, but that doesn't mean you should hold back from asking me whatever you want to know."

"Then why do I feel like things got weird," I whisper, searching his face for any sign that he's hiding something in his reply.

He exhales sharply. "It's my fault, I brought him up. And I can't stand to think of any man having his hands on you or talking about kids or a future with someone else, especially not him. I walked away so you wouldn't see how much of a caveman it turns me into when I'm reminded of the fact that you haven't always been mine."

My mouth falls open. And Max lifts one hand to gently cup my chin and close it slightly, before leaning in to kiss me.

"Things aren't *weird*," he whispers against my lips. "I just can't seem to control my reactions where you're concerned. And the last thing I want to do is scare you off. Got it?"

He kisses me again, and this time I wrap my arms around his waist and fully return his embrace. We might have avoided the topic of what our relationship actually is for tonight, but then again, he's telling me in other ways that this is serious for him.

"Got it," I say when we finally separate. "But for the record, you losing control and going caveman could be kinda sexy. Don't worry about hiding it next time." I wink at him, and he shakes his head.

"I've said it once, and I'll say it again. You're trouble." He leans back in and nips at my neck before kissing the same spot. His lips trail down, across my collar bone to my bare shoulder, then he straightens and presses a kiss to the tip of my nose.

He pushes away from the counter, and I immediately miss the warmth that radiates from his body.

"Now, are we good? Because I'm hungry." He looks over his shoulder at me with a sexy smirk. "And you need your strength if I'm going to let my inner caveman out."

I let my breath out in a low whoosh. His sex appeal is so freaking potent. "Am I going to need to start calling you Fred Flintstone?" I say flippantly as I make my way into the kitchen and start washing some vegetables.

Out of nowhere, I'm yanked back, spun around, and tossed over his shoulder, all before I can even shriek his name.

A large hand lands on my ass, and not exactly gently. "You'll be calling me something, sweetheart, but it won't be that."

My laughter trails after us as Max carries me down the hall and dumps me onto his bed.

"What happened to eating first?" I ask in between giggles, but my laughter dies out when he pulls off his shirt and drops his pants, letting that beautiful cock of his spring free.

"Me caveman. Me hungry for woman. You woman." He grins lasciviously at me before reaching for the hem of my sweats and yanking them down, along with my panties.

His tongue hits my pussy and I moan out his name. He doesn't waste any time, diving in and eating me like he's a dying man granted one last meal.

"I guess dinner can wait."

Hours later, after two orgasms, a very late dinner, and then another orgasm, we get ready for bed. But as we climb under the sheets, and he pulls my back to his front, wrapping his large body around me, my eyes land on the button-up shirt I pulled on to wear while eating dinner earlier.

When I walked out of the bedroom wearing it, the stare Max gave me from the kitchen could have set a puddle on fire, it was so hot. Dinner was almost delayed — again — because he needed to lift me onto the counter and figure out if I was wearing panties or not.

Spoiler alert — I wasn't.

"I need you to start wearing baggy scrubs to work."

Max's hand pauses in the torturous, gentle stroking he was doing up and down my bare thigh. "What?"

"When you wear collared shirts at work, it's torture. So, to save me from my pain and suffering, please start wearing baggy scrubs."

His warm chuckle sends shivers across my skin. "Quid pro quo, Heidi. What do you think you do to me when you show up in those fitted scrub pants? Back in my day, we had hospital-issued scrubs and that's all."

"Back in my day?" I giggle. "You're not that old, Max."

"No, but med school was a long time ago for me."

Our laughter fades into a comfortable silence. I don't want to ruin the moment, but under the cover of darkness, I feel bold. Safe to say what's on my mind.

"I know you're worried about my reputation at the hospital, but it really sucks not being able to act the way I want around you when we're there together."

"Are you saying you wish you could suck my cock at work?" he says and I reach a hand back to slap his hip. He just laughs and presses his lips to the back of my neck.

"No, you dirty man. I'm just saying it's difficult trying to differentiate between how we are at work, and how we are when it's just us. I hate feeling like I'm always on edge, worried I'll slip and mess up."

Max shifts onto his back, the sheet sliding down, revealing more of his delicious torso. God, I want to run my tongue over every divot of muscle.

"I know. It isn't exactly a walk in the park for me, either, constantly battling a hard-on every time you get too close. Last thing I need is to traumatize a patient with a hard dick."

I snort-laugh at that incredibly inappropriate idea.

"What are you doing tomorrow?"

I let my fingers trail up his stomach, starting at his belly button. "I'm not sure, probably some laundry and finishing up the reading I need to do for the seminar. Why?"

"Come to family dinner at the Donnelly house."

I push up onto my elbow. "You want me to have dinner with your entire family?"

He nods. "Sure, why not. Kat already adores you, you've met Sawyer and Beckett, all that's left is my parents, and I know they're going to love you, too."

"But they'll know we're together."

His gentle smile says it all. "That's fine with me."

Well okay, then.

Chapter Twenty-Three

Heidi

I lean against the inside of the car, feeling the wind rushing through the open window. It's invigorating, freeing, and brings a smile to my face.

This is what I've always wanted my life to be. Full of moments in time that are balanced, happy, peaceful, and with someone by my side who trusts and treasures me, the way I do them.

Turning my head, I look at Max's strong profile. His hand is on the wheel, holding it confidently, the way he holds me. His face is relaxed, and I love that I get to see this side of him. We're heading to Dogwood Cove, and while I've been there before this still feels brand new. Because I'm experiencing it with him.

We decided not to hide. The chances of someone from the hospital seeing us are slim, and we're willing to take that risk now, when we weren't before.

Neither one of us is saying it, but I'm certainly feeling like things are growing deeper and stronger between us. I'm falling in love with him, the more I learn about who he is. And today, having the chance to be in his hometown and spend time with his family, I suspect I'll only fall even more.

"So, we'll grab lunch at Camille's, then head to the beach for a walk before dinner at my parents' house. Does that still sound good to you?" Max glances quickly over to me, catching me staring at him, and quirks his lips up in a smile. "Sweetheart?"

"Mm-hmm."

His throaty chuckle makes my smile grow even wider. "Heidi, if you don't stop looking at me like that, I'll be finding the nearest dirt road to pull off, so I can distract you the way you're distracting me."

I inhale sharply at the lust that drips from his words, squirming in my seat to ease the ache that's suddenly present between my legs.

"You'd like that, wouldn't you?" he murmurs, his eyes glued forward. A hand suddenly lands on my leg, and I automatically part them. "Oh babe. You're a dirty girl."

The car suddenly veers off the highway and onto a bumpy gravel road. Max maneuvers down the road expertly, turning into a wooded area that I would have never noticed from the road.

He puts the car in park, then presses the button to release both of our seatbelts. Then his hands are tangled in my hair as he holds my head possessively but gently. His lips find mine and I no longer care if anyone sees us. I only care about how good he makes me feel.

"Max," I murmur as his lips trail down my neck. "What about our plans?"

"There's no one waiting on us, sweetheart. Besides, do you really think I would give a shit about anything other than you? Especially when your pussy needs my attention?" he says gruffly as his fingers make quick work of unbuttoning my shorts.

His thick fingers slide under my panties, zeroing in on the already damp juncture of my thighs. "Wet for me? Good girl. You're gonna come on my fingers, sweetheart, and maybe then I'll let you suck my cock so we can both know beyond a shadow of a doubt that what we have is worth any risk."

His dirty words speak to all my buried — and not so buried — insecurities. I moan out his name as he pinches my clit lightly before rubbing slow circles, soothing and tormenting me at the same time. It's cramped trying to do this in a car while I'm still, basically, fully dressed.

Max clearly feels the same way. "Lift your hips, sweetheart." I do, and somehow, we manage to shimmy my shorts down slightly, giving him much better access. "That's a good girl. Fuck, I need to taste you."

Don't ask me how a big man like Max manages, but he somehow folds his body in half. The next thing I feel is his tongue licking up my slit, then swirling around my clit, sucking gently. When he sits back up, I whimper at the loss of his mouth, but then he's pressing his lips to mine. The taste of me, mingled with the taste of his mouth, is beyond hot.

"Goddamn, you're sweet. Perfect. You ready to come for me?"

I nod frantically, my head thrown back against the headrest of my seat. I'm breathing heavily, full of desperate need.

"Look at me, Heidi."

My eyes fly open at the exact second that he plunges two fingers into my greedy pussy.

"Christ, you are perfection. Can you feel your body squeezing me tightly? Fuck, I wish it was my dick in there."

He doesn't stop mumbling dirty things in my ear, and I am loving every second.

"Oh God, Max, I'm gonna come," I cry out, and he doubles down on the flicks of his fingers until I start to tighten and clench around him, one hand gripping his arm and the other the door handle, so tightly my knuckles are white.

"Yes, baby. Yes," he croons, kissing me softly as I come down from my release. I slowly blink my eyes at him as he pulls his fingers out, lifting them to his mouth, and staring at me as he licks them clean. Good Lord, that shouldn't be as hot as it is. "You're so fucking delicious."

I trail my hand over his legs, brushing the bulge straining against his shorts. "You seem tense, Max. I feel bad that I'm so relaxed, and you're so...hard."

He groans, his hand returning to the back of my head, gripping my hair tightly. The slight bite of pain is delicious.

"Are you offering to help me?"

I nod eagerly as he opens his jeans and pulls out his cock, stroking it a couple of times.

"This won't take long." His words hold a delicious warning. "Watching you come always gets me halfway there."

"Well, I better finish you."

I drop my head down and take him in my mouth in one smooth motion until the tip hits the back of my throat.

"Fucking Christ!"

His hoarse curse motivates me. I waste no time, bobbing up and down on his cock, swirling my tongue under the mushroom head before sucking him in deeply once again.

"Good God woman, I'm gonna explode like a fucking rocket if you do that again."

I look up at him and wink, then do it again. I swirl and suck in a repetitive motion until his hips jerk underneath me and I feel the warm jets of his come hitting my throat. I manage to swallow it down, squeezing every last drop out of him before releasing him with a pop.

"I'm not the only one who's delicious," I whisper, winking at his hooded expression. I tuck him into his pants, then lift my thumb to the corner of my mouth and wipe away a drop of his release before sliding my thumb into my mouth and licking it off.

"Christ. You are the perfect blend of filthy and sweet, aren't you?"

"Only with you."

I can see his mind wrapping around that confession, taking it in fully and acknowledging just how big of a deal it is. I am me when I'm with him. Fully, completely, me.

Hours later, after hunting for sea glass on the beach and enjoying a picnic lunch from Camille's café, we pull up in front of Max's childhood home, and he shuts off the car.

"Here we go. Time to experience the full force of Donnelly chaos."

"You're not doing a great job of settling my nerves, Max," I mutter, eyeing the innocent-looking house.

"You have nothing to worry about. You've already met my

siblings, and they love you. And my mom will be thrilled to see I'm happy and in a relationship."

I twist my hands together in my lap. "Doesn't this feel a little fast? We've only been dating a short while and I'm already meeting your family. Are you sure you want to do this?"

Max covers my hands with one of his, then tips my chin up with the other. "I am very sure. I don't need more time to know you're important to me, Heidi. But I would never want to push you into something you aren't ready for. So just say the word and we'll leave. You're in control, sweetheart."

Those three words, that acknowledgment of my feelings, and the support I feel flooding from him is all I need.

"I'm nervous, but I'm excited. Let's do this."

His wide grin tells me just how happy he is. Max climbs out of the car and jogs around the front to open my door. He helps me out, but instead of just taking my hand and leading me to the house, he pulls me in close, tucking my head under his chin.

"I mean it, Heidi. If you feel uncomfortable at any time, just say the word, and we can go."

"We don't need a safe word for dinner with your family." I laugh. "Come on, let's go."

He kisses the top of my head, and I can feel that his lips are tipped up in a smile when he does so. But he does as I ask, and takes my hand, leading me up to the front of the house.

When he pushes open the door, the smell of home cooking and the sounds of family assault me. Something delicious is clearly being prepared in the kitchen, and there's laughter and animated conversation. He leads me down a short hall and into the room that's filled with people.

"Hey, guys."

The conversation stops so suddenly, I clench Max's hand. Then, just as fast as it fell silent, sound fills the room again.

"Heidi, you're here!" Kat is the first one to hug me. "I knew you guys would be perfect together. My matchmaking at country night totally worked, didn't it?"

I squeak out a sound, but she's squeezing me so tightly, I can't properly reply. Max does it for me, instead.

"Kat, let her go. And I'm not going to dignify that matchmaking comment with a proper response."

Kat releases me, but shoots daggers at her brother, prompting me to laugh. "Sorry, Kat. The dancing that night was a good push in the right direction. How about that?"

"I'll take it," she concedes.

"Hey, Mom," Max says, and I pivot just in time to see him hugging an older woman. Coming up behind her is who I assume must be Max's dad. And if his rugged, silver fox good looks and easy smile are what Max has in his future, then I'd be lucky to be around at that time.

"Dennis Donnelly. Nice to meet you, Heidi." His handshake is warm, strong, and steady. But I notice the limp Max has mentioned, and my practiced eye can see the lines in his face that must be from chronic pain. My heart thuds against the walls of my chest, thinking of how Thad's carelessness almost made it so this man wasn't standing in front of me today.

"Thank you for having me," I say, just as Max's mother slides her arm over my shoulders.

"Heidi, we're thrilled to have you here." She starts to guide me into the kitchen, and I cast a panicked glance over my shoulder at Max, but he's in conversation with his brother and doesn't see me. Kat does and gives me a wink as she follows. "It's been so long since any of my boys brought someone for dinner, I was starting to worry."

"Mom, don't freak her out," Kat chides before passing a large — thankfully — glass of wine my way. She sits down on a stool lining the counter, and I do the same.

"Can I help with anything?" I ask, desperate to shift the conversation away from mine and Max's relationship.

"Oh no, you just sit there, and we'll chat while the boys get everything set at the table."

Max walks into the kitchen at that moment, and I feel his lips press a kiss to my head, then he's moving to a drawer, pulling out some silverware, and heading back out of the kitchen. Sawyer and Beckett cycle in, each grabbing dishes, glasses, napkins, and then leaving. It's been so long since I was around a family this closely connected, and the normalcy of how everyone knows their role and just chips in is comforting.

"Now, all Kat has told me is that you and Max work together. Are you a nurse? Or a therapist?"

I gulp down my wine. Shit. How the hell do I answer this? Why didn't Max and I discuss what to say?

"Actually, Heidi used to be a nurse on the peds ward years ago, but now she's doing her final residency rotation with us. We've been working together closely for a while now, and it's clear this is her calling. Clarence has already decided he wants to hire her when she graduates. I've told him he'd be a fool not to; she's a great doctor."

I twist around on my stool, unaware that Max had come back

into the kitchen. My heart feels like it might burst at his easy answer to his mom's question. First, because he's so forthcoming about who I am, and second, because of what he said about me. About my work and my future. He might have said it all so casually, but every word of support and praise falls on me and sinks into the part of me that has been craving a partner who builds me up, instead of tearing me down.

"Well, Westport General is lucky to have you back, I'm sure." Claire pats my arm. "Now, who's hungry?"

And just like that, the moment I was dreading is over. Max's family didn't bat an eye at finding out we're not just dating, but that we also work together.

Dinner is delicious and loud. The Donnellys are an animated group, everyone with stories to tell and teasing to be done, but all of it lovingly. At the end of the evening, I'm left wondering why I was ever nervous. As Max and I say our goodbyes, his dad surprises me by folding me into a gentle hug.

"You're good for him, Heidi." When he pulls back, he winks, then turns to give Max a hug before I can say a thing.

As we drive away, Dennis's words sit with me. He may think I'm good for Max, but I *know* he's more than good for me.

And when I look over at the man who's holding not only my hand, but also my heart, I can't help but send out a desperate prayer to the universe.

Don't let this be too good to be true.

Chapter Twenty-Four

Max

"I have to go away this weekend," I say casually as Heidi finishes brushing her hair. I'm leaning against my bathroom counter wearing nothing but my boxer briefs. It should be weird watching her go through her nighttime routine, but I'm so enthralled by this woman, even the mundane tasks are addictive to me.

"Oh."

The pretty frown that mars her face makes me grin. And she sees it, which only makes her frown even deeper.

"Sweetheart, you're coming with me."

Heidi whirls around, her toothbrush sticking out of her mouth. "What?" she mumbles around it.

"I planned a little weekend escape for us. We leave tomorrow morning." I give her my most satisfied smirk, and I'm rewarded by a little squeak of excitement. She rushes through the rest of brushing her teeth before throwing her arms around me. My hands instantly go to her delicious ass, lifting her up to sit on the bathroom counter.

"Where are we going?"

"Ah, that's a surprise," I tease, running my hands up her thighs.

"Max," she wheedles, but I just shake my head with a grin. Lifting her off the counter, her legs wrap around me as I carry her into the bedroom and set her down on the bed.

"You'll find out tomorrow. Now, we better get some sleep, it's an early departure."

"That's mean, Max," she pouts as I pull her into my arms.

"Let me do this, sweetheart. Please." I can't explain why it's important to me that this be a surprise, but it is. Thankfully, Heidi seems to see that etched across my features. Because she eventually nods, and with a sweet kiss to my lips, she lets it go,

I should have known she gave in too easily. All morning she has continued to try and to get me to crack, but I've stayed strong.

"Just one hint, Max? Please?"

I run my thumb over her pouting lips. "Where's the fun in that? Hurry up, sweetheart, we need to leave."

An hour later, we're pulling into the parking lot of Harbour Air, a small charter company that flies seaplanes back and forth to the mainland. I turn off the car and look over at Heidi. Those eyes I'm rapidly becoming obsessed with are sparkling as they look everywhere, taking in the plane that's taking off and the other that's parked at the dock.

"Are we going in one of those?"

I nod.

She grabs my hand, squeezing it in excitement. "I've always

wanted to take a seaplane. Always."

I can't help it; her joy is infectious. Leaning over, I kiss her cheek, inhaling the uniquely feminine and alluring scent of her. "Perfect."

We get out, go to the small office located on the dock, and check in. Then, in what feels like no time at all, we're seated in the small cockpit of the plane, listening to our pilot. He introduces himself as Rourke and has a faint accent as he goes over the safety protocols. Heidi's hand is clutching mine tightly, and I can hear her gasps of amazement as we taxi out over the water and lift into the air.

Her reaction is everything I hoped for. We both need this — a chance to be together farther away from home, away from anyone who might see us and question what we're doing. Even if we never leave the hotel room, which if I have my way, we won't, except maybe to eat. We need a break from real life and a chance to just *be*.

The flight to the mainland is over far too soon, and I can tell from Heidi's wistful glances at the plane she feels the same way.

"We're flying home the same way," I whisper in her ear as we walk up the dock.

"Really?" she breathes. "Thank you, Max." Her head drops to my shoulder, and it's effortless for me to turn and kiss the top of her silky hair.

There's no denying, I'm at the point where I'll do just about anything to make her happy.

By the time we get checked into our hotel in downtown Vancouver, neither one of us seems capable of holding back much longer. The second the door to our suite closes, I've got

Heidi tossed over my shoulder and I'm walking us into the large bathroom. Then slowly, I lower her, relishing the feel of her body sliding against mine, setting alight all my nerve endings.

"I need you."

Those three words echo around my head and my heart. My need for her is just as strong and just as deep. I cup her face in my hands and steal her breath with my kiss until she sags against me, her hands placed on my chest, gripping my shirt tightly.

"I'm yours."

The rough truth in my reply hovers between us. I never thought I'd say that to someone ever again, but here I am, ready to give her everything.

"Heidi," I start, my thumbs stroking over her cheeks. Desire and lust pulse in the air around us, but everything else is frozen in time. It's just us. And three more words I suddenly need to say. Immediately.

"I love you."

She lifts her hands from my chest and wraps them around my wrists, turning to press a kiss into each of my palms. When she finally meets my eyes again, I see the sparkle of tears.

"I love you, too. I can't believe I'm saying that, but I do."

Heidi must see the slight frown flash over my face because she shakes her head, and those tears spill free, tracking down her beautiful face to her tremulous smile. My thumb wipes them away as I force my nervous heart to wait for her to clarify.

"I don't mean it's unbelievable that I love *you*. You're the most amazing man, Max. Despite how we started and what you might think, you're easy to fall for, easy to love. I just meant, after Thad, I told myself I was giving up on love. At least until school and residency was over and my life was settled. I didn't want to tie myself to another person and risk losing everything I've worked for. But you don't take anything from me I don't want to give. You stand beside me and push me to be better instead of holding me back."

Her arms snake around my waist and she hugs me tightly, her head coming to rest under my chin.

"You're making me redefine what I thought a partner could be, in the best possible way. So yes, I love you. And I can't believe I'm lucky enough to say that, and to know that you feel the same way."

God, she's so fucking sweet. A part of me still lingers on this fear that I'll taint her somehow. That being with me will end in pain for one or both of us. But in this moment, I don't give a shit. All I care about is being with the woman I love.

Slowly — slower than I think I've ever been with her — I guide her arms up so I can lift her shirt over her head, revealing her porcelain skin. Dipping my head down, I kiss my way across the swell of one breast, then over to the other, infusing her skin with everything spoken and unspoken between us.

The desperate passion that's normally present is gone, and in its place is a desire to worship her, revere her, and love her.

I reach behind her, turn on the shower, then return to my mission of uncovering every inch of her. I drop into a crouch as I slide her shorts down over the curve of her hips, leaving nothing but a triangle of lace covering her. Leaning in, I deeply breathe in her scent.

"Beautiful."

Suddenly, her hands are under my armpits and Heidi's

pulling me up to stand, her fingers fumbling with the button on my shorts.

"I need you *now.*"

And just like that, the urgency is back. Clothes fly all over and we can't stop kissing everywhere our lips reach. We stumble under the hot spray of water, letting it cascade down between us. I spin us so that her back is to the wall, then lift her hips and press into her. Heidi responds instantly, wrapping her legs around my waist, her nails scraping along my scalp as our tongues tangle together.

"Is this what you want? You need me to take you right here against the wall, claim you as mine?"

"Yes," she cries out as I begin to thrust my hips forward, pressing her harder against the tile wall. My dick is sliding back and forth, so close to where I want to be. But in our desperation, we made a critical mistake.

"Damn it. Condom."

Heid grabs my head, forcing me to look into her wild eyes. "I want to feel you inside me, Max. All of you."

My body freezes. I've never gone bare with a woman. Ever. But now that she's planted the idea in my head, all blood has rushed south, and my cock is throbbing with need. "Are you sure?" I grind out, holding myself perfectly still. She's amped up from desire. I need to know this is really what she wants.

Heidi's gaze softens, and she tucks a piece of hair back, wiping away the water that is still pouring down our faces. "Yes. I'm sure. I trust you."

It only takes the slightest adjustment to line myself up, and then, with an exquisite control that hides the desperation I feel,

I slide into her hot wet heat. My forehead falls to her shoulder as my arms shake. Not from holding her up, but from the pure pulsing pleasure I'm experiencing from being bare inside of her.

"Heidi," I groan, biting down on her shoulder as I slowly start to rock my hips back and forth. She's peppering kisses all over me, murmuring words I can't make out over the pounding of my own heartbeat in my head. "This is going to be fast," I gasp as I feel her clench around me. "Fuck. Babe. God, you feel like heaven. Like home. Like everything good." I draw back, then slam back in, earning a garbled cry. "Heidi. Mine." I do it again. And again. Until she's tightening around me, and my own orgasm is rushing through me, and I'm spilling inside of her as our cries of pleasure echo in the steamy air.

"Sweetheart, if you don't stop looking at me like that, we'll miss our dinner reservation," I mutter under my breath, hoping the other couple standing in front of us in the elevator doesn't hear me.

Heidi's soft yet sultry giggle only makes matters worse, and I try to discreetly adjust myself. Not easy in the slacks I'm wearing. When we decided to go out for dinner, I made a few calls and got us into one of Vancouver's hottest restaurants. But we have to be there in twenty minutes, and it's at least a fifteen-minute walk from the hotel. I had to lock myself in the bathroom to get ready just so I didn't strip the lacy number Heidi put on under her dress right off her.

As it is, I'm not sure how I'll manage to get through an entire meal knowing what my dessert will be.

"I can't help it. You know how I feel about your shirts," she whispers back, her hand sliding down from its respectable position on my waist to squeeze my ass.

"Woman," I growl, turning my head to glare down at her. But the second my eyes land on her lips, perfectly coloured with some plum-coloured stain, my resistance dissolves. My hand goes to the back of her neck, and I pull her roughly up to meet my lips. "Stop. Tempting. Me."

"Never," she whispers back, and I feel her mouth curve up into a smile.

I set her down, shaking my head at her while my own smile reflects the giddy high of confessing the feelings I think we're both experiencing. Not to mention the ability to be affectionate in public and not worry about who might catch us. Suddenly, I realize the doors are open to the hotel lobby and the other couple are nowhere to be seen. Taking her hand, I lead her out, all the way onto the bustling sidewalk. Tucking her under my arm because I crave as much contact as humanly possible, we walk toward the restaurant.

I suppose a smarter man would keep some degree of his guard up, even after telling someone how you feel and having the most searing sex of your life. But I'm clearly not very smart.

I'm too wrapped up in Heidi, in the feel of her foot sliding up my pant leg under the table as we eat our entrées and the sexy little smirks she gives me when she catches me staring. In the elegant curve of her neck as she sips her wine and the ease with which she seems to understand me and *know* me.

So wrapped up, in fact, that I don't sense danger coming until it's too late. After our plates are cleared and we're enjoying one final glass of very expensive wine, a voice I had hoped to never hear again finally penetrates the bubble we've built around us.

"Heidi?"

The blood drains out of her face. I know if I turn around, I'll be looking at the man responsible for so much pain and suffering in my life.

"Thad," she whispers. I place my hand over hers, squeezing lightly, partly to show her I'm with her, but also to ground myself. He walks into view and my stomach revolts, making me feel as if I might lose the entirety of the delicious meal I've just enjoyed.

In the ten years since I saw him standing with Heidi at her going away party, I've managed to forget how powerful my body and mind react to the site of Thad Marshall. I was there with my mother through all the lawyer meetings about settlements and who was at fault. I held her while she cried when she saw Dad in the hospital the first time. I stood there, looking at my father in a hospital bed hooked up to ventilators, and wondered if he'd ever open his eyes again. And when he did and he recovered, I was the one who had to tell him Thad managed to escape any serious repercussions, earning a slap on the wrist — a fine and license suspension. The settlement he paid our family was paltry, and if it hadn't been for my father belonging to a union with excellent benefits, my parents would have struggled financially, thanks to his forced early retirement.

None of that mattered to Thad. He was more angry about the damage to his car than he was upset about injuring a human being.

Looking at him now, I find it difficult to believe the amazing woman sitting across from me was ever with him. A woman who, as I watch, seems to be sinking in on herself. Anger bubbles inside of me, turning into a boiling pool of molten rage.

His eyes find mine and I see recognition dawn in them. I don't look away. I don't even blink.

"I see you found your way back to that little hospital," he sneers. "And straight into the arms of a Donnelly."

I push my chair back and move to stand, but Heidi's quiet voice stops me in my tracks, surprising me with it's steel. "Don't. Don't say his name. Don't you dare speak to him or me like that. You're nothing but a vile, horrible, selfish little man who preys on anyone he can."

Out of the corner of my eye, I see two men in suits walk up behind Thad. But he's so focused on Heidi he doesn't seem to notice. Her eyes are ablaze, and I watch in wonder as she stands up to the man who hurt her so badly. Her bravery, her strength, all of it is stunning to see.

"You ruin people, Thad. That's what you do. You almost ruined me, just like you almost ruined Max's family. How could you hit a man while driving drunk and not take responsibility for it? What kind of monster does that? You almost killed his father and you walked away, as if nothing happened."

"Is this true, Thad?" one of the suits interrupts. I watch Thad's face and get no small amount of satisfaction from watching his body shrink with dread. The suit turns to me. "You're Max, I assume? Is what she said true? Did this man injure your father and wasn't held responsible?"

I nod, somewhat confused by what's going on. The suit looks

to his partner, then back to Thad, examining him critically. I take in the sweat beading on Thad's brow. I might not know exactly who these men are, but they're important to the asshole, and that alone makes me want to ensure they know exactly who he is.

"Yeah. Twelve years ago, he made the decision to drive drunk. He plowed through a crosswalk and hit my father. His leg was broken in three places and he had a serious brain bleed. Thad was fully at fault but got by on a technicality. His lawyer claimed my father was not actually at the crosswalk but just in front of it, and therefore was jaywalking."

Suit number two lets out a snort of derision. Heidi's hand is still warm and steady underneath mine, and I glance down to see she's flipped hers over to thread her fingers with mine, binding us together.

The suit turns to face Thad. "Our deal is off. There's no room for you with Klein Golder. I told you we were a company with strong values and morals, and if there's even a shred of truth to what these people claim, you have no place with us." He looks back to Heidi and me. "I'm very sorry to have interrupted your evening. Your dinner will be placed on our tab."

The suits walk away, and their leaving seems to wake Thad from whatever trance he was in. "Wait!" he cries out, chasing after them without sparing Heidi and I a second glance.

"What the hell was that," I say, bewildered.

Heidi's light laugh draws my attention. "That was Thad Marshall getting his ass handed to him. Klein Golder is the name of the investment firm he wanted a position in when we moved to the mainland. I guess he finally got his chance, and we just ruined it for him."

A wide, vindicated grin stretches across my face. "Well, okay then. Not how I envisioned our night turning out."

Her eyes are twinkling as Heidi pushes back from the table and reaches out for my hand. "Me neither. But we got a free dinner and a show out of it. Now let's go back to the hotel for dessert." She winks at me, her intentions clear.

I stand and take her arm in mine. "Isn't there a cheesy quote about revenge being sweet?"

Heidi leans in close. "Yes. But I'm sweeter."

Chapter Twenty-Five

"No, don't do it. No. No. No!"

My eyes fly open to a body thrashing next to me. Max is in the throes of a nightmare from the looks of it, his skin glistening with sweat, a deep line between his eyebrows.

"Max," I say softly, barely dodging his flying arms. "Max," I try a bit louder. But then he bolts up into a sitting position, looking around wildly, his fists clenching the sheet that is now bunched at his waist.

"Max, you're okay. You're safe."

His head whips around to me. "Heidi?" he croaks, and that one word is laced with complete anguish. Cautiously, I reach out and take his trembling hand in mine.

"I'm here. You're okay."

His entire body sags back down onto the bed. He stares up at the ceiling, his chest heaving up and down for several minutes.

"Did I hurt you?" he asks hoarsely, and I lean into his side automatically.

"No, not at all. I'm fine." My hand is running up and down his arm, hopefully soothing him as he comes down from the adrenaline rush. "Do you want to talk about it?"

The pain etched into every line of his body makes my own heart ache in return. I hate that seeing Thad brought up so much emotion for Max. I hate that while I was internally celebrating how unscathed I felt after seeing him again, Max was suffering deeply enough for it to come out in his dreams. I know, instinctually, there's more to his story than just Thad. I just don't know what.

Max takes several slow breaths, but the tension still radiates off him in waves. "Seeing Thad tonight. I guess it brought up a lot of crap."

"Were you dreaming about your dad's accident?"

He starts to shake his head, then nods partially, then sighs. "Sort of. It's complicated."

"Well, talk to me. I love you and I'm here for you." I stroke my hand over his hair, smoothing it away from his face.

"The day Thad hit my father was also the day I found out that my girlfriend at the time betrayed me."

"What?" I whisper, aghast.

Max rolls onto his side, burying his face into my shoulder. "I need you close if I have to talk about her."

I squeeze my arms tightly around him in silence.

"In med school, I dated a fellow student. Cara." He pauses, shaking his head. "I think I loved her. It's hard to say now because what I feel with you is so different. But back then, I thought I loved her. Fuck, I was such an idiot."

I can't stand to hear him beat himself up. I tip his head up and kiss his lips softly, infusing comfort, support, love, whatever I can. He kisses me back, his hand gently cupping the back of my head. When he pulls back, I let him, knowing there's more he needs to share. Thankfully, his eyes are a little bit clearer and there's less torment brewing in their beautiful blue depths.

"Do you remember what I told you about my friend's brother dying when we were kids?"

I nod.

"When Cara and I were doing our residency, the U of V research program was still pretty new. Dr. Nguyen was heading it up then, and he put out the word that he wanted to mentor someone to co-lead the research and eventually take over. And he wanted someone fresh. Pulmonology was my planned specialty, same as Cara at the time."

"Wait. You're talking about Cara Andrews?" I interrupt, surprise and understanding filling me. "What you said that night in the on-call room about finding your way to pediatrics later by accident. She was the accident, wasn't she?"

"Yes." He tilts his head back. "Not a lot of people know this, but when I entered med school, my original goal was to be a pulmonologist. I was dedicated to CF research and treatment because of Callum's death. Cara and I talked a lot about our plans, about taking over the field, both in research and practice."

Max is silent for a minute, his hand rhythmically running up and down my back. "Cara knew my story, about losing Callum and how that loss is what drove me to medicine. She also knew I never shared that because I didn't want sympathy to affect anyone's opinion of me. I felt my work would stand alone and show who I was as a doctor and what I was capable of. But I guess Cara thought differently."

There's a bitterness in his voice and his hand pauses its movement. I hold my breath.

"I interviewed for the position on the research team and so did Cara. We agreed it wouldn't matter who won the spot, we'd be happy either way. And I would have if she hadn't done it the way she did. Unbeknownst to me, Cara went to her interview with Dr. Nguyen and passed my story about Callum off as her own." He lets out a harsh laugh. "Apparently, sympathy was the right angle. I had no idea what she did until the announcement was released. By then, it was too late. I felt trapped and couldn't do anything to defend myself without being painted in a bad light. Not to mention, a couple of hours later, my attention was ripped away from her betrayal and onto my dad's fight for his life."

"Oh, Max." My heart is breaking for him. To suffer such a betrayal and then be smacked with the fear of losing his dad, all in the same day. It's little wonder seeing Thad triggered the nightmare. But my current anger is focused entirely on his ex-girlfriend. "How dare she be so callous and use your personal pain for her own gain. God, I want to expose her to everyone. What a fraud."

Max's lips cover mine, interrupting my rant. "Sweetheart, I love you and your anger on my behalf, but it's not worth it. It's in the past."

"But it's not, is it?" I whisper. "Not really. She's the reason you don't let people get close to you. She's why you're so afraid to be vulnerable."

His deep sigh is layered. Relief, acceptance, and love all in one. "Yeah. She is. But you're changing all of that for me, Heidi."

I twist and shift until I'm straddling him, my knees resting on either side of his legs. I cup his face in my hands, draw him in and kiss his forehead, letting my lips rest there for a moment.

"I'm not changing anything. You're doing that, just by being willing to trust."

His fingers thread through my hair, crashing me into him. "I love you."

The energy turns explosive in a heartbeat. Gasps and moans fill the air, and I don't know if they're mine or his. All I know is that soon, he's lifting my hips, lining us up so that all I have to do is sink down, and then I'm being stretched and filled in the most delicious way.

"Yes. Don't stop."

His grunt is matched with a perfectly timed thrust, the angle making his cock hit all my walls with every single movement. My head falls back and the only thing holding me up is my grip on his biceps. When I feel his mouth close over my nipple, I almost fall, my hands letting go, but he's there. His large hands span my back, supporting me, lifting me up. The parallel between the physical action and the deep-seated knowledge I have in my heart settles around me.

He will support me.

He will hold me.

He will lift me up.

He loves me.

I wish I could say riding the float plane home to the island was as magical an experience as it was coming over just yesterday. But it

was vastly overshadowed by the magic of knowing that the man sitting next to me — solid, warm, and strong — loves me.

I'm still floating on that cloud when I walk into the hospital the next day. We didn't spend last night together, not for lack of wanting, but for the practical reason that I needed to do laundry and prepare for a week of shifts, and my car was at my apartment.

It feels incredibly unfair that we still have to keep everything a secret. I want to shout from the rooftops that Max Donnelly has healed my heart and shown me that a partner can walk beside you and not in front.

My first glimpse of him standing at the nursing station fills me with resolve. It's not against the rules for us to be together, but my career comes first. The fact Max understands that and is willing to fight for it only serves to strengthen my commitment.

He's worth waiting for.

"Dr. Morgan, I hope you had an enjoyable weekend off?" he asks, perfectly poised and cordial in his delivery. If I weren't staring at his deep blue eyes, I would have missed the twinkle in them, the slight smirk of his lips, and the rapid perusal of my entire body. Then again, I probably wouldn't have missed it, given how strong my visceral reaction is to his voice and attention.

"It was very *pleasurable*," I reply, biting my lips at the flare of his nostrils to the word "pleasurable." "And you?"

"Yes. Same. It was quite *satisfying*."

I fight back the smile threatening to break free. Thankfully, Ginny starts her morning report at that moment, giving us both the distraction we need to focus our attention back where it needs to be.

After report, Max gestures to the patient rooms. "You'll be taking the lead today, Dr. Morgan. I'm here to consult, but you're in charge."

His open statement of his trust in me and my work feels amazing, like one more piece of proof that Max is the partner I need. I want to show him how much that means to me, but I can't. I also want so badly to make a flippant remark about him getting off easy and having a lazy day, but we haven't reached that level of teasing at work. It would raise questions from our coworkers, who seem to have just barely accepted Max is no longer biting my head off.

If only they knew the other parts of my body he's been biting. Sucking. Licking.

I trip over my own feet as images of Max devouring my body flash in my mind.

"Everything alright?" he murmurs, his hand coming briefly to rest on my lower back.

"Mm-hmm. Fine, just thinking about something and not watching where I'm going." My voice is far too chipper, and he knows. Oh that man, he knows I'm lying. I hear the barest huff of a chuckle and then we're at the first patient's room. It's time to work. But not before one parting shot from Max, delivered in a low, husky tone that sends shivers down my spine.

"Something tells me you were thinking something dirty, Morgan. I look forward to hearing about it later."

Chapter Twenty-Six

Max

The last month of Heidi's residency is going to steal my sanity, I just know it.

Four weeks until I can claim her as mine.

Four weeks until I don't have to hide how I feel.

Four weeks.

We've started talking about how we'll handle it at work, the plan being to meet with Clarence first. A niggling voice in the back of my head has been saying we should've gone to him right away. Because even though I know there's been absolutely nothing he could question in terms of our professional boundaries so far, the right thing to do would have been to be up-front from the start and have Heidi reassigned.

Except I was selfish and wanted her to myself. Thank God my role with Heidi is purely as supervisor and mentor. If she were an intern, or anyone I had to evaluate somehow, this would have been a disaster. But aside from a few situations when she was just too fucking tempting and we risked it in an empty conference room for a few stolen kisses, we've kept it very professional. No preferential treatment, I openly challenged her on a judgment call I disagreed with, and she has continued to push back and question me.

Granted, now those challenges and pushback moments act as a torturous form of foreplay. There's nothing better than getting her home after a shift when she's pushed my fucking limit of control. The sex is always amazing between us, but those days it's even more explosive.

I knew I needed someone who could keep up in bed. I've got an appetite, for all that it hasn't been fulfilled in a long fucking time. And Heidi meets me every goddamn time, giving me what I need and taking what she does in equal measure.

I would have never though I'd be the kind of man to say this about someone, but she's perfect.

Four more weeks.

Maybe I got cocky. But I don't see the freight train coming until it hits me.

"Hey, buddy," I say, walking into the patient room. We've known Carson for almost as long as we knew Teagan. The two of them were friends, and I know her death likely hit him hard.

While not a cystic fibrosis patient, Carson has pulmonary hypertension that, sadly, went undiagnosed for too long. I've wanted to submit paperwork for a long time to have him assessed for a lung transplant, but he's managed to have lab results just good enough to make him ineligible.

"Hey, Doc," he says, giving me a weak smile from the bed. The kid doesn't look good and my gut sinks. I'm not sure how our team could handle another loss if that's where this goes.

"I know you missed the food around here, but we gotta stop meeting like this." I try to inject some levity, and I'm rewarded with a laugh. We fist bump and I turn to his mother, who sits at his bedside. "You know the drill, we'll get some updated images, keep the high flow oxygen on, and start some diuretics to remove the fluid buildup."

Carson's mom nods in understanding, just as Heidi and the bedside nurse walk in to join us. I pass my orders on to the nurse and step back to let Heidi greet Carson.

The rest of the day goes by and part of my mind is still in that room. I flash between seeing Carson, to seeing Teagan in that bed. And the desperation builds in my mind — *I can't lose another patient.*

"Max, what's wrong?" Heidi's worried whisper has me jerking my head up from the lab results I've been staring at for way too long, wishing they said something different.

I lean back and rake my hands through my hair. "Aside from Carson being back and me not knowing how we're going to help?"

She sits down beside me and lets her hand subtly brush my side. I know she means it to be comforting, but it isn't.

"We need to give the treatment protocol time. We can get this under control."

"For how long?" I ask, the words coming out sharper than she deserves. "For a month? Two? Then he's back, and all we've done is give him two more months of waiting for the next episode."

"We've given him two more months of living," she replies firmly. "You know that, Max."

I push back from the desk and stand up. "I need to... I just... I'll be back." I walk off the unit without looking at another person. She doesn't follow me, and I'm glad. But on the heels of that relief is guilt. I was unfair to her; I took my worries out on her and was a fucking asshole. Again.

After grabbing a coffee from the kiosk in the main lobby, I head outside. The warm sunshine feels like an insult, as if it shouldn't be a beautiful day out here, when inside the building behind me so many people are suffering.

I walk briskly around the large block the hospital sits on. And every bird chirping, every person laughing, every dog barking, all of it fuels the injustice boiling up inside of me. How can life go on out here when there are children dying inside that hospital?

In the distant recesses of my mind I know my thoughts are irrational. So much has happened in the last few months, all of it has me on edge and not thinking clearly.

When I eventually return to the unit, I check in with the nurse in charge to let them know I'm back. There's no sign of Heidi or any of the other residents, for that matter.

Something crossed my mind when I was outside. I didn't give it any thought at the time because I know it's wrong. I know what I fleetingly considered doing would break so many rules. But now, surrounded by sick kids and scared parents, listening to the background noise of beeping monitors and hushed conversations, I can't shake the idea from my head.

Before I can think too much about what I'm doing, I grab Carson's chart and head for an empty meeting room that has a computer.

It takes me less than a minute to pull up the website. Two minutes to scan the criteria, making note of anything pertinent to Carson. And it takes only seconds for me to save the document I need to my desktop and start filling it in. I'll finish it later, print it out, and submit it.

If I go through with it.

My phone is sitting on the desk next to the keyboard, so when it vibrates with an incoming call, I can easily glance at it.

It's Heidi. I ignore it and the pang of guilt I feel in doing so. But shortly after the call, she sends a text.

HEIDI: Where are you?

I pick up the phone and thumb out a short reply, knowing that if I don't, she'll get worried.

MAX: Busy. Everything okay on ward?

The "..." comes and goes. Perhaps I should wonder why it's taking her so long to respond, but my attention is drawn back to the screen in front of me.

My focus is split between my warring conscious that's telling me what I'm doing is wrong and my increasingly stronger need to see this through to completion. I don't hear the door behind me open until Heidi's shocked whisper makes me jump in my seat.

"What are you doing?"

Spinning around, I cast a furtive glance behind her, but there's no one else in the room.

"Close the door." I turn back to the computer. I sense her come closer, and I tense, knowing what she's going to see on the screen in front of us.

"Max. Those aren't the right numbers. Carson's levels are not that high."

"I know that."

"Are you..." Her voice trails off, but it's clear what she's hinting at. And she's right.

"I have to, Heidi. He deserves to be on the list. If he doesn't get assessed, and soon, he'll die." I keep my eyes pointing forward, refusing to meet her gaze, even though I can feel her penetrating stare.

"What happens when the transplant team comes to assess him, and his results are different from what you put down? They'll know you lied. You'll get caught and it'll cost you your medical license."

The condemnation in her tone is clear. But I'm committed. This must happen.

"He's only going to get worse, Heidi. You know it, I know it, and he knows it. By the time the team actually makes it over from Vancouver to do his review, he'll meet the criteria."

"He might, he might not. Are you really willing to risk your career like this? My career? Because I'm tied to you right now, Max. Isn't that the whole point of us staying secret? What happens to you, happens to me, and vice versa?" Her voice is rising in volume and pitch, and I finally look at her, narrowing my eyes.

"Shh. Quiet." My harsh whisper makes her wince, and I almost give in and admit she's right. This is a bad idea. I know the risks. But I also know I can't *not* do this. No matter the cost. "You can walk away now and pretend you never knew. Plausible deniability. This is why we kept our relationship a secret, isn't it? So your career wouldn't be affected. You'll be fine. I won't say a word."

"Max, you can't do this. He isn't Callum or Teagan. You can't save them all."

I scoff. "I can fucking well try. I have to help him. And if you don't want to be a part of this, fine. I respect that. Just keep your mouth shut."

An outraged gasp escapes her. "You really think you need to say that to me? God, Max, no. I would never betray you like that. But I also can't stand by and let you do this without at least trying to get you to see you're wrong. You can't do this."

"I have to. If you can't understand that, then you don't understand me. I think you should leave."

The scrape of her chair pushing back is too loud in the void that has suddenly appeared between us. Because she knows, just as well as I do, that what I said affects more than just this moment right here.

"I thought we trusted each other. Respected each other. This isn't okay, Max, and you know it. If you do this, you're risking more than just our careers. You're risking us. Is it really worth it?"

A small part of me hears the hurt in her voice and cringes at the fact that I'm causing her pain. But a larger part of me is set in my resolve. This has to happen. I'm a doctor; I became a doctor to save lives, and I'll do whatever the fuck it takes to do that.

Her footsteps echo across the room and across the empty space where my heart used to be as she carries it out with her.

But it's better this way. I don't think she'll betray me and tell Clarence what I'm doing, but just the same. It's better to know now that she isn't the woman I thought she was, the one who would be by my side, no matter what.

I look back at the computer screen, at the intake form for the provincial transplant team staring at me.

This is where my responsibility lies.

With my patients.

Not with a woman.

Chapter Twenty-Seven

Heidi

I make it back to the nursing station feeling numb. Part of me can't quite grasp the fact that Max pushed me away so easily. I thought what we had was real, and when he said he trusted and respected me, he meant it. But his actions just now prove that wrong.

When he eventually comes out of the room where I found him falsifying reports to try and get Carson assessed by the transplant team, he doesn't even glance my way.

Which is a blessing in disguise, since I'm barely holding on. I want to scream at him not to throw everything away, not to throw *us* away. Of course, I understand his deep desire to save his patient. What health-care worker wouldn't want to do anything possible to help? But there's a line that should not be crossed. And he's pretending that line doesn't exist.

I get that he's probably terrified to lose Carson. I know how he feels when he thinks he can't protect someone or save them. He might have had therapy in the past, but it didn't come close to fully healing the damage done by his father's accident, or by Callum's death.

The rest of the shift goes by in a blur. Max and I barely

exchange a handful of words. It's as if time has rewound back to when my residency first started and Max was keeping me at a distance. Only this time, it hurts so much more.

Because now I know what it's like to be cared for by Max Donnelly. I know what it's like to see the softer side of him, the part he doesn't show to many people.

"What the heck is up his ass," Tina huffs, dropping down into the chair next to me and crossing her arms. I look up to see her glaring at Max, who's standing across the hall from where we're seated.

"I don't know what you mean," I reply woodenly. It's a lie, and I can only hope she doesn't see through me.

"He just snapped at me for being ten minutes late hooking up antibiotics for room five. Ten minutes. Does he realize I haven't taken a single break all day, that we're down a nurse and overcount on patients? Please don't ever get like that as a doctor. Don't ever forget what it's like for the nurses."

The exhaustion is evident in her voice, and it's an overwhelm I remember so clearly from my nursing days. I wrap my arm around her shoulder and give her a sideways hug. "I promise you, I will never lose sight of how hard you work. Nurses are the real heroes here, and we all know it. Even Max."

"He sure isn't acting like he remembers," she grumbles. I give her one more squeeze, then let go, picking up my phone and stethoscope.

"He knows. Maybe it's just a bad day." I can't help but defend him, even as my heart is hurting from what we said to each other in the conference room.

Tina stands up with me, lowering her head to rest on my

shoulder briefly. "Thanks, Heidi. You're probably right. I just needed to vent."

I watch her walk away, and a part of me wishes I was in her shoes. If I were still a nurse, I wouldn't be in my current position. I wouldn't be heartbroken and scared, and uncertain of what the future looks like.

Because I wouldn't be with Max.

My heart stutters at that thought. Despite the last few hours, despite my fear that he's ruining his life over one patient, despite the hurtful words he said, I love him. That isn't something that just goes away.

At least, not for me.

Tina and another nurse try to convince me to go out with them after our shift ends. But after watching Max disappear from the unit without even saying goodbye, I can't fathom the idea of being around people while my heart is aching so deeply.

Instead, I go home to the apartment I haven't spent much time in, aside from grabbing fresh clothes on my way to Max's house. I immediately take out the bottle of wine that's one of the four things still in my fridge. Next, I go to the bathroom, turn the taps on for the large tub that was the selling feature for this rental, then head to my bedroom to strip out of my scrubs. I toss my phone on my bed, sighing at the jab of pain that comes from seeing not one single message from Max.

I sink into the deep tub, all the way, until only my face is out of the water. Closing my eyes, I turn my focus internally, trying to practice some of the breathing exercises the therapist taught me after leaving Thad. I don't need grounding right now, but anything that helps me calm my mind can't be a bad thing.

But in the muffled silence, with no sound but the water swirling around me, the voices in my head are loud. Clamouring at me that I should have tried harder, said something different, forced him to walk away from the computer.

Even though I know all of that would have been futile.

I saw the determination in his eyes. I saw how committed he was to this path, regardless of right or wrong. Regardless of what it meant for his future, for our future.

And nothing I could do or say would convince him otherwise.

I had no choice but to let him do what he was going to do. The only thing left for me is to try and protect myself from the inevitable recourse of his decision.

When I get out of the tub, the water is cold, and my skin is wrinkled. But my mind is no less conflicted than it was before.

I pull on my favourite cozy pajamas and walk out to the living room, taking my phone with me but not looking at it until I'm on the couch, under a blanket, with a freshly filled glass of wine in hand.

Still nothing from Max.

But there is a missed video call from Skye. I call her back instantly, needing the comfort only my best friend can give.

"Hey, gorgeous!" she answers the call from her own bed, and I can't hold back my laughter at the picture on the screen.

"What the hell is on your face?"

"It's called a sheet mask. Not all of us are blessed with a

perfect complexion."

I settle back into the couch and take a sip of wine.

"Sorry I missed your call; I was in the bath."

I think she waggles her eyebrows at me, but it's hard to tell under the bizarre-looking thing draped over her face. "With your man candy, I hope?"

"Um, no. I'm home alone tonight."

Skye scrambles to sit upright and peels the mask off her face. "Wait. I need to see you clearly. Did you say you're alone? Have you *been* alone since you started dating Dr. Hottie? It seems every time I call, you guys are together."

It takes me a second to decide how much I should tell her. But in the end, my need to confide in someone wins. Besides, she's the one person in my life right now that I *can* talk to without fear of any repercussions — for me or for Max.

"I'm not really sure what's going to happen with us," I start, and instantly my eyes fill with tears. It's the first time I've allowed the emotions to bubble to the surface all day, and now that the seal is broken, I can't stop it. Somehow, I manage to get everything out, maintaining Carson's patient confidentiality, of course. But I tell her what I caught Max doing, and how he reacted, the things he said, and the way the rest of our shift together went.

"Damn. That man is a fucking moron."

I choke out a laugh, even as I'm grabbing another tissue to wipe away the tears. "He's not. He's really smart." I sniffle.

"Not right now, my friend. Right now, he is a fucking moron. Not only is he breaking all kinds of rules, but he's also pushing away the best thing to ever happen to him. That is the *definition* of a moron in my book."

I give her a watery smile. "Thanks."

"Don't thank me yet," she says, lifting one hand. "Because you're also a moron."

My brow furrows. "Excuse me?"

"Hear me out. You love this man. Don't say anything, you haven't told me that, but I've been your friend long enough to be able to read between the lines. You love him."

I simply nod.

Skye tilts her head at me and continues. "You love him, and yet, you're letting him throw away everything that's ever mattered to him."

"I'm not, I tried," I start to protest, but Skye starts shaking her head, interrupting me.

"No, babe, you didn't try hard enough. Think about Max. Think about the things only you know about him. Is it possible something else is triggering him, or motivating him to do this dumbass thing? I'm guessing the answer is yes. Which means he needs you, the woman who loves him, to help him take a step back and *see* he's been triggered and he's letting the wrong things influence his actions."

My mouth opens, then closes. There is no reply. No rebuttal. Because she's right. Without knowing half of the story, Skye is so freaking right.

Teagan dying. Carson being readmitted. Thad bringing up all the trauma from his past. No wonder Max is spiralling.

Fear is driving him, yet again, to make the wrong decision.

"*You* are a genius," I say, lifting my glass to salute her. "Maybe you need a career change. Become a relationship counsellor or something."

Skye visibly shudders. "Good grief, no. That would require fixing my own mess of a love life. How about I just tell you like it is and live vicariously through your happiness when you get that Dr. Hottie of yours to smarten up?"

I laugh again, this time already feeling much lighter. "Deal."

Eventually, we hang up and I go to bed, determined to confront Max tomorrow and work even harder to get him to realize what he's doing isn't right, even if it comes from good intentions.

I just need to figure out how.

CHAPTER TWENTY-EIGHT

Max

Rolling over with a groan, I slam my hand over my phone to try and shut off the alarm. How is it 7 am already when it feels like I just went to bed an hour ago?

That's the thing with insomnia. Time passes interminably slow, and yet, all too quickly at the same time.

I drag my ass out of bed and into the shower, the same as I have every day this past week. Ever since I printed out the paperwork that still sits on my kitchen counter, haunting me. It's almost complete, false lab reports and all, but something has stopped me from uploading it and submitting to the provincial transplant team.

Each time I walk into Carson's room and see him lying in that bed, knowing his body is failing him and feeling as if I, too, am failing him, my resolve grows to send in the forms and give him the one last chance he has to live. Then I walk out of his room and see Heidi across the unit, and that resolve dissipates as the memories of what we said to each other come roaring back.

"They'll know you lied. You'll get caught and it'll cost you your medical license. Are you really willing to risk your career like this?

My career? Because I'm tied to you right now, Max. Isn't that the whole point of us staying secret? What happens to you, happens to me, and vice versa?"

"I have to. If you can't understand that, then you don't understand me. I think you should leave."

"I thought we trusted each other. Respected each other. This isn't okay, Max, and you know it. Why would you do this?"

The hurt in her eyes, the tears I knew were building, every single one was a dagger to my heart. I know I fucked up when I told her to leave. She might have been the one to question our trust and respect in each other, but it was my words and my actions that ripped apart the foundation of what we were building together. And the worst part is, I can't make up my mind as to whether it was worth it. Whether I was right to say what I said and do what I did.

Sure, in the moment, I felt like I was right. It's what I've always done, trusting only myself. Showing no weakness, protecting myself above all else. At the time, it felt as if pushing her away was my only option if she was unable to understand my actions. But as time goes on and the hole in my heart grows wider and wider, I question that belief.

I have the day off today, and for the first time in a long time, I resent that fact. Not because work has been a pleasant place to be, quite the opposite. I've been a grumpy ass to everyone, and I know the nurses are starting to give me a wide berth because of it. But at least work makes me feel like I have a purpose. Like I can still somehow make a difference, at least somewhere. I might feel even more conflicted about Carson when I'm there, but I am nothing, if not an expert at compartmentalizing. And every other patient that I *do* help, helps me to hold onto what little sanity I still have left.

When I get out of the shower, I pull on some sweats and a T-shirt I pick up off the floor and stagger out into my living room. I come up short at the sight of all three of my brothers sitting on my couch.

"Jude? What are you doing here?" I say gruffly, my attention focusing on the one brother I don't often see at my apartment early in the morning. Granted, none of them make a habit of showing up early, or barging into my apartment uninvited, but Jude doesn't even live in the same country. Which makes his presence extra surprising.

He looks at me quizzically. "Aside from the fact that I told you I was planning a short trip home, these guys told me I was needed to help you pull your head out of your ass about something, so I got an earlier flight." He gestures to the twins. Sawyer just lifts his coffee cup in acknowledgment, and Beckett has the decency to look a little sheepish.

"I don't know what the fuck you're talking about."

Sawyer pushes himself to standing, walks to the kitchen, and returns with another cup of coffee that he hands to me. "Neither do we. But Kat, apparently, ran into Heidi, and something she said made Kat worry about you. The timing of Jude's visit is purely coincidental. But helpful if you don't want to listen to me and Beck."

I should be angry at the idea of Heidi going to my family, but I'm not. If anything, I'm relieved she had my sister to turn to. Even if it does mean I now have to face the Donnelly brothers' inquisition.

"I need to get some training in, so we're heading out on a hike," Jude says, unfolding his large body from my couch. "Go get changed."

Even I know it's useless to try and argue against all three of them. I take my coffee back into my bedroom and change into some clothes that will be comfortable for hiking. When I return to my brothers, they're standing by the kitchen counter having a muttered conversation.

"Let's get this over with." I stride to the door, stopping only to grab a water bottle and my keys.

"Dude, is this part of what's got you all fucked up?"

I turn slowly to see Sawyer holding up the paperwork for Carson's referral.

"That's confidential."

"There's no name on it," he fires back.

I run my hand through my hair. He's right, I carefully didn't fill in any of the identifying information yet. Still, I feel exposed, raw, and I don't like it.

"Are we going to hike or not?" I grind out, opening my front door.

One by one, my brothers file out. It's Jude who stops, giving me a penetrating stare. "What are you doing, brother?"

I exhale slowly, closing my eyes against his inquisition. "I'll tell you about it on the trail."

Half an hour later, we all climb out of Sawyer's truck. I can't imagine ever living somewhere without nature within easy access. Just the sound of the wind rustling the trees has my stress level lowering. Not a lot, but it's a start.

After a brief discussion of which trail to take, we set off. To give them credit, my brothers don't instantly start interrogating me. Instead, the conversation turns to Jude's season, how well his team is playing, and their chances of going to the playoffs. He's not a superstitious guy, which is weird for a hockey player, so he's open and honest about how things are going.

"What about your head? All clear from the latest concussion?" I ask, earning a sharp look from Jude.

"Yeah. Of course. I wouldn't be on the ice if I wasn't."

"Just be careful, man."

He nods and silence falls again. I know I'm lucky to be friends with my brothers. There's no competition, no animosity. Don't get me wrong, as teens we were often beating each other up in the backyard, but there's no bad feelings between us, no matter the different paths we've all taken. As we hike, I realize this was exactly what I needed. Out here, far away from the hospital and Heidi, I feel like I can take a full breath for the first time in a week.

We hit the first summit of the trail, a viewpoint that overlooks the waterfall we plan on reaching the top of.

"Break?" Sawyer asks, sinking down on the bench and stretching his legs out. "Hiking with you bastards after a busy set is kicking my ass." He yawns, his head falling back.

"Anything serious?" Beckett asks him, sitting down beside his twin, pulling out his water bottle, and drinking deeply.

"Nah," Sawyer replies, folding his hands behind his head. "Just a lot of calls, that's all. But today isn't about me." He twists at the waist to look at me. "Maxy boy is in the hot seat."

I walk over to the edge of the lookout and lean against the railing, staring at the water that cascades over rocks, the same way it has for centuries. It's constant, never-ending, and there's something soothing about that.

It makes me think of Heidi. Of the calm she brought to me, the way I knew in a deep part of my soul that she would be constant in my life. At least, I thought she would be.

Pushing off the railing, I turn to my brothers.

"I fucked up."

"We already figured that part out," Sawyer remarks. "Tell us how."

Ignoring his snark, I do just that. I tell them everything, leaving out only the details about Carson that would identify him in any way. It's almost ironic; here I am, worried about maintaining the rules of patient confidentiality while also flouting the rules by falsifying reports to get him on the transplant list.

When I finish, there's silence for several minutes before all three of my brothers start shouting at once.

"You're a fucking idiot. I though you were the smart one."

"What the hell, Max."

"You broke her heart, bro."

It's Beckett's comment about Heidi that sinks in the deepest. "I know. I know, all of you are right, I know. That's why I haven't submitted the paperwork yet. You saw it sitting on my counter, it's been there for days."

"That's good, man. That means you can fix this," Beckett says quietly. "Don't submit it. Rip it up, as if you never started down this path in the first place."

I nod, knowing that's exactly what I'll do when I get home. "I can fix that part of it. But can I fix things with Heidi?"

"That depends. Why the fuck did you push her away when

she was trying to get you to see reason?"

Jude's gruff voice is surprisingly free of judgment. Nonetheless, I keep my eyes focused on the ground in front of me.

"Honestly? I don't know. I was consumed by the need to save this kid."

"You can't save everyone, Max."

I look up at Sawyer, to see an uncharacteristically serious expression on his face. As a firefighter, he knows what it feels like to save someone, and to fail to do so.

Out of nowhere, tears start to well in my eyes. Okay, not out of nowhere. I know damn well it's the realization that, yet again, I let my past influence my present actions in a stupid way. It's realizing I assumed the worst of Heidi, instead of trusting her. And it's realizing I might be more broken inside than I ever let myself admit.

"I can't..." My voice trails off. I can't what? Lose another patient? That's the sad reality of my job and I know that. I can't not try to save everyone? That's not the point. Of course, I can try to save every patient, that's why I'm a doctor. But I have to be realistic and work within the legal and moral boundaries of right and wrong. "Filling out the paperwork was a dumb fucking idea. I think I've known that all along, and that's why I took the papers home instead of submitting them."

"Right. So you're not a fucking idiot, just a regular one."

I glare at Sawyer, even though he's not wrong.

"Max," Beckett starts, his voice a soft contrast to Sawyer's harsh one. "When Dad had his accident, we all got counselling to help deal with the fact that he almost died. But you missed most of the sessions."

I drop my head in acknowledgment.

"Maybe you need some help to finish working through that? Maybe that incident has affected your ability to cope with pain and loss."

A teardrop splashes to the ground, followed by another.

"Beck, man, you should've been a therapist, not an accountant." Despite the teasing tone, no one laughs at Sawyer's joke.

"You're right," I say hoarsely, finally lifting my head to look at each of my brothers in turn. "I do need to work through some shit. But I don't know if I can do that without fixing things with Heidi first."

"So fix it."

Jude's simple statement hangs in the air between us, settling over me like a weighted blanket, offering comfort and hope.

The next day when my alarm goes off, I don't feel quite as wrecked as I did yesterday. After coming home and shredding the paperwork into tiny pieces with my brothers as witnesses, we had some beer and pizza and just hung out. And I finally told them the truth. I told them about Cara and I told them about Heidi's connection to Thad. I told them everything. And with the weight of those secrets finally lifted from my shoulders, I slept last night. Deeply, dreamlessly, restfully.

Finally getting some sleep should make me feel better about going in to work today. But when I pull up to the hospital, I don't get out, ready to take on the day and right my wrongs. Instead, I sit in my car and stare at the building that defines so much of who I am.

I don't *want* my work to be the primary thing in my life anymore. This place, this job, it might be fulfilling, but it's also heartbreaking in equal measure. I love my job, it is my calling. But I want to be more than Dr. Donnelly, or Max Donnelly, son and brother. I want to be Max Donnelly, love of Heidi Morgan's life. I want to be her husband someday. I want to talk about having kids with her. I want to spend my life worshipping her and trying to prove to her that I deserve her love.

Which means I have to start today with apologizing and telling her I never submitted the paperwork. She was right, I was wrong, and I have my work cut out for me in begging for her forgiveness. Begging her to trust me again.

I make my way up to the ward, only to be met by Clarence getting off the elevator at the same time.

"Ah, Dr. Donnelly. Good to see you. How's everything going?"

"Fine," I reply curtly. He's not the person I want to see right now, with the guilt over my near-transgression so fresh in my head. We reach the nursing station and my eyes dart around, looking for Heidi. Instead of finding her, I see Carson's mother step out of his room and head toward Clarence and me.

"Dr. Donnelly, could I have a moment?" she asks quietly. I turn to her, grateful for the distraction.

"Of course."

She twists her hands together, her eyes downcast. When she looks up, I see the moisture pooling, and my stomach drops. "Carson told us last night he doesn't want to proceed with getting assessed for a transplant. We talked all night, and we want to respect his decision. I know you said you were working on his application, and I'm sorry to have wasted your time."

I hold up a hand to interrupt. This is not good. I can feel the weight of Clarence's stare at my back. "It's fine, don't apologize. Carson's choice is the most important thing, and if you are all in agreement, that's all that matters."

She lets out a muffled sob, her hand coming to cover her mouth. "Thank you. We...I...I need to go, but we'll see you when you come to his room. He'd like to talk with you."

I nod and she turns to leave, hurrying back to her son's bedside.

"Dr. Donnelly, let's go to the conference room to discuss something."

Clarence's tone leaves no room for discussion. At that exact moment, I see Heidi just down the hall. Judging by the look on her face, she heard everything.

I move to follow Clarence down the hall and she falls in step beside me. "You don't need to come," I whisper quietly.

"I do. You're not alone, Max."

Her fingers brush against mine and I let out a shuddery breath.

When she follows me into the conference room, Clarence's eyebrows raise, but he doesn't say anything. His attention is fully on me, as it should be.

"Ginny approached me last week to ask about submitting an application for the transplant team. I reviewed Carson's most recent results and concluded he didn't qualify, which is exactly what I told her. So, could you please explain to me why his mother is still under the belief you were putting forth the application?"

I sit down in a chair across from the man I respect as my superior, but also as the person in control of my future. And Heidi's future, since she foolishly followed me in here. All I can do in this moment is tell the truth. I look him straight in the eye and fold my hands on the table in front of me. I'm the picture of calm, at odds with the roiling sea of emotion and stress inside of me.

"I was considering submitting the application with the hope that by the time the team came to assess him, his numbers would've reached the point to qualify him."

"You were going to falsely report his lab results."

I nod, then shake my head. "I was going to, yes. But I didn't." I hear Heidi's sharp inhale. But I keep my eyes trained on Clarence. "It was wrong to even consider it, I know, especially to give Carson's family false hope. I had a moment of weakness, desperation, even." Finally, I turn my attention across the table, to Heidi. She's pale, her arms folded around herself. "But I couldn't do it. It was wrong. *I* was wrong. I can't save every patient. I couldn't save Callum, or Teagan, and I might not be able to save Carson. I have to be okay with that because the alternative, the risk of losing my career and losing the opportunity to help countless more kids, isn't worth it."

"You didn't submit the paperwork," Heidi whispers as Clarence asks who Callum is. But he hears her and frowns, as if he's just now trying to piece together why she's here. I know that's another conversation we need to have with him. But in this moment, I'm trying to focus on containing the cautious flicker of hope inside of me. Hope that she could forgive me.

I move my head back and forth slowly. "I didn't. It took my brothers verbally smacking me in the head to really get it to sink in. Breaking the rules like that wouldn't be worth the loss."

I don't have to say what that loss would be. She knows.

She knows the loss would be her.

CHAPTER TWENTY-NINE

Heidi

"What on earth are you two talking about?" Clarence's bewildered voice filters into my head, but just barely. Instead, it's Max's words that are claiming my attention.

"The loss..." I echo quietly, as I walk around the table. He stands up when I reach him, and the cautiously hopefully expression etched onto his face is all the confirmation I need to know his remorse is genuine. I lift a hand and cup his cheek, smiling slightly when he turns into my touch. "I knew you'd do the right thing."

My words are quiet, meant only for him, but I've apparently managed to forget that our boss is sitting right here. The man who holds the power to destroy everything I've worked for.

"This is very touching, and whatever dynamic is between the two of you is most certainly something we need to return to, but if I could draw your attention back to the important matter, please?" Clarence says drily, but not without some criticism. Max and I both startle apart and turn to him.

"I-I'm s-sorry, sir," I start stammering out, suddenly unsure of how to proceed. I've known Clarence for years and we've always had a good working relationship, but now I feel unsure, like I'm on rocky ground and could fall at any moment. "It was my fault. We developed feelings for each other, but Max wasn't going to act on them. I pushed him —"

"Heidi, no," Max interrupts. His hand reaches out for mine, our fingers tangling together in a very obvious display of what our relationship truly is. I glance up at him to see those blue eyes I adore shining at me, full of love. I know we've still got a lot to work through, but in this moment, we're united. He turns to face Clarence. "Clarence, the only person who's at fault is me. I knew that entering a relationship with Heidi was unwise. It crosses all kinds of professional boundaries and disrupts the power balance between us. But the truth of our feelings for each other took over all rational thought. Still, I recognize the responsibility lies with me to proceed appropriately, and I didn't. I take full blame. Heidi is an exemplary physician and at the start of her career. She should not suffer any repercussions for something I should have handled better."

I should be happy to hear Max stand up for me, not shy away from his feelings, and try to protect me. But instead, he's making it sound like he made some catastrophic error in judgment all on his own.

"Stop. You're not the only one involved in this," I say, turning to face him. "I know you're trying to shield me from any consequences, but that's not fair. We were both equally at fault. We knew what we were doing."

"I can't let you lose everything," Max murmurs, his eyes worried and darting up and down my face.

I squeeze his hand gently. "Neither can I."

"If you'd both just stop and listen to me for a moment, I would like to move on from this," Clarence yet again interrupts us, and I drop Max's hand guiltily.

"Sorry."

We both say it at the same time, and I fight the instinct to smile.

Clarence steeples his hands in front of him, then gestures to the two seats in front of Max and me. "Please. Sit down."

We do, and I fold my hands on the table in front of me in an effort to avoid reaching for Max. My body aches to touch him, but my heart is still warning me to wait.

"As I assume you both know, seeing as you are two intelligent, rational adults, it is not exactly against hospital policy for relationships between staff to occur. However —" Clarence pauses and frowns at Max "— the power dynamic between the two of you, with Dr. Donnelly being your supervisor, does complicate matters. Max, you should have come to me the minute your relationship turned from professional to personal, so we could adjust course. The fact that you continued to supervise her was ill-advised and inappropriate, to say the least. The only silver lining is that you have not conducted any formal evaluations yet. Nonetheless, we will have to immediately reassign Dr. Morgan to a different attending for the remainder of her residency period."

I nod quickly and out of the corner of my eye I see Max do the same. I expected as much, and he's not wrong. That is what we should have done right from the start, but I wanted so badly to remain working with Max, to learn from him, that I ignored my conscience.

"I won't go to the university with this," Clarence continues, this time directing his sharp look at me, "purely based on your performance thus far and based on the professional respect I have for you, Dr. Morgan, dating back to your nursing years. As Dr. Donnelly said, you are an exemplary physician. That is evident to anyone who has worked with you. A stain on your record would do a disservice to many. And since there have been no reports of your relationship affecting your work, I am willing to overlook this."

"Thank you, sir," I say on a shaky exhale. I'm fully aware I just dodged a major bullet. Hospital policy or not, when Max and I started dating, we should have come to Clarence and had me reassigned. I don't know why we ever thought it would be okay for him to continue supervising me and sleeping with me at the same time.

"However, as I said, I would like to move on from that topic and get back to the more important issue. The transplant team referral."

I suck in a breath and sense Max's entire body tightening as well.

"Had you gone ahead and filed the paperwork, Dr. Donnelly, this would be a very different conversation. The fact that you came to your senses and did *not* file a falsified application is the only thing saving you from a formal reprimand. Or worse." Clarence pauses, leaning forward. "You understand what I'm saying? This could have gone very poorly had you gone down the path you started. I'm shocked and disappointed in you. I don't know what got in your head to make you ever think falsifying patient reports would be a good idea, but I'm telling you once, and once only. Figure it out, and don't ever let yourself go down that track again."

Max nods stiffly. "Understood. It won't happen again, I promise. It was a moment of weakness, brought on by multiple stressors. I will not let things get so out of hand again."

Clarence's eyes bounce over to me, then back to Max. "I trust you can determine what those stressors were and avoid them in the future."

"Yes."

Oh God. I'm one of those stressors. I know it. Being with me is what triggered the nightmares, the memories of his father's accident, and Cara's betrayal.

Clarence pushes back from the table and stands, but I'm frozen where I am. "Right. Well, I'll give you two a few minutes to collect yourselves. In the meantime, I'll work on having Heidi reassigned to Dr. Sloan. Might I suggest the two of you not let it come to light how long your relationship has been going on? I'm not at liberty to ask you to lie, but I trust you understand me when I suggest that it would go over better with your colleagues if they believed this to be a newer development."

"Understood," Max says stiffly. "Thank you, Clarence, and again, I'm sorry for my transgressions."

Clarence nods briefly. "It's over and done now. Let's move forward."

He walks out of the room, and the snick of the door closing behind him echoes in the heavy silence.

I don't know what to say. How to act.

"I'm so sorry," Max starts quietly, and those three words make it impossible for me not to touch him. I cover his hand in mine. His head darts up and again, there's that hope I saw earlier in his eyes. "Heidi, truly, I don't know how I'll ever show you just how sorry I am. The things I said, the way I acted. It was horrible. Shit, no, it was worse than horrible. It was cruel, and wrong, and the worst possible way I could've handled things."

"Max," I start, but he shakes his head.

"No. Let me say this, please. Because I know your beautiful heart wants to tell me it's okay and that you understand, but I can't move forward unless I get this out. You deserve better than me, but if it's me you decide to give a second chance, I need to earn it."

It's my turn to hold up my hand to interrupt. I know Max is determined to earn my forgiveness. And in my heart, I've essentially already given it to him. That doesn't change the fact I was likely a large part of the reason Max was under so much pressure.

"But you heard Clarence. He had a good point. You did what you did as a reaction to the stress in your life; stress that includes your relationship with me and all the baggage I bring."

Max grabs both of my hands in his. "No, sweetheart, no. You are not the cause of any of this. You've made me feel safe and capable of opening my heart to someone for the first time in a really long time. I can't begin to describe how much that means to me. The only stress being with you caused me was my own worry. Worry that being with me would somehow screw things up for you." He lets out a harsh, self-deprecating laugh. "And look how well I managed that. Fuck. I almost *did* screw everything up for you." He shakes his head and looks back at me. "Our relationship makes me stronger. Better. It was your voice, telling me what I was doing was wrong, that got through the fog in my head."

"I thought you said it was your brothers," I say on a shaky laugh.

His answering smile is more relaxed and open. "It was both. They're the ones who smacked me upside the head and told me to listen to *you*. To trust and respect you, and what we have together."

"Smart brothers."

He half chuckles, half groans. "I hope you won't mind if I do *not* tell them you said that. Otherwise, the next time they see you, it'll be all they can focus on. Especially Sawyer."

A giggle escapes me. "That's fine."

Max's tone sobers. "I know I've got a lot of work to do. I need to find a therapist to help me deal with how I process grief and loss. It's not going to be easy, but it would be easier with you by my side. So, I'm really hoping you'll give me a chance to win you back."

"You don't need one. I'm not going anywhere. When I said I love you, I meant it."

His lips are on mine before I can take another breath, and everything in my world turns right side up again. A happy sense of rightness settles in my soul, and all the rips and holes in my heart begin to mend.

CHAPTER THIRTY

Max

Somehow, I get through the rest of my shift without making a fool of myself over Heidi. Even so, I guess the abrupt change in my attitude from tense and grumpy to relieved is pronounced enough for others to take notice. Because as I'm tidying up some charts, my head already on needing to find Heidi and ask her to come over tonight so we can finish talking, Ginny corners me in the office where I'm working.

"Alright Mister Sunshine, what's up with the one-eighty? Don't get me wrong, we're all glad you're back to your usual self, but as your friend, what happened to turn you into Eeyore, and what happened to change you back? I'm assuming it has something to do with a certain resident." She sits down in the chair behind me.

I spin my chair around and let out a huff. "You always were too smart for your own good."

Ginny just rolls her eyes. "Tell that to my four kids who think they know better on a daily basis. I swear, if one of them tries to tell me to retire again, I don't care if they're grown adults, I'll whoop their butts."

A chuckle escapes me. "No, you won't."

She narrows her eyes at me, then her face softens into a smile. "Fine, no, I won't. But this conversation isn't about me. It's about you and how we can prevent you from becoming a grump again."

I lace my fingers together behind my head and give Ginny a sly smirk, just to mess with her. "I make no promises. I might be a grump, or what did you call me? Eeyore?" She nods and I shrug. "Yeah, I might become that again. Not planning on it, but hey, I'm human, and I'll probably screw up at some point. If I do, I'll need you to whoop *my* butt because it'll mean I screwed things up with the love of my life."

"Oh, Max."

I lean forward, resting my elbows on my knees. "I hope that 'oh, Max' is a happy one. Because I'm happy." I pause, considering what I said. "Well, I will be once I make damn sure she knows I don't deserve her, but I'm not letting her go. She's the best thing to ever happen to me. I almost lost her, but somehow, I'm lucky enough to have earned another chance."

Ginny's hand moves to cover mine. "It's definitely a happy one. Because I'm thrilled for both of you that you found your way to each other. I always thought you two would be good together, even when she was with that useless twit Thad." We both chuckle. Then she takes on a serious tone, her eyes narrowing and focusing on me intently. "But listen to me, Max. You might be human, and yes, we all make mistakes. However, that woman deserves nothing less than your very best. So, *don't* screw it up again. Understood?"

"I think he understands, Ginny."

We both startle at the sound of Heidi's amused voice. The

open and raw love I see radiating from her has me sighing out loud.

"Yes, I think he does. Alright, you two, we'll see you tomorrow. Don't be late." Ginny pats my hand, then stands to leave. On her way out, she squeezes Heidi's shoulder. "I don't need to know what happened this time, but if he gives you crap ever again, you come straight to me."

"Thank you."

The two women exchange small smiles, then Ginny's gone and Heidi's closing the office door behind her. The blinds are partially drawn across the window, but it's still possible for anyone to look in and see us. That doesn't seem to bother her as she walks up to me, lifts one leg up and over mine, and sits, straddling my lap.

"We're at work, Dr. Morgan," I can't help but tease, even as my hands come around to cup her perfect ass.

"We are. And I heard Clarence say it was fine, as long as we were discreet and you weren't my supervisor anymore. Seeing as I just spent the day listening to Dr. Sloan drone on as if I were a first year, I'd say I've earned the right to sit on my boyfriend's lap if I want to."

Laughter escapes me as I draw her in closer. "I'm sorry, love. At least there's only a month left." I tuck the tiniest piece of hair behind her ear. "And then this is all behind us."

"One month," she sighs. "One month until I'm a fully qualified doctor, working at my favourite hospital."

"With your favourite coworkers," I supply with a smirk.

Heidi giggles. "Yeah, the coworkers are a pretty good perk."

I push off the chair, bringing us both to standing. "Are you done for the day?" She nods. "Good. Then let's go home. I have hours of naked groveling to get started on."

Her brow furrows, but only for a second before she registers what I just said.

"That's right, sweetheart. How many orgasms will it take to earn your full trust and forgiveness again? Five? Ten? More?" I force my tone to stay casual, unlike my cock, which is already hardening just from the very thought of being with her again.

"I already told you I forgive you." She says the words, but the breathy tone to her voice betrays her.

I give her a wicked grin. "Are you saying you don't want orgasms?" Her head shakes back and forth so quickly I can't hold back a laugh. "Then let's go."

The entire drive back to my place, I keep looking in my rearview mirror, as if Heidi is going to suddenly disappear.

I know she's not. I know she's following me, just as I know I'll do whatever I can to never let her go again.

Still, when we pull into the parking lot for my building and she climbs out of her car and gives me that sunny smile I'm addicted to, I have to close my eyes against the intense wave of happiness — and anticipation — that hits me.

It might have only been a week since I last had her, but that week felt like an eternity.

Apparently, she feels the same way because the second my front door closes behind us, she pushes me toward my couch. I sit down and she straddles my lap again, just like she did at the hospital. Only this time, there's no risk of prying eyes catching us.

Our scrub tops go flying, in between frantic kisses. I'm filled with an insane need to feel her surrounding me, holding me inside of her.

But I've got groveling to do first.

I stand up, taking her with me, spin around, and deposit her back down on the couch before sinking to my knees in front of her. I grasp the hem of her pants and peel them down her legs slowly.

"I missed you this week. As messed up as I was over Carson, the worst part of it was knowing I'd hurt you. I never want to hurt you again. And to prove it, I'm going to spend the next several hours earning your forgiveness and your love. One lick, one kiss, one touch at a time. Okay with you?"

Heidi nods frantically.

I lower my head and start to kiss her inner thighs, running my hands lightly up and down her legs. Her hands come to the back of my head, and I feel her try to guide me where she wants me.

"Uh-uh, none of that, my love." I lift my head, reach for her hands, and bring them to my lips. Kissing both of her wrists, I rise up on my knees and place her hands across the back of the couch. "I'm in control tonight. Do you trust me?"

"Yes," she says, half sighing, half moaning the word.

"Good girl."

I lower my head slowly to see if she can actually keep her hands where they are and give up control to me. I want to earn back her trust in all parts of our life together but starting here feels right.

I gently nip at her inner thighs again, this time moving higher, closer to where we both want me to be.

"Mmm." I ghost my lips over her glistening pussy. "I missed this, as well. A lot."

"Max, please," she pleads. I glance up, and her eyes are wild with passion, but like the good girl she is, she's keeping her hands up. I reward her with a soft kiss to the tip of her clit.

"I've got you."

I flatten my tongue and lick her entire slit. Her legs clamp around me instantly, and I use one arm to lift them over my shoulders before diving in and eating her perfect pussy with the reckless abandon that's been stored up inside of me for too long.

Her first orgasm comes on fast. But I'm not stopping at one. Even as she's pulsing around my tongue, I lift my hand to her mouth. She opens, sucking my fingers in deeply. I pull back from sucking on her clit and slowly work one, then two fingers into her, turning my hand so I can curve them over and hit that sweet spot inside of her.

"Ohmygod." Her hips lift off the couch and her hands grab fistfuls of my hair.

I freeze. "Hands, babe."

Her whimper is almost my undoing, but she does as she's told and returns her hands behind her head. Only then do I start moving my fingers again and lower my head to flick my tongue over her clit again.

"Oh God. I can't, I'm going to— Max. Max. Oh my God, yes, yes, yes!" Her words are garbled but seconds later she's coming again, this time squeezing my fingers and flooding my mouth with her essence.

My cock is throbbing, angry and desperate to feel her. She's still panting, her head thrown back, eyes closed, and I swear I've never seen someone so beautiful. I withdraw my fingers and tug my scrub pants down far enough to free my cock. Then I'm pulling Heidi off the couch and turning us at the same time, so I'm leaning against it and she's exactly where I need her to be. Her hands come to my shoulders, and a dreamy smile stretches over her face as she slides down my dick.

"You're a magician, Max Donnelly. An orgasm magician."

I let out a low, hoarse chuckle, holding back from thrusting up into her. "You're still riding the high, sweetheart. Open your eyes. Look at me."

She does, and the honest love beaming out at me is blinding. I crush her to my body, cementing us together. Heidi starts to move her hips back and forth. My head starts to swim with sensation overload. I lift my head to look at her, filled with a possessive need to claim her. My hand comes up to bracket her throat as I lean forward and suck the skin just above her breast, biting down gently.

"Mine."

"Yes."

That one word of submission is enough to send me over the edge, thrusting up and down, rocking my hips until I'm spilling everything I have inside of her.

Eventually our movements slow, heart rates return to normal, and I become more aware of our surroundings. The hardwood floor underneath me isn't exactly comfortable, I never did get my scrub pants all the way off, and we're both sweaty and sticky from work and from what we just did.

"Shower," I announce. "Then we're doing that again."

Heidi giggles, climbing off me carefully. I stand, kick off my pants, and take her hand.

"Don't you want to clean up?"

"Nope. I want to get even dirtier with you first."

Her laughter follows us into the bathroom and straight into the steaming hot water of the shower. We take turns soaping each other up, the action loving and caring, not sexual. But as the water rinses away the suds, my eyes drop to her breasts and the mark I left there earlier. As the water cascades over us, my dick starts to harden again just from being near her naked body. And just like that, my cock is hard again.

"Mmm, already? I guess when you said several hours, you meant it." Her hand wraps around my length, stroking me gently.

I groan as her thumb sweeps across my tip. "I did." Heidi drops to her knees, running her tongue up and down. I gather her hair in my hands and stare down at her, pouring every ounce of love I feel for her into my words.

"I know I was in charge earlier, but this time I want you to take what you need from me. Fuck my fingers, fuck my mouth, fuck my cock. Everything I am, everything I have, is yours. Whatever it takes for you to believe I'm in this with you. For you. For us."

"I already believe that, Max. I love you. I never stopped loving you. I don't need orgasms to know I forgive you and I trust you. I just need you to forgive yourself, so you can be here with me."

I drop down into a crouch, so I'm on her level.

"I'm here. And if you'll have me, I always will be."

CHAPTER THIRTY-ONE

Heidi

"I'll never get tired of this view."

"Me either."

I look over my shoulder at Max's wicked smirk. "Behave."

He lifts his hands up in a gesture of innocence. "Hey, I'm just saying my view is spectacular." He closes the distance between us and cups my butt as he leans down to kiss my neck. "Fucking perfect."

I shiver, despite the heat of the sun beating down on us. "Max."

"Yeah, babe?"

"We can't." Even as I say the words, his hands are trailing around my hips, dipping down underneath my shorts and teasing me. He slides one finger all the way down and under my panties, swiping it quickly through the moisture already pooling between my legs.

"Hmm. Something tells me we could if we're fast."

Voices up ahead have him pulling his hand out quickly, moving to stand beside me but turning slightly, I assume to hide the bulge I feel hardening under his shorts. But as the other hikers pass us with casual greetings, Max lifts his finger to his mouth and sucks it in deeply, his eyes locked on mine.

"You're so bad," I whisper as soon as the other people are far enough away.

Max just gives me an unrepentant grin. "Sorry, babe. Not my fault you're so delicious. Let's just get to the hot springs so I can hide what I'm doing under the water."

"Because that worked so well for you last time?" I can't resist the tease.

His shoulders lift and fall in a carefree shrug. I am so in love with him. "Seeing as you're here with me this time, I'd say it worked pretty damn well."

He takes my hand, and we walk the rest of the way to the hot springs, side by side — the way we've gone through everything the last few weeks. Any worries we had about people at the hospital finding out we were together were quickly proven unfounded. Sure, there were a couple of questioning looks from my fellow residents, but nothing like the judgment we feared. Clarence was right to suggest we not draw attention to how long our relationship had been going on. I think my move to Dr. Sloan's service was part of what made it easier for everyone to accept Max and I as a couple.

We reach the first pool fairly quickly, and just as Max said it would be, it's full. He winks and draws me farther along the path, until we're ducking off the trail in between some bushes. We traipse through the forest a little longer, the voices from the hot springs fading behind us, until we reach the pool where I stumbled upon him, naked, all those weeks ago.

It feels like a lifetime has passed since the day everything started to shift between us. Being here again, together, is the perfect full circle moment for our relationship.

Wasting no time, Max pulls his T-shirt up and over his head.

"Are you planning on joining me or just staring?" he asks, reaching out a thumb to swipe at the corner of my mouth. "You've got a little drool right there."

I swat him away, rolling my eyes. "Stop it." Turning around to give him my back, I do the same, peeling off my tank top slowly.

"Heidi."

"Mm-hmm?" I ask, innocently peeking at him over my shoulder.

"Where's your swimsuit?"

I don't answer. Instead, I slowly shimmy my shorts down, step out of them, and kick them to the side, along with my socks and shoes.

"And you said I was bad." All of a sudden, two strong arms are wrapped around my waist, and I'm lifted in the air.

"Max," I squeal. "Put me down."

"Not a chance. Not out here where anyone can see what's mine." He walks into the water and sinks down instantly. Only when we're submerged up to our shoulders does he loosen his grip enough for me to turn around in his arms.

I run my hands up his torso. "I like you saying that I'm yours."

"Good." He leans down to kiss my bare shoulders. "Because you are. Just as everything I am belongs to you." His lips trail across my collarbone, and my hips rock into his pelvis automatically.

"Take me, Max."

A low groan is the only answer I get. But then again, I don't need anything else. I don't need anything except this man.

"Why am I nervous? I've already met everyone. I've already done the Donnelly dinner." Max's hand comes over to cover both of mine, which are twisting nervously in my lap. We're parked outside his parents' house for family dinner, and there's a lot of cars in the driveway. "Are there more people here than just your family?"

"No," he says, his voice filled with love. "Just Kat and Hunter, Sawyer, Beckett, Leo, Serena and Violet, and my parents."

"That's a lot. Serena and Leo weren't here last time."

"No big deal. My family loves you almost as much as I do, and Serena and Leo will be just the same." He lifts my hand to his lips and presses a kiss there, melting away most of my tension. Most, but not all.

I take a deep breath in and out. "Okay. Let's do this."

Max's warm chuckle precedes the brush of his lips across my temple. "It's going to be fine. But if my mother starts with any baby talk, just smile and nod."

I twist in my seat, leaning back against the side of the car. "Baby talk?"

The impossibly handsome man I love more than anything just smiles, his blue eyes dancing with mirth. "I'm joking, Hei-di."

He might have been joking, but now the idea of being pregnant with Max's baby is in my head. And I kinda really like it. Still, I shake my head slightly. "No baby talk yet. Please."

Max opens his door, climbs out, and walks around to open mine. Reaching a hand in, he pulls me up to stand and straight into his strong arms. "Deal. Not *yet*." He winks on the emphasis of the word "yet" and I shiver.

"Hey lovebirds! Mom won't let us start eating the appetizers till you're inside, and I'm hungry."

I peer over Max's shoulder to see Sawyer with his hands in his pockets, leaning against the porch railing, grinning at us.

"Just ignore him. Sometimes it works to make him go away."

"I heard that," Sawyer calls out.

Max drops his forehead to mine. "I swear if he and Beckett weren't identical, I'd wonder if he was actually related to me. He's a menace."

"Don't worry. Someday, someone will come along and turn him into the man he's meant to be." I mean that in a teasing way, but Max gets a solemn look on his face as he cups my cheek.

"Just like you did with me. I didn't even know I was living half a life until you came along. Even when I was trying to make myself hate you, I couldn't, simply because everything felt richer, fuller, better when you were around."

Another voice interrupts our moment, this one too cute to ignore.

"Unca Maxy, I'm hungwy."

I feel Max's silent laughter as he turns us both around. "Okay, Vi. We're coming."

As soon as we get in the door, we see Sawyer standing in the living room, drinking a bottle of beer, wearing a satisfied smirk.

"Low blow sending a kid to do your dirty work," Max remarks, shoving his brother lightly with his shoulder.

"Hi, honey," Claire Donnelly comes bustling out of the kitchen, wiping her hands on her apron. Max gives her a kiss and a hug before turning her loose on me.

The next thing I know, I'm being folded into a hug that is way stronger than I expected from such a small woman. But I guess raising five kids will do that.

"Lovely to see you again, Heidi. I'm so happy you came for dinner." She backs up slightly, her hands resting on my shoulders. "Is it safe to assume you'll be at more family dinners in the future?"

Max wraps his arm around my shoulders. "She'll be at all of them if I have anything to say about it. But can you not scare her away with the interrogation about our future just yet? Our family is a lot to take in, even without you dreaming about grandchildren."

Claire just gives us an impressive eye roll. "I didn't mention grandchildren, *you* did. And you make it sound like we're a firing squad."

"I mean, sometimes it feels that way," Hunter comments as he and Kat come into the kitchen at that very moment. Kat beelines to me, and I'm pulled into yet another hug. This family doesn't shy away from affection.

"I'm so glad you're here. Ignore Hunter, he's still scarred from when my brothers gave him shit about us dating. Be glad you avoided *that* fun. Although, wait, hang on." Kat backs up and raises her voice, pitching it into the living room. "Hey, Sawyer. How come Max and Heidi didn't have to put up with your crap when they got together?"

"Because you're my little sister, and Max is my older brother."

It's comical how both Kat and Claire narrow their eyes in identical ways. But it's Claire who speaks first.

"Sawyer Donnelly, get your behind in here right now and apologize for being a brat."

He comes in, a sheepish smirk on his face. "Sorry, Mom."

"Don't apologize to me." She points a finger at Kat and then at me. "These two ladies are who you're in trouble with."

"Not me." I hold my hands up in defense. "I'm fine."

Kat stands with her hands on her hips. "Run."

Sawyer takes off out the back door, and Kat races after him. Hunter, Max, Claire, and I just watch them race around the yard. Eventually, Kat catches up to Sawyer. That woman is fast. She takes him down, and then all we hear are shouts of laughter.

"Is she tickling him?" I ask, confused about how a petite woman like Kat managed to topple her much larger brother.

"Yup. He's extremely ticklish," Max says affectionately. "Hunter, my man, you better get out there and give some back-up. When Sawyer gets up, he's gonna be out for revenge."

Hunter heads outside just as more people file into the kitchen.

"What's going on?" Leo asks.

"Sawyer was an idiot."

"Kat has him pinned."

"Yep."

"Good for her."

I watch the back and forth between siblings, cousins, and partners. And I can't help but wonder why on earth I was nervous about tonight. This family is filled with nothing but love and affection for everyone.

Just the way I am for Max.

He might not have been completely serious when he talked about me coming to all the family dinners in the future, but a part of me can't help but wish for that to come true. I'll even face talk of grandchildren.

Because with Max, I've found more than just love. I've found a future.

Epilogue

Max

The arena is packed. Makes sense, seeing as it's the first home game for Jude's team. They were introduced as league champions at the start, and when Jude skated out onto the ice, the roar became deafening. Guess he deserves it, seeing as he was named MVP after the final game last spring.

We've never been prouder to be his family than the moment we watched him lift the cup in the air. Pretty sure all of us Donnellys were crying from the box seats we managed to get for that game.

Just the same way we are now, from the box seats Jude got us for tonight.

"Gotta say, I didn't expect to be living the life of luxury when we got together." Heidi drops down into the seat next to me, passing over a beer. "Watching NHL games from fancy box seats is an unexpected bonus to our relationship."

I chuckle then take a sip of my beer. "You're welcome, except I can't take credit. This is all Jude." I lean in and kiss the side of her neck before whispering, "The bonuses I give you are not fit for public."

"I'm looking forward to some of those bonuses when we get back to the hotel." Her hand slides up my leg, dangerously high.

"Heidi," I say warningly, covering her hand and moving it to a safer position. Wicked temptress that she is, she just giggles and leans her head down on my shoulder. I turn and press another kiss to the top of her head.

It's hard to believe a year ago, she was nothing but a memory. A woman I'd once been attracted to but never had a chance with. And now she's the center of my entire world.

She's been looking at buying an apartment, and I've been trying to convince her to just move in with me. She says it's too fast; I say it makes sense. We work together, we spend just about every single night together, it's pointless for her to have a separate place just to store her clothes.

Jude's team scores a goal, drawing our attention back to the game. The arena erupts in cheers, and we're all on our feet, as well.

"Damn, this is gonna be a good season, I can feel it," Sawyer announces, dropping his hands on my shoulders and shaking me.

"C'mon man, I almost spilled my beer," I complain, but only half-heartedly. Because we all feel the same excitement. After last season's championship win, Jude told me he was worried he'd never reach that high again. But seeing him tonight, flying across the ice with the large letter *C* emblazoned on his jersey, I have faith he will.

No matter how much I worry that every game could be his last. That's a fear I'll keep to myself, no matter what.

"How do I always forget how much more intense it is watching them barrel into each other live, as opposed to on the TV." Mom sinks down in the seat next to Heidi. "It was so much easier when he was younger. Don't get me wrong, the collisions still happened, but I don't know, they weren't as big or brutal back then."

I bite my tongue. She's right, it is a lot more intense watching a game live, in more ways than one. The energy is up as the crowd feeds off each other. But when it's your family member on the ice, the stress is also up. Because out of everyone sitting in this box, I'm the one who's all too aware that injuries happen way too often in professional sports. And that's not only because I'm a doctor. That's because I'm the only one that Jude confides in about his own injuries.

Only Heidi knows that in the championship final this spring, Jude had a fall that gave him yet another minor tear to his already battered ACL. He skated through it, and no one in our family knew until he called me to say he wouldn't be meeting us after the game for a brief celebration. He begged me to lie and tell everyone he was tied up with the team, when in reality, he was being treated by the team doctors, given painkillers, and dropped off at his hotel.

The next morning, he made it to breakfast with us, and I saw the tight lines of pain around his eyes. But everyone else only saw the hockey star hero of our family. That's the way he wanted it, and I respected his wishes. The doctor in me couldn't help but try to talk with him about retirement, however, he wouldn't even hear me out.

The buzzer sounds for the first intermission, and the team files off the ice to make way for the Zamboni. If Violet were here, she'd be enthralled. That big, slow machine is her favourite part of a game. But she's back home in Dogwood Cove with Leo and Serena. They're the only family members who couldn't make it down to Montana for tonight's game, but Leo's texting all of us in the group chat, so I know they're watching.

"He looks good, doesn't he," Mom says, leaning forward to look at me. "Strong. That extra training over the summer paid off, even if it did mean we didn't have him home as much."

"Of course, he does." My dad is a man of few words, just like Jude. But when he speaks, those words hold weight. He's standing behind my mom's seat, his own beer in hand.

The intermission ends, and then Jude's back on the ice with his team, flying on his skates as if he was born with them on his feet. The minutes tick by without another goal, just a flurry of activity too close to the Blaze's net for my comfort, and then the puck goes flying down the ice, shot free by one of the defensemen on Jude's team. Except there's no one there for it. Play stops, and I lean back against my seat, only just realizing I'd been on the edge of it for the last several tense minutes.

A loud cheer goes up from the crowd, and I glance up at the jumbotron to see what has everyone excited, just in time to see a guy drop down on one knee in the aisle next to another guy, who I assume is his partner. The team's mascot is dancing behind them, and everyone in their immediate vicinity has excited and shocked looks on their faces. The guy being proposed to nods, then they're hugging, and the cheer gets even louder.

"Don't get me wrong, I'm happy for them, but good God, that's my nightmare." Heidi shudders next to me. "I would hate having all that attention and pressure on me. Like, he's surrounded by strangers, being watched by millions *more* strangers. What if he said no? Ugh."

"Are you taking notes, brother? No public proposals." Kat turns around in her seat in front of us, smirking at me.

"Maybe Hunter should be taking notes," I fire back, glaring at her, hoping my nosy little sister gets the message. The last thing I need is a conversation about proposals right now. If Heidi's hesitant to move in with me so quickly, she sure as shit isn't going to be ready for me to propose marriage any time soon.

Not that it feels too soon for me. Nope, I'd marry her tomorrow if I thought she would say yes. The ring hidden in the top of my closet is proof of that.

The sound of someone slamming into the boards pulls our eyes back to the ice.

"Oh my God."

My mother's panicked cry confuses me for a second, until I scan the jerseys on the ice and don't see the number I'm looking for. It's in that second I realize with a sinking feeling in my gut that the player lying on the ice, surrounded by other players, is Jude.

And he's not getting up.

Did Max ever give Heidi the proposal of her dreams? Read their extended epilogue to find out: **bit.ly/JuliaJarrett_HTWY_ bonus**

Acknowledgments

Writing a book can be an incredibly solitary process. Unless you find yourself lucky enough to have found friends in the writer community.

I consider myself very lucky.

This book was one of the hardest I've ever written. I knew what I wanted Max and Heidi to feel and say and do, but translating that onto paper was incredibly challenging.

If it weren't for the amazing people who kept me on track, helped me clarify where things were not working, and figure out what had to change, this book would not be in your hands.

Thank you, Chelle, Alex, Theresa, Amy, Molly, Carolina, Chris, Kelly, Erica, and Mr Jarrett for telling me I wasn't allowed to give up on this story.

I owe you more than I can say.

tard series

About Julia Jarrett

Julia Jarrett is a busy mother of two boys, a happy wife to her real-life book boyfriend and the owner of two rescue dogs, one from Guatemala and another one from Taiwan. She lives on the West Coast of Canada and when she isn't writing contemporary romance novels full of relatable heroines and swoon-worthy heroes, she's probably drinking tea (or wine) and reading.

For a complete listing of Julia Jarrett books please visit www.authorjuliajarrett.com/books

Follow Julia:
Instagram @juliajarrettauthor
Facebook Reader Group: Julia Jarrett's Nutty Muffins
TikTok @julia.jarrett.author